RICHARD HARTZER

A Test of Faith
By
Richard Hartzer

ISBN: 978-1-959788-50-8

Author's note: in the very first prints of "A Confession of Faith", Faith's best friend was named Rebecca. Later versions of "A Confession of Faith", and now in "A Test of Faith" her name is Audrey.

PROLOGUE

Now that my journey is over, and I'm able to look back and absorb everything, I decided to write these stories as a way of coming to terms with the whole thing. I wrote the majority of my first book in prison, and I decided to leave it as it is. It's not perfect, but it perfectly captures my mindset and emotions in that moment. This book, and the one after it, were written once things had settled down and I realized that my story was one that could impact others. As you read further, you will notice that I include scenes in which I was not present. I recreated these scenes after conversations with the people who were there, and I included them to give the readers a more detailed description of the overall action.

Looking back, I am amazed at the turns my life has taken so far. If you had told me this story a few years ago, I would never have believed it. It's a perfect example of the way God uses anyone as long as they are available. You don't have to be perfect or possess some sort of special ability. Just listen to His voice, and no matter what happens, always keep the faith.

I was in the room with a madman. A madman with the will, dedication, and resources required to overthrow the government of the United States and take over for himself. A madman who was so threatened by my knowledge, there was no telling what he would do to silence me. I had to find a way to escape before I lost my freedom, and maybe even my life. I sprang out of my seat and lunged toward the door, but he stood up to stop me, holding his hands out like he was about to keep me from scoring a touchdown. Lowering my shoulder into his chest, I knocked him off balance and sent him flying over a chair. I reached for the door, but it was still locked. I turned around in time to see him pick himself up off the ground and start walking toward me, growling like a wounded animal.

I took a step back, but the door prevented me from moving any farther. "Get back! Get back or I'll..."

"Or you'll what?"

My eyes darted around the room, searching for something I could use as a weapon. "I'll make sure you're sorry."

He moved closer, a hungry tiger stalking his prey. "Faith, listen to me. You don't want to go this way. If you stop now, I can still help you. If you don't reconsider your allegiance, I'm afraid you'll wind up paying for your transgressions."

"It's you that needs to reconsider your allegiance. You may have an army, but there are plenty of people out there who'll fight you."

"Do you seriously think I'm afraid of them? They're no match for the power at my fingertips."

Cornered, with nowhere to go, I let out a primal scream and lunged once more at my enemy.

CHAPTER ONE

I sat down next to Jakob on the sofa and looked around the living room of the bunker we had called home since I was executed.

Dad's brows furrowed at me. "Okay, now that Faith's finally here, let's get started. Paul, is there any new information this morning?"

"Not really. I'm having trouble getting any inside information. All my former colleagues on the Chancellor's staff either think I'm dead, or they're looking for me because they know I helped you all escape. No doubt they discovered long ago that I only injected everybody with enough sedative to appear dead, and I'm sure they've found the van and realized we weren't really inside when it exploded."

My father nodded in agreement. "I'm sure you're right. We have to rely on instinct rather than information. Based on your experience working with Chancellor Sloane, what do you think he's planning?"

Paul sighed. We had been over this countless times already, but when you've been trapped in an underground safehouse for as long as we have, you run out of new things to talk about. "While his agents are still searching for us, the Chancellor is carrying on as if nothing happened. He's counting on the fact that the American people forgot about the protests. He has no intention of legalizing religion, so he's trying to stall until the fervor dies down."

Mom jumped into the conversation for the first time. "How can he do that? There were thousands of people out there protesting.

How can he just ignore that?"

Her question was rhetorical, but that didn't stop Paul from answering anyway. "People have short attention spans. Once the shock of Faith's impending execution wore off, everybody just went back to their daily lives. Everybody thinks Faith's gone, and without somebody like her to unite the people, the momentum just fizzled out." He then turned to my father. "If REFUGE had acted when they had the chance, the Chancellor would have given in by now."

My father had heard this line from Paul before and was quick to respond. "Duncan told me we caught him off guard so they couldn't mobilize quickly enough."

Paul scoffed. "Off guard? How can someone in a position like that be caught off guard? You have to be ready for anything."

Dad's voice remained steady, although his face was becoming flush. "Faith had no way of warning him before she posted her last message and asked the people to protest. They're regrouping and coming up with a plan."

Paul had a point, but so did my father. The night before I was to be executed for posting the truth about Chancellor Sloane and his ban on religion, I secretly posted a message on my website calling on the citizens to protest in their local parks. The fact that Chancellor Sloane was willing to execute an 18-year-old girl struck a chord with people, and they spilled into city parks across the country in protest. Sloane had no choice but to make a speech telling everybody to go home because their voices had been heard, but he had yet to make any changes.

"Why can't I just go public and tell everybody that I'm not really dead?" My tone carried my frustration about the situation.

My father and Paul shook their heads at me, but only Dad spoke. "Faith, we've been through this. Any communication with people on the outside could give away our location. We're safe in this bunker, and we need to keep it that way."

"But you've been in contact with Duncan. He's on the outside." My mouth was about to get me in trouble again.

"That's different. Those are secure telephone conversations and I made them out of necessity. I had to inform him that we were alive after all, and I had to request more supplies."

Paul took this opportunity to take another jab at my father and Duncan. "Speaking of supplies, when are they sending more food?

We've been down here nearly 3 months and, based on my estimates, we will run out of food in less than two weeks unless we take drastic measures."

My father sighed. "I know. Duncan said he can't risk a supply delivery. We need to make the food last longer."

Paul stroked his beard for a moment before pulling his hand away from his face. We didn't have a boar hair brush and beard oil in the bunker, so his immaculate beard had become a shaggy mess. One day he grabbed a razor and threatened to shave the whole thing off, but he changed his mind. "What do you have in mind? The adults have already cut back to one meal a day so the children can eat two."

"I hate to say it, but the adults may have to eat every other day."

"I can help, too," Jakob announced. He had been silent during this conversation, so his declaration startled me. At nineteen and eighteen, he and I were technically adults, but we had been allowed to eat twice a day along with my 12-year-old sister Hope, and 9-year-old brother Alex. "I can cut back to one meal a day."

I grabbed Jakob's hand and nodded in agreement. "Yeah, me too."

My father studied us for a few moments to convey the gravity of our situation, but he knew this was the right choice. "Are you sure? We wouldn't let you do this if it weren't an emergency."

My eyes met Jakob's for a moment, then we nodded our heads at the others. It felt good to contribute to the cause, even though it would be uncomfortable for us. We had always sat in on these meetings, but we were usually content to let the older people do most of the talking. We were happy just sitting close together on the sofa, allowing our arms to rest alongside each other. The contact was soothing in the midst of such tense discussions.

Dad sensed that this was a good place to end the meeting. "Okay. But in the meantime, I'll keep asking Duncan for more supplies." He then turned to my mother and smiled. "Emily, what are we cooking for lunch today?"

— • ● • —

"Mac and cheese again? We just had that!" Alex stomped his feet and folded his arms for emphasis.

Mom was running out of patience, but she still remembered how young Alex was. "I'm sorry. We don't have very many options."

"Why can't we go get more food?"

"You know why. We have to stay in here until it's safe to leave."

I continued to stir the pasta without looking up. I had heard this conversation countless times and refused to get involved.

My younger sister, Hope, shuffled past me and took this opportunity to gang up on my mom. "And when's that gonna be?"

Alex now had an ally in the fight against Mom. "Let's just order pizza!"

I couldn't stay silent anymore. "What are we gonna do? Call Luigi's and say, 'Hey, can you deliver three pepperoni pizzas to this rickety-looking cabin out in the middle of nowhere?'"

Mom glared at me. "Faith, you're not helping."

You're not helping was practically my last name. I heard it all the time, along with "Stop arguing with your sister" and "Stop talking back."

My father, sensing everyone's growing frustration from the living room, came in and tried to de-escalate the situation. "I know this is tough on everybody, but we have to be patient. We'll get through this."

Hope looked up at him with a mixture of pity, frustration, and boredom on her face. "Daddy, we've been in here forever, and there's nothing to eat."

My father knelt down and looked Hope in the eyes. "We have plenty of food and we're completely safe in here. You know what? I downloaded a new game on the computer. Why don't you guys go play for a few minutes?"

Hope and Alex ran off, arguing over who got to play the new game first. It would probably end up in another fight, but at least they forgot about food for the time being.

Mom kissed Dad on the cheek. "Thank you."

I wrinkled my nose at such a nauseating display of affection. "Eww. Not in front of the children!"

Mom kissed Dad on the lips just to spite me and left the room.

Dad blushed for a moment, then regained his composure and turned his attention to me. "Are you doing okay, Jellybean?"

For some reason, that question hit me like a ton of bricks. I wanted to tell him, "Actually, I'm not okay. I'm still stunned from being nearly executed a few months ago. I'm depressed because we're hiding with no end in sight. I'm tired of eating the same food from the same boxes and cans. I'm tired of having no privacy. I'm tired of sleeping on the floor in a room with my sister and brother. Alex is bouncing off the walls because he can't go outside and play. Hope complains too much. I can't stand sitting near Paul when we eat because his jaw makes this stupid clicking sound when he chews. I never get to watch what I want to because one of the grown-ups always hogs the TV. Jakob and I never have any time alone by the lake like we used to. I miss my best friend, Audrey. I miss our home. I miss freedom. Sometimes I secretly hope we get caught, just to put an end to all this." I wanted to say all these things, but I couldn't. I just smiled my most cheerful smile and lied through my teeth. "Yeah, I'm good."

We all shared the same frustrations, so there was no use talking about it. It wouldn't fix anything, and it would only bring everybody else down too. Sure, I was thankful to be alive after everything we had endured, but once the initial relief wore off, and the reality of our situation sank in, it brought depression along with it. I wore a cheerful mask during the day, but I silently cried myself to sleep most nights. I couldn't confide in anyone since we were all going through the same things. I almost spilled my feelings to Jakob one day when he noticed my bloodshot eyes, but I mustered enough strength to hold it in. He and I were as close as ever, but this experience was putting a tremendous strain on our relationship. We still talked and sat next to each other all the time, but we didn't enjoy our time together as much as we had in the past. We couldn't spend enough time together enjoying the outdoors in the months leading up to our capture, and in a cruel twist of irony, we now lived in the middle of the woods, but we couldn't go out and enjoy them.

A shriek from the next room snapped me back to reality.

Dad bolted out of the kitchen. "What happened?"

I followed Dad into the living room and saw Mom holding a hysterical Hope.

"Alex pushed me!" Hope screamed.

"Whoa, that's a lot of blood!" The words escaped before I could stop them.

My father looked at me with a scowl. "Faith, you're not helping."

There it was again. "I'm sorry."

Dad brushed Hope's matted hair away from the injured area. "What happened?"

Hope answered in one-word sentences, punctuated by sobs. "Alex… pushed… me… off… the… chair!"

Alex heard his name and decided to defend himself from Hope's reckless accusations. "She hit me first!" he screamed.

"No, I didn't!"

"Yes, you did, you big fat heifer!"

Mom whipped her head around and yelled, "Alex!"

Hope wasn't about to give Alex the last word. "Yes, you did, you little turd!"

Dad whipped his head around and yelled, "Hope!"

"Mommy! Hope said 'turd'!" Alex proclaimed in true younger-brotherly fashion.

"So what, you just said it too!" she retorted with blood dripping into her eyes.

Even though Hope's head was pouring blood, I couldn't help but snicker at the childish name-calling. I held my tongue though because I didn't want to hear my unofficial last name for the third time.

Dad didn't think it was as funny as I did. "That's enough!" Everyone stopped in their tracks. "Emily, take Alex into the other room and deal with him while I take care of Hope."

My mother dragged Alex out of the room, but he couldn't help but whisper one last insult at Hope before he left. "Heifer."

Dad shook his head and sighed, before turning his attention to Hope's injury.

"Is it bad?" she whimpered.

Dad brushed her hair out of the way again and tried to survey the damage. "Faith, grab a flashlight and the first aid kit for me."

I knew exactly where everything was, so I was back in an instant. "Here you go."

My father, the doctor, put on a pair of gloves, blotted the blood away with some gauze, spread a portion of hair apart, and pointed.

"Shine it right here… OK, let's see what we're dealing with."

I knew better than to stare at the injury, but something compelled me to take a glimpse anyway. That was a mistake. Once I saw how deep the cut was, my stomach began to churn. I held my tongue, though, because Hope had actually calmed down a bit and I couldn't make it worse.

Dad must have sensed my queasiness, and now he had two patients to calm down. "Head injuries bleed a lot, so they always look worse than they really are." He continued to look things over and looked at Hope. "Well, I have good news and bad news."

"What's the good news?"

"You can keep your head."

A slight smile appeared on Hope's face. "Gee, thanks. But what's the bad news?"

"The bad news is that you have a pretty serious injury. Normally I would take you to the hospital for something like this, but that's not an option, so I'll have to make do with what we have here. You'll be okay, though. Faith, I need your help. Put some gloves on."

The gloves were reluctant to stretch over my sweaty hands, but I finally convinced them to cooperate. Dad pulled a tube of glue out of the first aid kit and looked at me. "I need you to put your hands on each side of the wound like this. Then gently push the skin together while I glue it shut."

Again, my mouth acted before my brain could stop it. "Are you really using glue? I guess we're all out of staples."

Hope's ears perked up. "You're gluing my head shut?"

Dad glared at me and I dropped my head. "I know, I know. I'm not helping."

Dad rolled his eyes and turned his focus back to Hope. "No, girls. This is special medical glue. It's non-toxic, so it's safe to use on people. Maybe I'll use it on Faith's mouth to prove how well it works."

Dad was probably joking, but I wasn't about to find out, so I bit my tongue. I would have to look at the wound to hold it shut. That realization caused some bile to rise in the back of my throat, but I gathered my courage and faced my fears. The cut was about half as long as my pinky finger and still bleeding. I took a deep breath, placed my fingers on both sides of the wound, and pushed her skin back together. When I closed the wound, another large spurt of blood escaped the area and covered my fingertips. My dad wiped it away and applied a line of skin glue along the cut. During times like this, it was nice to have a doctor in the family.

Dad put the glue in his shirt pocket and looked at me. "Hold it shut for two minutes. It's imperative that you don't move while the glue sets."

"OK," I said. Over the next two minutes, every part of my body itched. It was only because I had been told to keep my hands still, so I tried to think about something else. I somehow held it together until my father gave me the signal.

"Now let go slowly."

I moved my hands apart with the steadiness of a brain surgeon, and to my delight, the skin held together.

"Hope," my father said. "You need to take it easy for a few days. No running around, skydiving, or fighting with your brother. Can you do that?"

Hope nodded. "Daddy?"

"Yes, Pumpkin?"

"Do we have any ice cream?"

After playing "Medical Assistant" that afternoon, I didn't have much of an appetite at supper time. That was convenient since I had already eaten my allotted meal for the day anyway. While everyone else was in other parts of the bunker, Jakob and I stole a few moments of alone time in the living area. Jakob sat close to me with one hand on the TV remote and the other hand in mine. He and I had experienced a very unique dating experience in which he planted a listening device in my living room, told me my father was involved in a plot to overthrow the government, kidnapped me, and turned me over to Paul, who at the time worked with Chancellor Sloane, and was pretending to be Jakob's father, and helped me try to rescue my family. My father didn't trust Jakob for a long time, but now that my father knew Jakob was firmly one of the "good guys", he welcomed him with open arms. He probably suspected that Jakob and I would eventually get married, but he had so much on his mind that he and I avoided that subject for the time being. Despite our current situation, I was confident that we would eventually have our "happily ever after" because our love was strong enough to handle any obstacle that came our way.

Jakob was scrolling through the program guide for the third straight time, watching everything and nothing, and I was listening to my mind as it went 1,000 miles an hour, trying to process everything that had happened, and everything that needed to happen. We all knew our first priority was to stay alive long enough to get out of the bunker. Beyond that, we had no idea what would happen next. I was Public Enemy Number One, and as long as I was alive, I posed an immediate threat to Chancellor Sloane and his ability to maintain control of the United States. Before Sloane sentenced me to be executed, I had built a loyal following on the internet, and I had convinced hundreds of thousands of Americans to protest Sloane's policies against religion. Now, like Paul had said earlier, the American people had forgotten about me and didn't know what to do next. Despite my father's apprehensions, I could regain the lost momentum and finish the job we set out to do, but I couldn't act without his and Duncan's permission. Growing bored with Jakob's scrolling, I stood up and walked over to the computer desk.

My best friend Audrey and I had spent countless hours causing trouble with our computers, and I was at home on the Internet. I thought about Audrey for a moment, then logged into my e-mail account. When I was imprisoned, I wrote my story and secretly e-mailed it to Audrey so others could read about it. Even though she thought I had been executed, she replied to my e-mail anyway, thinking I would never read it. On the contrary, I had read her reply several times, and I read through it again that day. It said:

Dear Faith,

I can't describe how I feel after reading your story. I was only involved in part of your life, so I was surprised to read about everything that was going on. I know why you had to keep everything a secret from me, and I'm not mad at all. It's been a week since you sent me that e-mail and I miss you more every day. I can't believe you're gone, and I can't believe Sloane could kill you and your parents. He really is a monster and I hope somebody finally gives him what he deserves. I haven't shown your story to anybody else because I know nobody around here would dare publish it. And besides, I wouldn't know where to go with it, anyway. I don't even know why I'm typing this e-mail because I know you'll never read it. I just had to let you know that I got your message and I miss you so much. Thank you for being such a great friend. I'll always remember you.

My "Drafts" folder was full of reply e-mails that I had typed up but couldn't actually send. Sloane's people had to have known I sent that original e-mail to Audrey, and they were definitely monitoring her account for any response from me. I was confident that my computer prowess could mask my location, but I couldn't take that chance. My father and I had several arguments about this subject, and although I wanted Audrey to know I was alive, it was safest for her and us to just keep her in the dark. I was closing my e-mail when something caught my eye on the security monitor that showed the video feed from outside the bunker. I stared for a couple of moments, then called for my father. "Dad… They're back!"

CHAPTER TWO

Three black SUVs flew toward the house and stopped out front. Agent Belford, and seven other agents, each wearing dark suits and dark sunglasses, exited the cars. Belford barked orders at his squad. "Remember, she's just a teenager, but she's still dangerous. She's not alone, so be on your guard. We take her alive." The setting sun cast long shadows through the trees, offering some camouflage for the agents while providing enough light for them to see.

The agents surrounded the home, guarding every door to prevent escape. Belford counted to three, and the agents at the front and back doors used their battering rams to smash the doors open, sending splinters of wood and agents into the house. The crash of the doors was followed by screams from the people inside. Within seconds, a terrified man and woman were lying face down on the ground with several guns pointed at them.

"What's going on? Who are you?" the man asked.

Ignoring the questions, Belford strode up to the couple and surveyed the room. "She's not in here. You two stay here and guard the parents. The rest of you fan out and find her."

"Answer me! What do you want?"

One of the agents moved his gun closer to the man's head. "That's enough out of you."

The other agents separated and began searching every room, shouting "Clear" every time they searched a room and found nothing. After a thorough search, the group reconvened in the living room. Belford squinted his eyes and strolled around the room, trying to imagine where a teenage girl might be hiding. He approached a door and opened it slowly, revealing a set of stairs that led down into the darkness. Motioning for some agents to follow, he began his descent. Belford made it to the bottom of the stairs, and his eyes caught a glimpse of his target. "There she is. With the computer."

The other agents raised their guns, but Belford left his in its holster as he approached the young lady sitting at a desk, listening to music with her earbuds, unaware of the danger that now approached. Belford laid his hand on her shoulder, and her eyes widened at his. Her mouth fell open as she saw the rest of the agents and their guns.

Belford smiled at his captive. "Faith Webber."

"What?"

"Faith Webber. We know she's been in touch with you, Audrey. You're her best friend, are you not?"

Audrey knew he was right, but her first instinct was to protect her friend. "I haven't seen Faith in months. I don't know where she is."

Audrey's dad shouted from upstairs, "Audrey, are you OK? If you touch her, I'll..."

Belford called back, "She's fine! We're just having a little chat!" He saw the terror in Audrey's eyes and signaled for the agents to lower their weapons. "Mind if I sit?" By the time Audrey shook her head, he had already pulled up a chair next to her. "Listen, I don't have a lot of time, so I'm going to be direct. We know she e-mailed her confession to you before her execution. She hacked into a phone belonging to one of our guards and sent a document to you. I'm not going to ask you where it is, because we've already read the entire thing. It took a while to decrypt it, but we finally figured it out yesterday. It's quite a story."

Audrey shook her head and raised her eyebrows. "So, what do you want from me?"

"We want you to come with us. As insurance."

"Insurance for what?"

Belford stood and took a few steps toward the stairs. "Faith's still alive."

Audrey's eyes widened. "She is? How?"

Belford wasn't in the mood for a lengthy conversation, so he gave Audrey a brief synopsis. "We found the cabin a while back because that was the location where Jakob's microchip shorted out.

We sent some agents to have a look around, but they saw nothing. Once we were able to read Faith's story, we found out about the safehouse under the cabin. We suspect that's where they've been hiding, and as we speak, a squad of agents is there to apprehend her. It's just a matter of time before we breech the cabin and arrest them."

Audrey shrugged her shoulders. "I still don't understand why you need me. Sounds like you have it all figured out already."

Belford turned around and grinned at Audrey. "We know how stubborn Faith can be, so we may need you to convince her to cooperate. If she knows that you've been arrested, she'll have no choice but to play nice."

The gravity of the situation descended on Audrey, and she plead with her eyes. "You can take me, but please leave my family alone. They didn't do anything. They don't even know about Faith's confession."

Belford scoffed at Audrey's naivety. "Fine. Just know that your parents are leverage to convince you to cooperate, just as you are leverage to convince Faith to cooperate. If you don't help us, we will arrest your parents. Now, let's go."

At Belford's command, the other agents guided Audrey out of her seat and toward the stairs. Once they reached the top, Audrey searched the room for her parents. The sight of them on the ground with guns on them made her knees buckle. "Mom, Dad, are you okay?"

Belford motioned for the agents to step away from the terrified family, and Audrey ran to them. They embraced for a moment on the floor, then Belford told them to sit on the couch. "Mr. and Mrs. Gibson. Allow me to explain our presence here today. Your daughter's best friend, Faith Webber, is a fugitive. She escaped from our custody, and we need Audrey's help."

Mrs. Gibson sat frozen, but Mr. Gibson took the opportunity to speak. "Help with what? She hasn't seen Faith in months. Whatever Faith did, I'm sure Audrey wasn't involved."

"You are correct. We have no evidence that Audrey was involved."

"So can't you just leave her out of this?"

Belford rubbed his forehead, trying to contain his frustration. "Mr. Gibson, I understand your concern, but I assure you, if Audrey does her part, you will all be completely safe. And you will have the gratitude of the United States government. Not a bad thing to have."

Mr. Gibson looked at his family, then back at Belford. "Why would you ask this of a teenage girl?"

Belford responded with a flat tone in his voice. "Mr. Gibson, we are not asking." He paused, to let the weight of that statement sink in. "Now, Audrey is going to come with us for a few days, and you two are going to continue to live your lives. If all goes according to plan, Audrey will return home soon, and your family will be well compensated for your assistance."

Mr. Gibson stood up and glared at Belford. "Compensated? We don't want your money! We just want our daughter!"

Every agent but Belford trained their guns on Mr. Gibson, but Belford waived them off. He smiled and took a step forward so both men were nearly touching. "Measure your words carefully. If you would like us to take your wife also, by all means, keep protesting."

Gibson looked at his wife's terrified face and admitted defeat. "Fine. Just give me your word that Audrey will be safe."

"We have no interest in harming your daughter. We only want Faith and her associates. You may say your goodbyes now."

The Gibson family stood up and squeezed each other with all their might, all three of them with tears running down their cheeks. Unmoved by the display of affection, Belford tapped Audrey on the shoulder. "It's time."

The family held on for a few seconds before finally letting go and taking one more look at each other. Mrs. Gibson wiped the tears from Audrey's face. "It'll be okay. Be strong and do what they say. You'll be back home soon."

Audrey couldn't muster the strength to say anything, so she simply nodded her head before turning around and walking with Belford out the front door. He opened the door of one of the SUVs and helped her step inside. She gave a half-smile and a brief wave before he shut the door. The dark tint of the windows prevented Audrey's mom and dad from seeing her, but they waved back anyway. Belford ignored the waving and sat in the back seat with Audrey. As the SUVs backed out of the driveway and headed down the street, Audrey thought about her family, and her friend Faith. "Faith!"

Belford's head snapped toward Audrey's. "What about her?"

"How is she alive? You said you'd tell me later."

Belford took a long breath in and let it out slowly. "Fine. One of our agents helped her and her family escape by pretending to execute them. He made them appear dead, but they were only sedated. He then burned the van they were traveling in, so it looked like they had an accident. Once we discovered the wrecked van and saw no signs of bodies inside, we realized they were all alive."

"So, her parents are still alive too? What about Jakob? Was he the agent that helped them escape?"

Belford grumbled under his breath. "No. We believe Jakob is still alive, but they had help from someone else. It appears that we had two traitors in our midst."

"Agent Cross? How could he help them? He was so mean."

Belford glared at Audrey with a fire in his eyes she hadn't seen before. "We don't know what happened to him. I suppose Mr. Webber offered him enough money that he decided to betray his country.

Audrey looked out the window as she processed all the shocking revelations. "Wow. I can't believe all this." She turned her head back to face Belford. "What are you gonna do if you catch them?"

"*If* we catch them? *If*? My dear, *when* we catch them, I will do what Cross should have done when he had the chance."

Audrey knew what that meant, and her heart pounded throughout the rest of the ride. She looked out the window and saw a building matching the description of the compound in Faith's story. Before long, she found herself alone in a sparse room that only held a table and a couple of chairs. It looked much like the room Faith was in during Cross's interrogation, but unlike Faith, Audrey had no secret agent-boyfriend to help her escape.

An eternity passed while she sat in the room. It felt like an hour or two, but there was no clock in the room, so Audrey didn't know for sure. Voices out in the hall met her ears on several occasions, but no one ever entered the room. She wanted to creep closer to the door so she could hear what was happening, but the camera mounted on the wall convinced her to stay put. Whatever was going on out there definitely had people on edge, so Audrey wasn't sure if she really wanted to know about it after all.

Finally, Belford entered the room and sat down. "Good news. My men are in position, and we will soon have the traitors in custody. Do you need anything? Restroom, food, water?"

Audrey shook her head. "I'm fine. Just ready to get this over with."

Belford stood and scooted his chair back under the table. "Suit yourself. I'll be back shortly." He left the room and left Audrey alone again with her thoughts.

Ever since Audrey read Faith's story, she had mixed feelings about the whole thing. Faith was her best friend after all, but if REFUGE really was trying to take over the country, maybe Faith was involved with some bad people that needed to be stopped. If this were the case, it would be difficult for Audrey to cooperate with Belford, but she really had to help the country. If Belford was wrong about REFUGE, Audrey knew she would still have to cooperate to keep herself and her parents out of trouble. Maybe Faith would still be able to stay alive, even with Audrey helping the government.

On some level, Audrey resented Faith for putting her in this situation. Yes, Faith technically broke the law, but maybe she was still a good person. A good person who hid a lot of things from her best friend. Maybe she was only protecting Audrey by keeping all these secrets. But if that were the case, why would Faith send her a copy of her story? Audrey's head hurt as she tried to make sense of Faith's actions and motivations. She gave up trying to figure out what Faith was really up to and laid her head down on the table.

CHAPTER THREE

Chancellor Sloane was a brilliant strategist, and his most significant legacy was Operation Oversight. He wanted the ability to monitor the locations of his soldiers during battle, so he had microchips implanted under their scalps. These microchips were so successful he had them implanted in all government workers. Many people were afraid of a loved one going missing, so these chips could also be found in many civilians. Only Sloane and a few other people knew the truth about these microchips. Not only were they useful for tracking, but he could also use them as a form of mind control. With these chips, Sloane could control government employees and manipulate elections to stay in office. As former government agents, Jakob and Paul both had these chips implanted in their heads, but they had recently been disabled through divine intervention. Paul's chip was fried when he encountered a mysterious man in a blue sweater vest, and Jakob was with me in the cabin above our bunker when I prayed for him, and a surge of electricity short-circuited his chip. Since the cabin was the last location Jakob's microchip had transmitted, several government agents had been out there to have a look. They usually came in groups of three or four and they never actually entered the cabin, content to peer in through the windows. Once they saw no signs of life, they likely thought Jakob was long gone, so they left. This was their third visit, and although their presence was unnerving, we felt safe in the hidden bunker that resided below the rickety cabin.

Dad heard my call and entered the room. "How many are there this time?"

"Three. They're just looking into the windows right now. I

guess they're trying to see if Jakob happened to come back here."

"Probably. We still need to remain quiet, though." My father left the room to spread the word to the others and instruct them to be quiet. During times like this, we were afraid Hope or Alex would give us away, but they had always cooperated.

Jakob had migrated from the couch and was now standing over my shoulder, watching the agents poke around the outside of the cabin. After a few moments, he finally spoke. "You ever get scared that our microchips will suddenly start working again and give away our location?"

My eyes opened wide, and I turned to look Jakob in the eyes. "Now I do. Do you really think that's possible?"

Jakob shrugged. "Nah. I'm sure God won't let that happen. Why would He have fried them just to make them work again?"

"I don't know. I never thought God would let my family get captured and almost executed, but it still happened."

The look in Jakob's eyes told me he wished he had never brought this up. "Well, you always say that God knows what He's doing, even if we don't understand it. I'm sure it'll be okay."

I had to convince myself that Jakob was right. "I'm sure it will."

At that moment, the agents outside the cabin did something we had never seen them do during their previous visits. Not satisfied to peek inside through the windows, they tried to pry the windows open with crowbars. "Dad?" I called in a loud whisper. "You need to come in here."

My dad trotted in from the next room. "What is it, Jellybean?" He then looked at the surveillance monitors and saw what was going on.

My heart was beating a little harder than usual. "Do you think they'll get in?"

Always quick to reassure us, my father shook his head. "No, the windows are bulletproof, and the walls are reinforced with steel. It may look weak on the outside, but they would need a battering ram to get in. And even if they get in, they wouldn't have any way of knowing about the bunker under the floor."

We watched in silence as the agents tried unsuccessfully to open every window, followed by the front door. Under different circumstances, it would have been comical to see grown men in nice suits trying to break into a dilapidated cabin in the middle of nowhere. They were much more persistent than before, so perhaps they knew more than we thought they did. When the windows and door wouldn't budge, one of the agents took a telescoping baton out of his jacket and approached one of the windows. He struck it with the baton several times, but it refused to break. All three agents then tried the same tactic on the other windows, but all of them were met with the same resistance. Thwarted by the bulletproof glass, they all met at the front door and discussed the situation for a couple of minutes. After some discussion, the biggest of the three agents tried to break through the front door with his shoulder. He achieved nothing other than injuring himself and creating a racket loud enough for us to hear downstairs. We could see the other two agents laughing at their partner, even though he was twice their size. After a few moments of laughing and bickering, they all walked onto the front porch and faced the door. Two of them took off in unison, and all hit the front door at the same time with all their might. The door held firm, but this time we could hear the loud "Wham!" where we were. This was enough to draw the other residents into the living area to see what was going on.

Hope's eyes widened when she saw the monitors. "Daddy? What are they doing?"

"They're just trying to get into the cabin. But they won't be able to. It's too strong."

At that moment, the agents had regrouped and assaulted the door again. Wham!

Dad squinted as he studied the monitors. "Paul, why do you think they're trying so hard to get in? They've never done this before."

Wham!

Paul looked around at everyone in the room. "Has anybody sent any transmissions?"

We all shook our heads, and I thought about the microchips. There's no way they would have given us away.

Wham!

After several unsuccessful attempts, the agents gave up and stood still on the front porch, plotting their next move. Surely, they wouldn't try to ram their SUV into the cabin. The number of trees wouldn't allow them to get it close. One of the agents took his phone out and began speaking with somebody.

My father looked at Paul. "You know these guys. Who do you think they're talking to?"

"My guess is that they're calling for backup. They can't fit a truck in between the trees, but we have a smaller, hydraulic battering ram that'll do the trick."

A look of concern flashed on Dad's face for the first time. "You really think it's strong enough?"

"Definitely. It's just a matter of time."

Mom walked closer and put her hand on Dad's shoulder. "How long will it take to get that thing here?"

Paul pursed his lips as he thought. "Given the terrain and the distance, I'd say three or four hours."

Mom took Hope and Alex to the other room to occupy their minds with something less stressful.

Dad thought for a moment, then stood up. "I need to call Duncan and let him know what's going on. I think we might need an escape plan." He left the room, leaving me, Jakob, and Paul behind to watch the action.

I turned to Jakob. "I don't like this. If they get in the cabin, we're sitting ducks."

"Nah. They don't even know we're down here."

"But what if they still find us? We're no match for that many agents."

Jakob squeezed my shoulder. "We have the element of surprise. Paul and I can easily take them out. Remember, we were trained for this."

"No, we need to get out. We just wait for them to leave and then we make our escape."

Paul shook his head at me and said, "No. How would we know they were really gone and not just hiding? And where would we go?"

I didn't have a good answer.

Jakob sat down on a nearby chair. "If we ambush them, we can take them out before they know what happened."

Jakob's plan was reckless and dangerous, and I couldn't allow it to happen. "I'm sure these agents have tracking chips, so if they all come here and don't leave, it's just a matter of time before more agents arrive."

My father entered the room with a smile. "Just talked to Duncan and they're sending a van. It can be here in 3 hours. By then it'll be dark, and we can escape."

"How are we gonna get out without the agents seeing us?" Jakob asked.

"There's a secret exit that leads into the woods. All we do is crawl through a tunnel for a couple hundred yards, then climb a ladder that leads up into a hollowed-out tree. The tree has a door built into it, so we just open the door and walk out."

"Why didn't you tell us about this tunnel before, Andrew?" Paul had a sharp tone in his voice.

"It wasn't an option until now. We couldn't take any chances until the situation became more desperate."

Paul scoffed. "More desperate? We've been eating one meal every other day of awful food and doing nothing but waiting for your boss to give us permission to leave. That's not desperate enough?"

Jakob stepped between the two of them before things came to blows. Even though Paul had left Sloane's security detail and accepted the Lord, he still had yet to be completely delivered from his fiery temper. Normally we all got along well, but the cramped living space had taken its toll on all of us, and our patience was wearing thin.

Paul took a step back and sighed. "Fine. Let's just focus on our escape."

<hr>

Paul checked his watch and sighed. "It's been three hours already. Where's the van?"

Dad shrugged. "Should be here any time now. Faith, did you finish cleaning the computers?"

"Just finished. I deleted anything that'll give away any of our secrets."

"Good. Is everybody ready to go?"

It was strange that my father asked us that. It's not like we had anything to pack. We went into the bunker a few weeks ago with nothing, and we were about to leave with nothing. We had no idea where we were going next, but they had to have real food and real space to spread out. While I was dreaming about freedom, we heard a rumble above us and felt the floor begin to vibrate.

Jakob looked up as if he could magically see through the ceiling. "Is that what I think it is?"

We all sprinted to the surveillance monitors and saw the cause of the ruckus. A few more agents had arrived with the battering ram Paul had spoken of earlier, and they were moving it into position near one of the cabin walls. Based on Paul's experience, he didn't think it would take long for it to make its way into the cabin. Where was the van?

Dad spoke in a whisper. "Everybody stay quiet. And pray."

Some of us prayed, while the rest of us held our breath and watched the activity on the screens. The vehicle looked like a heavily armored riding lawn mower with a metal arm extending out from the front of it. Despite its modest size, Paul said it packed a powerful punch. We weren't sure if the cabin walls would hold until we could make our escape, but we were about to get our answer. Once the battering ram was in place and anchored into the ground, the agents backed away. The onslaught was about to begin. It wasn't long before we heard the first strike. Even though we knew it was coming, the sound and the jolt made us all jump. We watched with nervous eyes and saw that the wall held firm. The first strike was followed by a second, and a third, but the cabin wall held. We began to feel more optimistic about our chances, but our relief would be short-lived. I don't know how many more strikes it took, but eventually, the end of the battering ram pierced the wall.

We all looked to my father for guidance. He gestured at us with his hands. "Everybody calm down. They won't even know we're down here."

We sat mesmerized as the battering ram continued to expand the hole in the wall, and several agents poured in. We didn't have any cameras inside the cabin itself, so we had no idea what was happening inside. My father held up his finger to his lips, and we all understood exactly what he meant. For the next several minutes, the only sounds we heard were the footsteps and voices a few feet above our heads. We could tell the agents were searching the cabin, but we couldn't make out what they were saying.

The sound of a ringing phone broke the silence in the bunker. Dad sprinted toward the phone and whispered into it. We watched him with anxious eyes as he held his quiet conversation. He hung up the phone and walked back to us, still whispering. "The van's ten minutes away. Paul, I want you and Jakob to go first, just in case we have any unwelcome visitors out there. I'll make sure everybody else gets into the tunnel, then I'll go last. Everybody grab a flashlight."

Paul nodded his head in agreement for one of the few times since we had been in hiding. "Okay, let's go."

In all the excitement of the phone call, none of us had noticed that the footsteps and talking upstairs had stopped. We were all suddenly aware of the silence above us, so we looked at the surveillance monitors. We only saw two agents outside, so we knew the rest were still inside. But what were they doing? Our answer came in the sound of an axe striking the floor of the cabin. Hope yelped as the rest of us flinched. The sound of the ringing telephone had given us away. The van may still be ten minutes out, but we had to leave.

Dad led the way to the bedroom area of the bunker and approached the tall dresser that stored his clothes. He turned the drawer knobs in a special sequence, and something clicked behind the dresser. The right side popped out a few inches, and he pulled the dresser away from the wall, revealing a short opening in the sheetrock. The dresser was attached to the wall with a hinge, so it swung out with ease. The hinge would allow us to pull the dresser shut, preventing the agents from discovering the passageway we would be climbing through. He crawled in and shined his light down the long, dark passageway to make sure the coast was clear. I never knew I was claustrophobic before, but the sight of the tight tunnel caused my stomach to ache. Even though we would have to crawl for a while, this would definitely prove to be more of a mental challenge than a physical one.

The chopping behind us grew louder, and we could hear chunks of debris falling into the bunker. It wouldn't be long before the agents were inside, so we had to hurry. My father backed out of the tunnel, and Paul led the way in, followed by Jakob, my mother, Hope, Alex, and me. I crawled in a few feet and flinched at the sound of the agents entering the bunker. They stomped down the stairs, barking orders at each other. I tried to turn around to make sure my father made it in, but the tunnel was too narrow for me to move that way. I ducked my head down and looked between my legs to see an upside-down image of my father climbing in and closing the door behind him.

After only a couple minutes of crawling, my hands and knees were begging me to stop, but we didn't have that luxury. Several agonizing minutes later, Paul finally reached the ladder. He climbed up and looked around for danger. Satisfied that the coast was clear, he signaled for the rest of us to join him. I climbed the ladder and emerged from the tree, filling my lungs with fresh air for the first time in months. It was great, but it would feel even greater once we made it to the van. We waited near the tree until my father appeared. He checked on us, then motioned for us to follow. "The van should be this way."

From that distance, we couldn't see the cabin or hear any of the activity, so we felt relatively safe. Until the sound of buzzing grew louder.

Paul and Jakob looked up and spoke in unison. "Uh oh."

We all looked at them, but only my father spoke. "What?"

Paul locked eyes with Dad. "Those drones are equipped with thermal cameras. They'll see us out here, even though it's dark. How far is it to the van?"

Dad shrugged. "I don't know, maybe a quarter of a mile. Are those things armed?"

Paul walked past us and approached my dad. "Not usually. I say we start running toward the van. All the agents are on foot, so even if a drone spots us, it'll take a minute or two before anybody can catch up to us. At least we'll have a head start."

Dad nodded in agreement. "Let's go."

We all began to sprint as fast as we dared in the dark woods. My father led the way with his flashlight, but we refrained from using the others. No need to call extra attention to ourselves. It only took a few moments before a drone spotted us and began flying our way, alerting the agents to our location by shining a spotlight in our direction.

"Just keep running!" my father said in a restrained yell.

Another drone joined the first, and they circled above us in perfect rhythm. Suddenly, several clouds of dirt and leaves flew up from the ground, followed closely by the sound of gunfire off in the distance.

"Start running single file!" Paul yelled. We formed a line and Paul dropped to the back of the pack to shield the rest of us from the incoming fire.

"Keep going! I see the van!" my father shouted.

More agents had joined the pursuit because we were soon met with even more clouds of dirt and flying debris from the gunfire. As we ran farther, the trees exploded around us, sending wooden shrapnel flying in every direction.

We finally saw a black van parked along the road with the side doors open. Despite our fatigued states, we somehow willed ourselves to run even faster. My mom, Hope, and Alex dove in through the side doors and climbed in the very back row, just as a fresh round of bullets peppered the side of the van immediately behind the doors. Jakob and I jumped in, and we all ducked down in our seats. Once my dad and Paul were on board, we took off.

We buried our heads down into the carpet as we heard more bullets hit the side and back of the van. Broken glass rained down on us, but we dared not brush it off because we didn't want to expose our arms and hands to the gunfire. The clamor finally subsided as we put more distance between us and the agents.

Dad sat up and surveyed the damage. "Is everybody okay?"

One by one, my mother, Hope, Alex, Jakob, and I reported our condition. Paul didn't say anything as he sat still, slumped over in the first row of bench seats.

Dad reached over and shook Paul's left shoulder. "Paul, are you okay?" There was no answer.

Dad shook him again. "Paul?"

Still no answer.

Dad pulled his hand away and rubbed his thumb and first two fingers together. It was dark in the van, but I could tell his fingers were covered in blood.

28

CHAPTER FOUR

Belford flung the door open, causing Audrey to lift her head from the table and look around the room. He was obviously upset about something, but Audrey was not about to ask what it was. She didn't know how long he had been gone this time, but it seemed like it had been at least an hour, maybe two. It was definitely enough time for something bad to happen.

Belford finally broke the silence. "Well, you'll be glad to know that your friends managed to escape."

"How did they do that? I thought they were trapped underground?"

Belford scoffed. "So did we. Apparently, they had an escape tunnel and a van waiting for them outside. Our drones followed them for a while, but then we lost contact with them."

Audrey tried unsuccessfully to keep her smile hidden. "Where are they going?"

Belford sat down at the table across from Audrey. "We don't know. Obviously, they had help from REFUGE, but there's no telling where they're going."

"Wait, does that mean I can go back home now?"

"Not yet. We will catch back up to them soon. But in the meantime, I have a job for you. Let's take a walk so you can stretch your legs."

They stood and crossed the dim room. Belford touched a sensor on the door, and a light turned green. "After you," he said as he opened the door. Audrey walked out into the hall and waited for Belford to lead her to their destination.

"Mr. Belford? I really need to go."

"I told you, I'll take you home when you're done."

Audrey tugged on his suit sleeve. "No. I really need to *go*."

Belford stopped in his tracks. "Oh. Fine. The restroom's this way."

They took a couple more turns, and Belford spoke into an invisible microphone on his collar. "Agent Nelson, meet us at the southwest first-floor restroom. Our guest needs to use the facilities." He paused as a reply came through his earpiece. "Okay, Audrey. Agent Nelson will join you to make sure you don't try anything."

"I sure hope Agent Nelson's a woman."

Belford let out a slight chuckle before regaining his composure. "Of course. Despite what you've read, we are not all animals like Agent Cross. Most of us agents are just doing our job and keeping the country safe. If Cross wasn't so close to the Chancellor, he would have been put out to pasture long ago."

Audrey had never heard that phrase before. A mental image of a man wearing sunglasses and a dark suit, grazing in a meadow popped into her head, but she was pretty sure that's not what Belford meant.

They turned one more corner and approached a brown-haired woman in a business suit. Audrey figured that was Agent Nelson.

"Hello, Audrey. I'm Agent Nelson. Come this way." Nelson opened the door, allowing Audrey to enter the restroom, and followed her inside.

Even though the stall had a door, Audrey was apprehensive about using the restroom in front of a stranger. Her overwhelmed bladder was enough to overcome her apprehension though, so she did what she had to do. Fortunately, Agent Nelson didn't try to make awkward small talk and left Audrey alone. Audrey emerged from her stall and washed her hands thoroughly as if she were scrubbing herself of the feeling of betrayal. She dried her hands and followed Agent Nelson toward the door.

"Audrey, would you like something to eat or drink?"

"No, I'm good. Thanks anyway."

Nelson opened the door and stepped aside so Audrey could exit. "Okay, just let us know if you change your mind."

Audrey nodded and joined Belford out in the hall. He turned and led her farther toward their destination.

"Want anything to eat her drink?" he asked.

"No, I'm good. Agent Nelson already asked me that."

"Oh, okay. If you change your mind..."

"I'll just let you know."

Belford shot her a confused look but shrugged it off and kept walking. He touched a door sensor, waited for the green light, and opened the door. "Come on in. This is where you'll be working."

Audrey stepped into a small office where a desk, two chairs, and a computer greeted her. "So, I'm gonna be doing something with the computer? But what?"

Belford sat on one of the chairs and motioned for Audrey to do the same. Once she sat, he continued. "We need you to help us locate Faith and her accomplices."

Audrey scoffed, then tried to cover it up with a cough. "How am I gonna do that? I'm sure Faith hasn't been online. She's too smart for that."

"You e-mailed her after she disappeared. Can you tell if she read it?"

Audrey shook her head. "Even if I could, there wouldn't be any way of knowing where she was. It's not like I can just come out and ask her."

Belford smiled, revealing a piece of broccoli between a couple of his teeth. "You're the computer expert. How do you suggest we do this?"

Audrey stared at the blank computer screen as if it somehow held the answer. "I don't know. Faith knows more about computers than I do. If I try to trick her, she'll see it coming a mile away."

Belford logged into the computer, stood up, and crossed the room toward the door. "I believe in you. You'll figure out a way to keep your family out of trouble." With that, he scanned his finger, opened the door, and left Audrey alone with her thoughts.

Tears welled up in both of Audrey's eyes, and for once she was relieved to be alone. What was she going to do? She had to keep her family safe but to do that she would have to betray her best friend. Neither option was very appealing. She had a feeling Faith had read her e-mail, but she also realized that Faith couldn't and wouldn't respond and risk giving anything away. She considered several options before finally coming up with a plan.

An hour later, Belford re-entered the room and sat down next to Audrey, who was typing away at the computer. "Looks like you had an epiphany."

"Just a sec. Almost done."

Belford resented the fact that he was taking orders from a teenager, but he gave her some slack. He watched her work for a couple more minutes and grew annoyed the longer he waited. He wondered if she kept typing just to make him wait longer. He was about to say something when she finally stopped and turned to face him.

"Okay, I'm done. What do you think of this?"

Belford studied the computer screen for a couple of moments before responding. "Think that'll work?"

Audrey shrugged and pursed her lips. "Don't know. But it's the best I can come up with."

Belford stood and patted Audrey on the shoulder. "Go for it."

A few clicks later, Audrey's plan was put in motion. No going back now. "Mr. Belford? When can I go home?"

"That depends on Faith's response. Audrey, I'm going to shoot straight with you. You're doing a great job, but I don't think we can let you go until Faith's in custody."

Audrey's face dropped and the tears returned.

Belford sat back down and sighed. "I know what Faith's story said, but we know the truth about REFUGE. We know what they're planning, and we know they must be stopped."

"How can you be so sure? Isn't there a chance they only want religion to be legal again?"

Belford's face showed the first sign of sincere sympathy, and Audrey couldn't help but feel relief that she wasn't dealing with Cross.

"Listen, Audrey. I know this is tough, and I wouldn't be asking this of you unless the situation demanded it. I can't go into specifics because they're classified, but trust me. We know things about REFUGE. Things Faith probably doesn't know about. Trust me, you're helping the good guys."

"It doesn't feel like it though."

"I know. I hate putting you through this." Belford lowered his voice to a loud whisper to avoid the microphones in the room. "We aren't supposed to talk about our personal lives with our...guests, but I want you to know something. I have two teenage daughters of my own, and I hate to think of them ending up in your situation. But if they were, I would want them to be treated with dignity, and I would want them to help their country."

Audrey sniffed and looked up to face Belford. "Really?"

Belford nodded. "I hope you realize how important this is, and how important you are. I wouldn't be exaggerating if I told you that the Chancellor himself would be grateful if you're successful."

Audrey nodded in return. "Thank you. I know you have a job to do, but I'm glad you're being so nice about it. If you're right about REFUGE, I wanna help. But I'd like a favor."

"What's that?"

"I wanna talk to my parents. I know it's late, but they won't mind."

Belford smiled and the broccoli reappeared. "I think we can manage that."

CHAPTER FIVE

"He's losing blood fast. They must've nicked his brachial artery." A note of alarm was in Dad's voice as he examined Paul's arm.

Jakob was in a panic. "What do we do?"

Dad stood up and laid Paul down across the bench seat, lifting Paul's left arm above his head. "We need a tourniquet. Is there a first aid kit in here?"

A voice from the driver's seat responded, "No, sir."

"How about a towel or some rags?"

"Check behind the back seat."

My mother leaned over the back seat and dug around the cargo area. "Found something." She threw a hand towel to my father. He pulled Paul's left shirt sleeve up out of the way and rolled the towel up.

"I need something to hold the towel in place. Is there a jack handle or tire iron back there?"

My mother searched around again and produced the jack handle. Fortunately, she refrained from throwing it to my father, opting to hand it to Hope, who handed it to Jakob. My father wrapped the towel around Paul's arm, near the shoulder, and used the jack handle to tighten the makeshift tourniquet.

"That'll slow the bleeding down some, but we need to get him to a hospital ASAP."

"No can do," the driver said. "You guys are still too hot to be out in public."

"We can't let him die!" Jakob exclaimed.

Dad tried to calm everyone down. "I'll do my best. But if we don't fix this wound, he'll bleed out before much longer. Faith, shine your flashlight over here so I can get a closer look."

I shined the light toward Paul's wounded arm and my father put his face down close to the injured area. "Good news is that the bullet went through and through. Bad news is that it did indeed hit the brachial artery. The flesh around the area is torn up, but not too bad. If I can find a way to close up the artery, he just might make it."

"Great," Jakob said. "Let's do that."

My father frowned. "I don't have any instruments. The tourniquet will hold for a couple hours, but anything longer than that could cause permanent damage."

Hope spoke up from the back seat. "What about the glue you used on my head? Do you still have it in your pocket?"

"Yeah, but that only works on skin. I can't use it internally. Driver, how long before we get where we're going?"

"Normally about four hours. But we can't take the shortest route because it takes us through Washington and Baltimore. We need to avoid major cities. And my name's Charlie."

Dad leaned toward the driver's seat. "Charlie, does REFUGE have any connections with any doctors or hospitals in the area? Four hours isn't going to work."

"I don't know of any, Mr. Webber. You can use my phone to call Duncan."

Dad took the phone from Charlie and made the call. "Duncan? It's Andrew Webber… Yeah, we're in the van now, but we have a problem. Paul's been shot, and he's going to bleed out if we can't get him to a hospital… I know, but you have to know somebody that can help us… I can't let him die. He saved our lives… OK… OK… Sounds good. Please hurry… OK, bye."

"What did he say?" asked Jakob.

"He's going to look for somebody that can help us, but for now, we keep driving."

Jakob's face wrinkled in disappointment. "What if nobody can help us?"

My father sighed and looked Jakob in the eyes. "He's stable enough to survive the trip, but there's a chance he'll lose his arm. We'll just have to see what happens."

We all sat in silence for the next several minutes, processing the situation and trying to recover from the chase. We were still sweaty, dirty messes from our sprint through the woods, and now that the adrenaline had left our systems, the sting of every scratch and scrape was now noticeable. I passed the time by peering out of the openings where the rear windows used to be, praying I didn't see anyone following us. I had seen a few sets of headlights here and there, but fortunately, none of them stayed behind us long enough to cause concern. I was still watching behind us when Charlie slammed on his brakes, sending us all lurching forward in our seats.

"Roadblock!"

I looked out through the windshield and saw a pair of cars blocking both lanes of traffic ahead of us. Several agents stood by the cars; guns drawn. I glanced around in all directions, looking for an escape route, but we were on a bridge, with nowhere to go but backward. Charlie realized the same thing and shifted the van into reverse. It wasn't long before another group of cars appeared on the road behind us. Charlie stopped the van, and we all looked at my father.

"Forward," he said. "Fast!"

Charlie looked like he wanted to object for a moment, but he shifted the van into drive and floored the accelerator.

My father had to yell to be heard over the sound of the wind whistling around the broken windows. "Aim for the rear wheels of the car on the left! Everybody duck!"

Charlie wasn't entirely convinced of this course of action. "Are you crazy?!"

Dad was unfazed. "If you aim for the wheels, it'll send the energy into the axle, which should push the car out of the way!"

We all stared at my father as if he were speaking a foreign language.

"What? I saw it on a TV show."

Finally convinced, Charlie continued to accelerate while we continued to duck… and pray. I could tell we were getting close because I could hear bullets as they ricocheted off the front of the van. It wouldn't be long until we made contact with the car, and my father's physics hypothesis would be put to the test. Jakob and I squeezed each other, and we both said, "I love you," at the same time. We were really close now because Charlie ducked down behind the dashboard to avoid the gunfire. We smashed into the car with a jolt that spilled us out of our seats. The van slowed but didn't stop completely. Charlie repositioned himself behind the wheel and floored the accelerator again. The van protested for a moment but soon got us back up to speed.

I didn't hear any more gunfire, so I peeked my head up and looked out the rear of the van. The collision had left one car undrivable and in a position that prevented the other vehicles from getting through. It looked like we were in the clear.

Dad looked around the van. "Everyone OK?"

One by one, we all examined ourselves and responded. Miraculously, no one else was hurt, and we were free to continue down the road.

Dad exhaled a huge breath. "We have to get off this road and out of this van. Charlie, may I use your phone?"

"No need. We have a plan. The rendezvous point is just ahead."

"Rendezvous point?"

Charlie laughed. "Yes. This isn't our first extraction, you know."

I don't know why, but we all laughed at Charlie's snarkiness. I can't say that I blame him for being a little testy in that moment, but he had maintained his composure during an intense situation.

"I have a question," my mother said from the back seat. "How did they find us? We didn't see them following us, yet they knew we would be crossing that bridge."

We all sat silently for a moment, trying to solve this new mystery. Finally, Jakob offered a response.

"Drones. Their drones are following us."

My father nodded his head in agreement. "You're right. And if that's the case, it's just a matter of time before we run into more agents. Charlie, you said you have a plan. Does that plan account for drones?"

A wry smile spread across Charlie's face. "Yes, sir."

As we approached a tunnel, Charlie's plan was about to be tested. He claimed to have performed several extractions before, but we wouldn't relax until our overhead visitors were gone.

Charlie pulled far enough into the tunnel to hide the van from the sight of the drones and flashed the van headlights three times. We watched as an SUV a large car sprang into action and approached us from inside the other end of the tunnel. The vehicles parked in front of the van and the driver of the SUV stepped out and approached the van, carrying what appeared to be binoculars. He walked out of the tunnel and scanned the sky with his binoculars. After a few moments, he approached Charlie, who rolled down his window.

"Looks like there's only one. I'll take care of it," the man said.

Dad raised his eyebrows. "He'll take care of it?"

Charlie smiled again. "Yep, you guys missed the 4th of July, so get ready for your own private fireworks show."

We looked at each other in confusion as the mystery man opened the back of his SUV and removed a gun of some sort. As he passed the van, I tried to get a closer look at the gun, but I didn't recognize it.

"What's that?" my mother asked.

Charlie turned around, and we saw his face for the first time. "That is an EMP."

Dad took this opportunity to show off his knowledge of acronyms. "Electromagnetic Pulse. It's designed to disable anything electronic."

We all watched through the back of the van as the mystery man hoisted the EMP to his shoulder, took aim, and recoiled as if he had fired a massive, invisible round from the gun. We saw several flashes of light, followed by an explosion as the drone crashed onto the street. The man surveyed the night sky with his binoculars again, but he must not have seen anything else, because he strutted back to the van and gave Charlie the "all clear."

Charlie nodded his head and turned back around to face us. "Let's go. We'll have to split up. They'll be looking for a vehicle big enough to hold all of us, so we brought two smaller cars."

Dad patted Charlie on the shoulder. "OK. Emily, you take the kids, and I'll take Paul and Jakob."

I squeezed Jakob's hand. "But I wanna go with Jakob."

My father looked at me, his eyes intense, but sympathetic. "I know, but I need him with me, in case something happens to Paul."

I considered another protest, but we were short on time.

Jakob and I climbed out of the middle row, then my mother, Hope, and Alex piled out of the back seat. Jakob and my father picked Paul up and removed him from the van, careful not to disturb the tourniquet on his arm. They approached the SUV with Charlie while the four of us walked to the car. This was the first time I got a good look at Charlie. He was an African American with short hair and a bit of a belly. Although he wasn't a physically imposing man, he carried himself in a way that made me sure he would be okay if he found his way into a tough situation.

We didn't have time to think about goodbyes, so we all simply waved to each other as we got in our vehicles. As we buckled our seat belts in the car, the brunette in the driver's seat greeted us. "Hello, Webbers. I'm Olivia."

We all greeted Olivia and watched as the SUV began to move. As it neared the edge of the tunnel, it stopped, and the EMP guy got out with his toy. He scanned the sky again with his binoculars but apparently didn't find anything. He looked disappointed because he wouldn't get to fire the EMP again. He got back in the SUV and it took off while we stayed put.

I whipped my head toward Olivia. "What are we doing?"

Olivia spoke in a reassuring manner so as not to escalate the already tense mood. "They're making sure the coast is clear. Then we'll split up and take different routes."

We sat in silence for a few moments until Olivia decided to make some small talk. "Faith, it's an honor to meet you. When I heard about this mission, I couldn't wait to volunteer so I could meet you. I have two teenage daughters and they wouldn't believe me if I told them about this."

I wasn't really in the mood to have this conversation, but I also didn't want to be rude. "Thank you. But it wasn't just me. I had help."

"I know. But you still had to go through with it. And that took courage."

I simply nodded my head in agreement.

Olivia glanced around again. "I think it's been long enough." She put the car in drive and drove us toward the edge of the tunnel. I half-expected to find another drone or some agents awaiting us, but the coast was clear. We left the road we were on as quickly as we could and made several random turns onto random roads. My mother kept asking if Olivia was lost, but she assured us that she had a plan. We had no choice but to trust her plan. I couldn't help but think this was a metaphor for life. All along the way, God has assured and reassured me that He has a plan. His plan may take us down some unexpected roads, and it may feel like we are lost, but we have to trust Him. I was still pondering this analogy when my fatigue got the better of me and I drifted off to sleep.

42

CHAPTER SIX

I opened my eyes and blinked them a few times to make them focus. The adrenaline rush from our escape was long gone, and fatigue was still gripping me. Off in the distance to my right, the lights of a city skyline appeared over the horizon. Olivia and I were the only people awake, so I would have to ask her for information.

"Where are we?"

Olivia smiled. "Don't worry, we're almost there."

I squinted, trying to find a building or landmark I recognized, but nothing. "Where's 'there?' Another safehouse?"

Olivia shook her head. "*The* safehouse."

My expression must have given away my confusion, and Olivia chuckled to herself. "We're going to REFUGE HQ. You'll be safe there."

"HQ? Where's that?"

"It's our headquarters."

I was mildly annoyed that she thought I was that dense. "Yeah, but what city is it in?"

"I can't tell you yet. The less you know…"

I rolled my eyes. "The better off we are. Yeah, I've heard that before."

The horizon was glowing orange, signaling that sunrise would soon be upon us. I took a deep breath, feeling a sense of optimism at the dawning of a new day. That optimism ended as soon as I thought of Dad, Paul, and Jakob. "Have you heard from the others?"

"Not yet. They were going to take a different route than we were, so we'll have to catch up with them later."

Olivia wouldn't tell me where we were, so I kept looking for some sort of clue. I had seen several Pennsylvania license plates, so we were probably near Philadelphia. Truthfully, our destination didn't matter that much. I had just had my fill of secrets over the past few months. I didn't have any luck prying information from Olivia, so I closed my eyes again; partly to get some rest, and partly because I wasn't in the mood for small talk. Olivia was nice enough, but I just wanted to be left alone. A low-flying helicopter broke the silence, and the sound took me back to the day after I was arrested. Paul Cross had loaded me into a helicopter, and I was flown to meet with Chancellor Sloane at the White House. The verbal barbs Cross hurled at me, the betrayal by Chancellor Sloane, the execution orders for me and my family, the needle—it all came flooding back to my mind like a tidal wave, sending my heart racing and my stomach sinking. I opened my eyes and tried to focus. The traffic was heavier now, and the bright lights of the passing cars blended together into one giant blur.

"Faith? Faith, are you OK?"

I jumped in my seat and looked back at my mother, who was now awake. "Yeah. Why?"

Mom reached up and rested her hand on my shoulder. "You're shaking. And look at your hands."

I was wringing my hands without realizing it. I pulled them apart and rested them on my lap. "Oh, I think I just got something on them and I was wiping them off. No biggie." Would she buy my excuse?

Mom studied me for a few moments before speaking. "Okay, just making sure."

Truth be told, that wasn't the first time something like that had happened to me. Several times since we entered the bunker, my eyes had lost focus, and I found myself wringing my hands or breathing heavily. It obviously wasn't normal, but what could I do about it? Everybody had enough to worry about, so I always just gritted my teeth and waited until I snapped back into reality. At first, it only took a few seconds, but the more it happened, the longer each episode lasted. Surely it would eventually end. And so would the nightmares. I would just have to stay tough until they did.

Olivia motioned toward the back seat. "Mrs. Webber, see that duffle bag on the floor? Open it and get the bags out."

Mom unzipped the bag and pulled out several plastic bags.

"Put those on. We're getting close to the city and we don't want the traffic cameras to identify you."

Traffic cameras? Just another reminder of the very real danger we faced. Mom handed me a wig, a pair of glasses, and a flimsy mask. It didn't look like a character I recognized, though. It was just a generic face. But I guess that was the point.

•◖●◗•

After another hour or so of driving and watching for unwanted visitors, we pulled into the parking lot of some sort of auto repair garage. One of the garage doors opened, and a mountain of a man in a set of dirty overalls ushered us in. He had a shaggy beard that was a combination of brown and gray, along with a ratty gray ponytail escaping through the back of a hat that had been gathering dirt and grime for quite some time.

I looked over at Olivia with squinted eyes. "*This* is HQ?"

Olivia smiled as she pulled the car into the garage and put it in park. "No, sweetie, we're just making a transfer."

I watched as the man in the overalls closed the garage door behind us. "A transfer? Transfer of what?"

"You."

Olivia opened her door, and the man in the overalls opened my door. Despite his rough appearance, he was truly a gentleman, after all. As I stood up, he turned his head, revealing the nametag that had been hidden under his beard. *Lenny*. I had never met a Lenny before. Was it short for Leonard, or was he just Lenny? He didn't look very chatty, so it was probably better not to ask him any questions about his name. I simply thanked him for opening my door, and he responded by grunting and spitting some sort of brown liquid at the ground. Most of it splattered next to his boot, but one huge glob clung to his beard and journeyed downward like a drop of dew trickling down a blade of grass. Maybe that's why his beard still had some brown in it, instead of being fully gray like his ponytail. Yeah, he was a true gentleman all right.

Sufficiently disgusted, we all got out of the car and looked around at our new surroundings. There was room for 4 cars, but the only other vehicle in the whole garage was a white delivery truck that said *Lennon Linen Service*. Maybe "Lenny" was short for "Lennon". I shook my head to clear my brain. My mind sure thinks of the most random things sometimes.

Olivia walked over to the laundry truck and motioned for us to join her. "All right, Webbers. Before we go to HQ, we need to put you in here." She unlatched the door, and it rolled upward, stopping at the top with a thud. We walked up and surveyed our new transport. It was filled with rolling laundry bins, each about twice as wide as a shopping cart. Each bin was filled with the kind of uniforms mechanics and cleaning people would wear.

Mom's protective side came out. "Olivia, you don't actually expect us to ride in here, do you?"

Olivia gestured to get Mom to calm down. "Don't worry, Mrs. Webber, it's a short drive, and all the laundry's clean. These trucks come and go at HQ every day, so this is the best way to sneak you in."

Clean… dirty… Alex didn't care. He climbed into the truck and flopped into the first bin he could find, burying himself at the bottom.

Hope craned her neck to see if she could see him. "Alex, can you breathe in there?"

Alex's hand popped out of the pile of clothes, giving us an enthusiastic thumbs up, accompanied by a few muffled giggles. Hope and I climbed into the back of the truck and looked around at the laundry bins. We were a little more selective than Alex. Mom still wasn't convinced, though. She motioned for Olivia to walk with her, away from our prying ears. We couldn't hear what Olivia said, but whatever it was, it convinced Mom to join us in the truck. Lenny must have been in a hurry to get rid of us because Mom had barely made it inside before he began to close the door. Olivia held up her hand to tell him to hold on, but he didn't like that. He rolled his eyes and spit on the ground, narrowly missing her shoe. I was beginning to like Lenny. We each found a suitable laundry bin and climbed inside, arranging the clothes to make sure we remained hidden.

Olivia called from outside the truck, "Don't come out until I tell you to. See you in a few minutes!" With that, the door slammed shut, and all I could do was wait… and wonder if we would ever see Lenny again.

The ride was dark and bumpy, but thankfully, it was short. The truck had stopped several times along the way, but this time the driver's door opened and then closed, signaling that we had reached our destination. As I waited in my laundry fort, I made a mental note to ask what brand of fabric softener they used. It smelled much nicer than the stuff in the bunker we had been living in. The back door rolled open, and footsteps approached my laundry bin. Whoever it was pushed me out of the truck, down the ramp, and onto the ground. Based on the sounds and echoes, it was obvious that we were in a large, open building of some kind. Despite my curiosity, I dared not peek my head out. We rolled for a while, through various hallways and eventually came to a stop. I heard several beeps and a slow whoosh that sounded like a spaceship door opening. We rolled a little farther, heard another whoosh, then stopped again. A bell dinged, and the sound of an opening elevator door met my ears. We rolled into the elevator and descended a few floors. Another bell dinged, and the doors opened again. We rolled out of the elevator, and Olivia told us it was safe to get out. Hope, Alex, and I extricated ourselves from our laundry bins with ease, but Mom took a little longer to get moving. Olivia held out her hand, but Mom was determined to do this on her own. A few groans and winces later, she too was standing on her feet. She caught me staring at her and furrowed her eyebrows at me. "You'll be this old someday too, you know."

Olivia and our other laundry chauffeurs left the room, and we were alone.

I'm not exactly sure what I imagined the REFUGE HQ would look like, but another underground bunker wasn't really what I had in mind. The room was sparse, to say the least. One side of the modest room featured a sofa, an oversized chair, and a television. The other side only held a large plastic table with several folding chairs around it. I glanced around for my dad, Paul, and Jakob, but they were nowhere to be seen.

Mom knew exactly who I was looking for. "I'm sure they're fine, Faith."

"Are you trying to convince me, or yourself?"

Mom smiled a half-smile and patted me on the shoulder. "Both."

I reached up and patted Mom's hand to reassure her. A door behind us creaked open, and a very tall, very elegant woman in a fitted business suit approached us. As she got closer, it became more obvious that she was older, even older than Mom and Dad, but it was also obvious that she had taken excellent care of herself over the years. She carried a tablet computer and moved with a confident grace. When she reached us, she held out her hand to shake Mom's. "Good morning, Webber family. I'm Mia, and I'll be taking over from here. We have much to talk about."

I couldn't contain myself any longer. "Where's everyone else?"

Mia looked at me and smiled. It wasn't a very warm smile, but at least she was friendlier than Lenny. "You must be Faith. The others have yet to arrive. They stopped along the way to tend to your friend's injury. You'll be relieved to know that Mr. Cross is expected to make a full recovery. Your father was able to cauterize the wound, and once Mr. Cross has received enough blood, they will be back on the road."

I exhaled a tremendous sigh of relief. "So, he's not gonna lose his arm or anything?"

"Not unless he somehow misplaces it between there and here." She was more amused by her little joke than we were.

Mom broke the awkward silence. "What is this place… besides HQ?"

"Three floors above us lies a facility that provides floor mats, uniforms, and a wide variety of laundry services for many businesses in the area. This is one of many companies REFUGE owns, but with whom we have no official ties." Mia then changed the topic. "You must be famished. Come, enjoy some breakfast, and your friends should be here before long."

The door creaked again. Olivia and the two men that had pushed our laundry carts entered, carrying several covered platters in their hands. The smells of sausage, bacon, and eggs greeted us, causing our eyes to widen. Mia gestured to a restroom door. "You may use the facilities if you wish. Enjoy your meal, and we will speak soon." With that, Mia glided out of the room.

We took care of our business and sat down at the table for our first meal in weeks that didn't come from a box or a can. Olivia and a man we had never seen before brought us our plates, overflowing with food. Alex looked at the plate, then looked up at Olivia. "No pancakes?"

Mom glared at Alex, but Olivia laughed it off and tussled Alex's already messy hair. "Those are on the menu for tomorrow. We'll leave you alone to eat, and then we'll be back in a little while to clean up."

We all said, "Thank you," and watched as Olivia and her friends left the room. I surveyed my plate, trying to decide what to eat first. I grabbed a thick slice of bacon, tore it in half, and tossed a piece in my mouth. I held it on my tongue for a few moments, savoring the smoky saltiness of the meat, and sucking all the juice out. I had almost forgotten what actual food tasted like. I scarfed down the other half of the bacon slice without savoring it, just in time to catch a look from my mother.

"Aren't you forgetting something?"

I wrinkled my forehead and stared back at her. "Thank you?"

Mom kept staring at me, waiting for me to come up with the right answer, but I was still oblivious. She finally whispered to me. "The blessing!"

I sucked the bacon fragments out of my teeth with my tongue. "Oh yeah. The blessing. Duh."

We all folded our hands and bowed our heads. Mom was sure to unleash one of her long, eloquent prayers that would last until our food got cold, so I spoke first. "Bless the eggs, bless the meat, thank you, God, now let's eat. Amen!"

Hope and Alex shouted, "Amen!", and we picked up our forks. We were just about to dig in when we all looked at Mom, who remained motionless. She didn't have to say a word; we knew what she was telling us. We put our forks down and bowed our heads again, giving her a chance to speak.

"Our gracious Heavenly Father, who has been faithful, and delivered us from so much, we thank you that your hand of protection has been on us, and we thank you for the wonderful people that you have sent to help us in our time of need."

Great. She was already 30 seconds in and hadn't even

mentioned the food, or the hands that prepared it.

She continued, "We ask that you continue to be with Andrew, Paul, and Jakob, and bring them to us safely. We ask for your protection and guidance as we take the next steps in our journey. We thank you for this meal that you have graciously provided for us, and we ask you to bless the food and the hands that prepared it. In your name we pray, Amen."

We all stared at Mom for a few more seconds to make sure it was safe to eat. Once she picked up her fork, we were free to pick ours up as well. Over the years, I had enjoyed some delicious meals, but this may have been the one I appreciated the most. Too bad the others weren't there to enjoy it with us.

CHAPTER SEVEN

I didn't count how many pieces of bacon I ate, but if I had to guess, the number would be high. Very high. My overindulgence was probably more a result of my anxiety than my appetite, but it was delicious either way. It had been a long, boring day. We had exchanged one small living space underground for another. Alex and Hope wanted to run around, but her head injury and the cramped space didn't allow very much fun.

Mia had disappeared right before breakfast, then returned a couple of hours later to ask us if we wanted any lunch. The thought of eating another proper meal was tempting, but we were still so full from breakfast we politely refused. Mia then disappeared again and had yet to resurface. Whatever she did for REFUGE, it kept her very busy.

Before Mia left, I asked if they had a computer I could borrow. At first, she was hesitant, but she finally relented and allowed Olivia to bring me one. I didn't know what I was going to do with the computer but having one made me feel more at home. I surfed the Internet for a while to see what was trending but soon became bored with that. There wasn't any news from back home, except for a minor explosion in a food plant. Fortunately, no one was injured, but production of canned meat was going to be reduced for the next several weeks. Good thing we were out of the bunker, and no longer depended on canned meat to survive.

A pit formed in my stomach as I thought about our home. It had been vacant for several months now, so there was no telling what kind of condition it was in. And what happened to all our stuff? Did the government seize the house and take all our belongings away?

What about my clothes and pictures? I closed my eyes and took a mental tour of my room. I saw my bed; unmade of course. I saw several pairs of shoes littered across the floor. I saw my desk. And on my desk, I saw the picture of me and Audrey from last Christmas. The smile on my face was so carefree and showed a young girl who had no idea of the fate that awaited her a couple of months later when Jakob moved in across the street. I compared that face to the face I most recently saw in the mirror and shuddered at how much I had aged in less than a year. The dark circles under my eyes, the pale hue of my skin, and though I would never have called myself overweight back then, I had definitely lost several pounds I didn't need to lose. Even though I loved Jakob, I found myself wishing I could return to that Christmas and spend time with my best friend again.

The thought of Audrey caused me to check my e-mail so I could read her message again. I couldn't respond, but perhaps reading her words would be of comfort to me. I scrolled through several new messages, and to my surprise, I had a new message from Audrey. The subject said, "I'm so glad you're alive!" That certainly caught my attention, so I clicked on it.

Hey Faith, it's Audrey. You're not going to believe what happened. A bunch of government agents came to my house and took me prisoner. They told me you were still alive and they wanted me to help them find you. They threatened to arrest my parents if I didn't help. I was scared and didn't know what to do. I couldn't believe you're still alive and I was so happy to hear that, but now we are in trouble. They still say that REFUGE is trying to overthrow Chancellor Sloane, and they want to stop them before a war starts. They said if I can't convince you to turn yourselves in, they're going to arrest us for helping traitors. I don't want to hurt you but I don't want to hurt my family either. You can't let them put us in prison. They said all you have to do is tell us where you are and it'll be over. They promise not to kill you or your family if you tell them everything you know about REFUGE so they can be stopped. I'm sorry to do this to you but I don't know what else to do. Please help us!

-   Audrey

The lump in my throat and the pit in my stomach grew larger with every sentence I read. How did they even know about Audrey? I let out an audible groan when I realized what must have happened. They must have figured out I hacked into Dan the Man's phone and e-mailed my story to Audrey. That means they've read my story and that's how they knew about the secret bunker under the cabin. I silently scolded myself for putting Audrey in danger, but I wanted my story to get out, so the truth wouldn't die with me. By trying to solve one problem I created countless more and put my best friend in harm's way. I hovered over the "Reply" button, but I realized I couldn't actually reply until I had spoken with Dad about it. I stared at the screen for a few more minutes, praying Audrey was safe. All the anxiety got the better of me, and my mouth felt tingly. I gagged and reached for a trash can just in time to lose my breakfast.

***

Now it was nearly supper time, and we still had not heard from my dad or Jakob. Mia had assured us that they were OK, but I wouldn't allow myself to relax until I put my eyes on them. Mom sat in the chair most of the day, trying to keep Hope and Alex somewhat calm, and I sprawled out on the couch, trying to find something on TV to keep my mind off Audrey and her family. The TV didn't get many channels, so there wasn't much to choose from. The channels they did get were based out of Philadelphia, so it looked like I was right about our location after all.

My finger was tired of changing channels on the TV, so I settled on a baseball game, just to pass the time. Hope and Alex occupied themselves by playing in the restroom sink, and I looked over at Mom. Hope and Alex always annoyed me, but they had to be getting on her nerves by now. "You OK?"

Mom looked over at me with dark circles under her eyes. "Yeah. Just tired."

"Me too."

She didn't have to energy to use many words. Neither did I. We sat for a few more minutes, watching the boring baseball game. Some guy I had never heard of hit a home run off some other guy I had never heard of, sending the crowd into a frenzy. How could people get so caught up in a silly game when there were so many more important things going on? I looked over at Mom to get her thoughts on the game, but she was asleep. I turned my attention back to the TV, then a voice from behind me caused me to flinch.

"That was quite a hit, wasn't it, Jellybean?"

I turned to see my father standing in the doorway. I sprinted to him, nearly knocking him over with my affection. We embraced for a few moments, then I glanced behind him to see if anyone else was there. "Where's Jakob… and Paul?"

"They're still being debriefed in another room. I told them I had to see my family before I could talk to them anymore."

Hope and Alex turned the sink off and joined Dad for their own hug. All the commotion couldn't rouse Mom from her sleep, so Dad walked over and knelt on the floor in front of her chair. He patted her on the knee and softly called her name. Mom lifted her head and rubbed her eyes, not sure whether she could believe what she was seeing. She touched Dad's face, and once she realized she wasn't dreaming, she reached out and pulled him to her. They laughed and cried for a few moments, and then kissed each other.

Alex stuck out his tongue to punctuate his disgust. "Eww, TBA!"

Hope smacked him on the arm. "It's PDA, dork wad."

Normally, my parents would have yelled at Hope for calling Alex an ugly name, but they were either too tired or too happy to say anything. Dad plopped down in the middle of the couch, and the rest of the kids joined him.

I glanced over at the door but still didn't see anyone. "Daddy, are they almost done?"

"Yes, Jellybean. They'll be here any…"

Before he could finish his sentence, Jakob and Paul stepped through the doorway. I sprinted to Jakob and planted a huge kiss on his lips. I had never kissed Jakob in front of my parents before, but my excitement got the better of me. Dad was probably a little mad, but he didn't say anything. I finally let go of Jakob and turned my attention to Paul. His left arm was in a sling, but other than that, you wouldn't have known that he had been shot the day before. I reached my arm around his good side and gave him a delicate hug. "I'm so glad to see you. Thanks for not dying on us."

Paul laughed. "The pleasure is all mine."

I looked at our reunited group and smiled. Then a thought hit me. "Well, we're out of the bunker. Now what?"

We all looked at each other, but no one spoke. Finally, Dad spoke up. "I guess I need to talk to Duncan."

Paul adjusted his sling, which was obviously bothering him. "We can't just sit around doing nothing, though. We need to go on the offensive. Regain our momentum."

Dad rubbed his eyes and shook his head. Apparently, this was the continuation of a previous conversation. "This isn't a military exercise."

Paul walked toward my father. "Sloane's treating it like one. If we are to survive, we should do the same thing."

Dad held his hands out, gesturing toward the rest of the family. "We're civilians. We aren't like you and Jakob."

Jakob's ears perked up. "What does that mean?" I had never seen him get confrontational with my dad.

We were all exhausted, and tensions were high, so Mom stood up and got between the men. "Look, we don't have to have this conversation right now. Let's all get settled, get cleaned up, and have a nice dinner. Then we can worry about what happens next. Deal?"

Dad and Paul looked each other up and down to see who would reach out first. A few tense moments passed, and Dad finally held out his hand toward Paul.

Paul took Dad's hand and shook it with a moderate amount of hostility. "Deal. Do you think they have any beard trimmers around here?" He adjusted his sling again and left the room to talk to someone.

I put my hand on my father's arm to get his attention. "Daddy? I need to show you something."

"What is it, Jellybean?"

I dragged him to the table that held the computer and showed him Audrey's e-mail. He frowned as he read it, then locked eyes with me. "You didn't reply, did you?"

I shook my head. "No, I didn't know what to do, but I knew I couldn't reply until I talked to you."

At about that time, Jakob came out of the bathroom and joined me and Dad. The tense looks on our faces caused him to stop in his tracks. "What's going on?"

Dad could tell I didn't want to talk so he answered for me. "Audrey sent Faith an e-mail. She said agents came to her house and threatened her. If Faith doesn't turn herself in, they'll arrest Audrey and her family."

Jakob turned and locked eyes with me. "You didn't reply, did you?"

I threw my hands up in the air. "You too?! Why do you both just assume I'll do something stupid?"

Jakob put his hand on my shoulder, but I shook it off. "Faith, that's not what I meant. You're not stupid."

"Wow, that makes me feel better. I can't believe you two. My best friend's in danger, and your first instinct is to protect yourselves." I stomped away, looking for a door to slam, but I didn't know my way around yet, so all I could do was lock myself in the bathroom. I cried alone for a few minutes, wondering who would be brave enough and stupid enough to try to talk to me. The answer came a short while later with the sound of a knock and my father's voice on the other side of the door.

"Faith?"

"Go away."

Dad sighed. "Faith, we need to talk. Either you come out, or I'm coming in."

"How? The door's locked."

"Just let me in."

I mumbled under my breath; half-hoping Dad heard me. "What are you gonna do? Send me to my room?"

"I want to help, but we have to be smart about this."

"Fine." I unlocked the door and let my father in. "What do you suggest?"

Dad shook his head. "I don't know. We can't give them what they want though. You know that."

I pleaded with tears forming in my eyes. "But what about Audrey? And her family? They didn't do anything wrong."

Dad brushed my hair with his fingers. "I know, Jellybean. This isn't fair. But I'll do everything I can to help them. I just need a little bit of time to think of something."

I hugged Dad and rested my head on his shoulder. "Promise?"

"I promise."

Our bunker underneath Lennon Linen had a full kitchen, but what we really wanted that night was pizza. We also wanted to get out and breathe some fresh air, but we all agreed that we should avoid any unnecessary risks. Besides, Olivia had told us that the employees of Lennon were unaware of the secret bunker, so we were forbidden from mingling with them.

My stomach had been growling off and on for nearly an hour as we waited for Olivia and Charlie to return with the pizza. Jakob had to have heard it since he was sitting right next to me, but he was too polite to say anything. He snickered once but tried to play it off by turning his laugh into a cough. He didn't fool me, but I appreciated the effort.

Mia hadn't checked on us since lunchtime. Even though she told us she would be taking care of us, she was content to leave most of the heavy lifting to Olivia. I had asked Dad about Mia, but he wasn't much help. He knew she worked closely with Duncan, but he either didn't know more or couldn't tell me more about her. Either way, her constant absence was mysterious.

The room grew silent as we all rested, and my stomach decided that would be a great time to growl loudly enough to shake the walls. Everyone's eyes widened at me, and I lowered my head to hide my blushing face. "I can't help it. I'm starving. Laugh if you want."

Jakob put his arm around me. "It's OK. I still love you."

We all cheered as Olivia and Charlie finally entered the room, carrying five pizzas and four bottles of soda. Hope jumped to her feet and held up her arms to hold everyone else at bay. "Better let Faith go first, or else she's gonna eat one of us."

My face turned red again, but I didn't try to hide it this time. "Yeah, I'm gonna start with a slice of Hope-peroni pizza." I stood up and ran toward Hope, who hid behind Mom.

Mom patted Hope on the shoulder and glared at me. "This took a dark turn, didn't it?"

I shot Hope a look. "She started it."

Olivia set the pizza boxes down on a table and opened the lids.

"We have cheese, pepperoni, and sausage. Help yourselves. There's plenty."

Mom went through the line with Hope and Alex first. Dad gestured for me to go next, and I didn't argue. Olivia had told us this was the best pizza place in the city and based on the smell, she was right. I started with two slices of pepperoni, and one slice of sausage. The pizza was so hot, the cheese stretched about two feet before finally letting go of the rest of the pizza. I poured a cup of root beer and sat down at the table. This was torture. I'd have to wait until everyone got their food, and then Mom would want to pray some long prayer again before I could eat. I couldn't wait. When she turned away to help Alex with his drink, I wolfed down a huge bite of pizza. It was amazing. I had just bitten off my next piece when Mom looked back at me, freezing me in my tracks. The hot cheese burned the roof of my mouth, but I couldn't swallow it.

Mom cocked her head. "Why are your eyes watering?"

"I'm just happy." But when I pronounced the *p* sound in *happy*, some pizza shrapnel escaped my mouth and landed on the floor. I swallowed the rest of the pizza and swished some root beer around my mouth to cool it off.

Mom could only shake her head. "Serves you right."

• ● •

Somehow, the nine of us finished all five pizzas. I think Jakob and I each ate an entire pizza by ourselves. I was miserable, but it was totally worth it. We sat around all evening watching TV and avoiding the conversation Paul had tried to start earlier. Eventually, he couldn't wait any longer. "Are we ever going to address the elephant in the room?"

Alex had been half asleep, but his ears perked up and he looked around. Mom patted him on the head. "There's not a real elephant, sweetheart. It's just a saying."

Dad leaned forward in his chair. "I haven't been able to reach Duncan yet. When Mia comes back, we'll talk to her and see what she says."

Paul frowned. "Where is this Mia, anyway? Is she ever coming back?"

Olivia chimed in to come to her boss's defense. "She'll be in here any minute. She's a busy woman."

Right on cue, Mia entered the room. It was nearly 11:00 at night, but she was still wearing the same business suit she wore earlier, and her hair was still perfect. "My apologies for being away so long. I trust Olivia and Charlie are taking sufficient care of you?"

We all nodded our heads.

"Excellent. I'm sure you all have questions, and I shall do my best to accommodate you. But first... "

Paul never found a beard trimmer, so he was still a little grumpy about his shaggy beard. "Yeah, I have questions. Who are you? What do you do around here? When do we get to see Duncan? What are we doing next?"

Mia remained calm and measured every word with care as she spoke. "Mr. Cross... our sincerest thanks to you and Jakob for being brave enough to come to our aid. The entire REFUGE organization owes you our deepest gratitude."

"You're welcome. But you still didn't answer my questions. We can't just sit around in hiding for the rest of our lives. We must take action."

"Mr. Cross, I understand your eagerness to act, and I assure you, that time will soon come. We must take a deliberate approach, though. Any missteps could jeopardize everything we have worked so hard to accomplish."

Paul scoffed but didn't say anything.

Mia closed her eyes for a moment before she opened them again and answered. "Mr. Cross, I am happy to answer all the questions I am able to answer. Firstly, no one meets with Duncan. His identity and location must be protected at all times. I serve as Duncan's deputy. He and I are of the same mind when it comes to strategic matters, so I am more than qualified to speak on his behalf. We are now going to discuss our options, and if you are willing, you and Jakob are welcome to join us. Your familiarity with the Chancellor should prove valuable to our endeavor."

We all looked at Paul to await his response.

"Fine. Let's get this ball rolling."

Again, Alex's head popped up, and he looked around the room. Mom patted him on the top of the head and whispered. "I'm sorry, sweetheart. There's no ball either." Alex laid his head back down, and soon he joined Hope in peaceful slumber, leaving us adults to discuss the important matters at hand.

Charlie gathered and discarded the empty pizza boxes to make room for us at the table. Everyone sat down in the folding chairs, except Mom, who stayed on the couch with Hope and Alex. She didn't want to risk waking them up, and besides, their dead weight didn't allow her much freedom of movement. She was content to use her one free hand to use the television remote and listen to our conversation.

Mia was in charge, so we all looked at her to start the conversation. "Everyone, I thank you for your patience, and I admire your bravery in the face of such extreme circumstances. I know the past few months have been challenging, but you rose to meet those challenges, and in so doing, you have come to this place. Not just this physical place, but this place in history. We stand on the precipice of something larger than ourselves. Duncan and I have conducted lengthy discussions about our next steps, and we are confident that we will emerge victorious. Now we must summon the courage to proceed."

Wow. I thought Mom talked for a long time when she prayed. Mia had her beat.

Paul wasn't much for pleasantries. He preferred action. "Nice speech. So, what's the plan?"

Mia smiled her strained smile at Paul. "I like you. You have spirit. Our goal remains the same. We are fighting for freedom. This country was founded on the concept of religious freedom, and we must return to our roots. Chancellor Sloane has reshaped this once great nation and used fear to extinguish the freedoms we once enjoyed. It is up to us to reignite that flame. We have invested years building financial support and manpower, but we never quite knew how we could accomplish our goal… until Faith came along."

"Me? What did I do?"

"You figured out the true use of the microchips. They control the mind of the person in whom they are implanted. As you told Duncan, it is how Sloane was able to convince the military to join his revolution, and how he has continued to serve as Chancellor, long after his term should have expired. It has been his greatest source of power, and soon it will be his downfall. If we take away his control over people, everything can return to normal."

Paul closed his eyes and shook his head. "You want to use his microchips against him? That sounds great in theory, but how do you propose to do this?"

Mia smirked. "I was about to ask you the same question. You know how he controls them. You must have some insight on how we can gain control of them."

"There are only two facilities with access to the Oversight program. The Pentagon and the White House."

I offered a potential solution. "Maybe we can hack in remotely. It would take some time, but it might work."

Paul waved off my idea. "The Oversight servers are not connected to the Internet, so there is no remote access. The only way to take control is to be at one of the computers."

Dad stood up and paced the floor. "There's no way we can do that. We can't just waltz into the Pentagon or the White House. Paul, not even you could do that."

"The Pentagon isn't an option anyway. The Oversight computer in the Pentagon only controls the military side. Sloane controls everything from the White House, using his office computer. The only way this works is if we're sitting at his computer."

Mia was the only one who didn't look defeated. "Well, I suppose that is what you will have to do."

Dad looked at Mia with an incredulous look on his face. "How would we, the most wanted people in the country, not only sneak into the White House but get on Sloane's computer?"

"I admit, it sounds rather challenging, but I believe there is always a way. Mr. Cross, how does the Chancellor's computer communicate with his microchips when they are spread all around the world?"

"Satellites. But it's a direct link between his computer and the main satellite, so there is no way to hijack the signal without being at the White House and controlling the satellite dish. But you're forgetting something. Even if we somehow get control of the microchips, we will need permanent access to them. How are we going to do that? We can't park someone at Sloane's computer until your mission is accomplished."

It sure seemed like Mia's plan was going to be over before it even started. She wasn't going to give up without a fight though. "Does the Oversight satellite serve any other function, or is it solely dedicated to that program?"

Paul frowned as he thought for a moment. "I'm pretty sure that's all it does. Why?"

"What if we could somehow get remote access to the Chancellor's computer without him knowing? Then when the time is right, we take control of the Oversight program on his computer, use that link to take control of that satellite, and free everyone under his control."

Paul continued to shoot down every one of Mia's suggestions. "I guess that would work. But I just told you, his computer isn't connected to the Internet. There's no way to hack into it from here. Someone has to be there."

Jakob snapped his fingers. "We could use a leech."

I wrinkled my nose at Jakob's interesting suggestion. "A leech? What in the world is a leech?"

"It's a device that you can stick on a computer, and it lets you control it from somewhere else. Paul, wouldn't this work?"

"Again, in theory, this sounds like a good idea, but someone still has to get into the Oval Office and stick it to Sloane's computer. I don't see that happening."

A lump formed in my throat, and my heart pounded harder than usual as a solution popped into my head. "I can do it."

Dad stopped pacing and stared at me. "You? No way. We almost lost you once. I'm not doing that again."

"Dad, think about it. I'm the only one that can get in there. It has to be me."

Jakob grabbed my arm as if I were about to march off to the White House at that moment. "No, Faith. Paul, don't you know anyone you can trust?"

"Jakob, think about it. Everyone that has access to the White House also has a chip in their head. There's no way they would go along with this."

I rested my hand on Jakob's. "See, it has to be me. I just need to get one of these leech thingies and get myself arrested again. No big deal."

Mia took a deep breath and spoke. "Faith, I admire your bravery. I wish there were another way, but I'm afraid you may be our only option. The way I see it, there are two phases to this plan. Phase one is getting Faith arrested, and phase two is installing the leech."

Dad was obviously upset about this plan, but he didn't say anything. He simply returned to his pacing, content to let Paul and Mia take the lead on the strategizing process.

Paul tapped his fingers on the table as he thought. "Getting Faith arrested is the easy part. Keeping her alive will be the real challenge."

Mia nodded her head in agreement. "Before she was executed, Faith was able to reach a large number of people and persuade them to protest in the parks. She has a following, so why not use that?"

Jakob sat up in his chair and snapped his fingers again. "What if she doesn't get arrested? What if she gets herself invited to the White House?"

"How am I gonna do that?"

"What if we made a video, showing that Faith's still alive? Then she could say that she wants to meet with Sloane to talk things out."

Mia and Paul thought about that for a while, then I continued Jakob's train of thought. "Yeah. I could use my followers as leverage, so he has to meet with me, or risk more protests."

Dad walked over and leaned toward the table. "For the record, this is a horrible idea. What's going to stop him from killing you when you get there?"

"That's the beauty of it. If everyone knows I'm still alive, he can't kill me, can he? The outrage would be too strong."

A tense hush settled in the room as we processed this possibility. It sounded good in our minds, but was there some angle we weren't considering yet? I couldn't risk my life again for a plan that wasn't fully scrutinized.

Mia was the first to break the silence. "This idea has merit. It would be simple enough to produce this video, but we must make sure she includes details that prove the video was not recorded before her execution, and we must have a large audience. I'm afraid the latter will be more difficult than the former."

Jakob looked around at the rest of us. "She's right. It won't do any good to make this video if nobody sees it. How do we get people to watch?"

As we thought, the television volume got louder, and Paul turned to Mom. "Can you please turn that down? We're trying to talk."

Mom didn't say a word, she simply pointed at the TV. The news had come on, and the TV station was showing a story about Sloane's upcoming address. Every year around this time he made a big speech about how great he was, and all the television networks were forced to cover it. Millions of people would be watching. We all sat speechless, thinking the same thought. After the story was over, Mom turned the volume back down, and we just stared at each other.

Mia unfolded herself from her seat and stood to her feet. She looked especially tall from this angle. "That speech is in two days. That does not leave us much time to prepare. "Where would we obtain a leech and the equipment to hijack this television signal?"

Paul and Jakob shared a strange look, and Jakob's face turned a slight shade of red. I squeezed Jakob's hand. "What's wrong?"

He looked down at the table, refusing to make eye contact with me. "Nothing. Why?"

"I don't know. You just got all weird all of a sudden."

Jakob continued to stare down at the table, and Paul stepped in to answer Mia's question. "I don't have any of those items, but I know who to ask."

Jakob looked at Paul, pleading with his eyes, but his pleas were denied.

"Jakob, we don't have a choice."

Jakob looked down at the table again and muttered, "No... Anyone but her."

CHAPTER EIGHT

Agent Belford opened the door and walked into Audrey's cell. She had waited in the computer room for a couple of hours after sending her e-mail to Faith, but Belford then relocated her to a more comfortable room to wait for a reply. She was able to lie down on a cot, but she was too nervous and upset to get any sleep. She sat up on her cot when she saw the agent enter the room. "Did Faith answer me yet?"

Belford shook his head. "No. I knew it was a long shot, but it was worth a try. At the very least, I'm sure it put pressure on her."

"So, what happens next?"

Belford dragged a chair across the concrete floor and sat down next to Audrey's cot. "Well, you've held up your end of the bargain, so I'm willing to do you a favor. How would you like to see your parents?"

Audrey sat up straight. "Really?"

"Yes."

"Does that mean I'm done?"

Belford took in a deep breath and let it out. "Not exactly. But you're trying to do the right thing, so I want to reward that. So, I'll take you home and let you visit for an hour or two. But we need to leave now before it gets any later."

Audrey sprang to her feet and marched toward the door. "Okay, let's go."

Less than an hour later, Agent Belford, Audrey, and two other agents pulled into Audrey's driveway. Belford had let Audrey call her parents, so they were waiting at the window when the SUV appeared out front. Audrey's parents sprinted out toward the SUV, but Audrey couldn't open the door from the inside. The agent in the front passenger seat opened the door, allowing the Gibson family to reunite in the driveway. They hugged and cried for a few moments before Belford asked them all to step inside the house. Once they made it to the living room, they all sat down.

"Mr. and Mrs. Gibson, I know this has been alarming, but I want you to know that Audrey has performed admirably. She has done everything we asked of her, and I have no doubt that her help will bring these fugitives to justice."

Audrey's dad replied with a slight amount of sternness in his voice. He tried to sound assertive but didn't press too hard. "Does that mean you're done with her?"

"I wish that were the case. Unfortunately, our plan hasn't worked yet. We still believe Audrey is the key to convincing Faith to turn herself in. We just need to put more pressure on her."

Mrs. Gibson spoke up for the first time. "More pressure? Haven't you put our daughter through enough already?"

Belford shook his head again. "No, we need Audrey to put more pressure on Faith. I know we came in here yesterday with quite a bit of force, but I assure you, we will be nothing but civil. Audrey's not a prisoner at this time, but we do need her to continue to help us. It's not an exaggeration to say that the security of the whole country depends on her success."

Audrey's parents looked at each other, and then at their only child. Belford's tone was much different now, and he genuinely seemed to care about their family. Mr. Gibson looked at Belford. "We don't really have a choice, do we?"

"Not really. I would much rather do this with your cooperation though. I give you my word as a father; Audrey will be safe, well-fed, and she'll have a comfortable bed to sleep in. We'll also give you a phone number to call, and we'll allow her to call you as well."

Audrey looked at her parents. "He's right. They're treating me well. He told me that if I get Faith to turn herself in, they won't arrest her. They're only after the people her dad works for."

I squeezed Jakob's hand even tighter than before. "Her? Who's her?"

"Faith don't make me do this. There's gotta be another way. We just have to keep thinking."

Mia was growing impatient. "Jakob, we do not have time. If this mystery woman is our best option, we must employ it."

Jakob stood up and stormed out of the room without saying another word. I pointed at the door to ask the others if I should go after him. Paul nodded his head, and I joined Jakob in the hall. He was leaning against the wall, shoulders slumped, head down. My mind was racing, trying to figure out what could be so bad about this person. I leaned up against the wall next to Jakob and nudged him with my shoulder. "I don't know what's going on, or what this person did wrong, but if she can help us, we have to try."

"I can't talk about it."

"Well, why don't you start by telling me her name."

"Her name?"

I nudged his shoulder again to try to keep the mood light. "Yes. She does have a name, doesn't she?"

Jakob nodded.

"Then what is it?"

Jakob had never been at a loss for words like this before. Whoever this woman was, he must really be afraid of her. But why?

Jakob's toes began to tap on the floor. He was more nervous than I had ever seen him. "Her name... her name is Corinne Maxwell."

"Corinne? That's a beautiful name. So, what's wrong with Corinne? Why are you so afraid of her?"

"Faith..."

I turned to face Jakob, lifting his chin so his eyes met mine. "Jakob, help me understand. Why do you hate this woman so much?" My heart was pounding, and a nauseous feeling was building in my stomach. I was bracing myself to hear some bad news.

Jakob sighed and tilted his head down again. "I don't hate her. We used to work together."

My heart slowed down, and the nausea subsided. "Oh. Well, that's not too bad. You got me all worked up for nothing. Let's call her tomorrow and see if she can get what we need."

"Faith? There's something more."

The nausea returned. "Something more?"

"Corinne was my girlfriend."

I folded my arms across my chest. "You mean ex-girlfriend?"

Jakob couldn't speak. He could only shake his head. Not the answer I was looking for.

Now I was the one tapping my foot on the floor. "*I'm* your girlfriend. You can only have one."

"This is a long story. Are you sure you're ready to hear this?"

"Not really but go ahead."

Jakob took in a deep breath and began to spill the truth. "Well, I guess you were bound to find out eventually, so here goes... Corinne and I used to work together. She's an expert in electronics, so she supported the field agents, like me, on our missions. She normally didn't go out into the field herself, but on one mission about a year and a half ago, I had to travel to another country, and we needed her technical expertise. We spent a lot of time together on this trip and kinda started developing feelings. Once we got back to the States, we began to date."

I didn't like where this was going, but I couldn't move. I just stood in silence, waiting for Jakob to tell the rest of this harrowing tale.

"We dated for a few months, and eventually fell in love, then a few months later we moved in together. We were young, but our line of work makes you grow up fast."

Beads of cold sweat formed on my forehead, and my legs went numb. I had to sit down on the floor to keep from falling out.

Jakob slid down the wall, and joined me on the floor, resting on his knees. "Faith, listen... you gotta remember, this was before I found God. Before I found you."

My nose began to run, but I didn't have the energy to care. "Jakob... I"

"I know. This is a lot to take in. I wanted to tell you, but when could I?"

I wiped my nose with my sleeve and looked up at Jakob. "Wait. She can't help us. Doesn't she have a chip in her head?"

"She used to. She got it removed when she left our agency."

"Left? Why did she leave?"

"The stress of her job weighed on her too much, and she became too emotionally unstable to keep working. Her boss told her to either resign or be discharged. She chose to resign, but she made an agreement that she would keep all her secrets if they removed her chip. She left her job, but she still has connections. Connections that'll lead us to the equipment we need. There's one huge problem though."

I scoffed and wiped my nose again. It was gross, but I really didn't care in that moment. "Only *one*? I'm seeing tons of problems right now."

"No, this is a really big problem."

I threw my hands up in the air, nearly striking Jakob in the face. "Jakob, just spill it. I'm already upset, so just tell me everything."

"Well, I wanted to break up with Corinne a while back, but then she started having problems at work. She was going through a lot, so I just couldn't make myself break her heart too. I planned on breaking up with her when I got back from this mission. When I never returned, she probably assumed I was dead."

I looked at Jakob with tear-filled eyes. "Wait a minute. If you show up at her house alive, she's gonna treat you like her boyfriend again?"

Jakob nodded his head slowly as I was processing the ugly truth. "Exactly. And I can't tell her about me and you, because then she won't help us. She may even turn us in."

My hands took on a life of their own and began to squeeze each other. The room became blurry. The walls began to move. I leaned over and sat on my knees, with my hands resting on the floor in front of me. My body wanted to throw up, but I had to hold it in.

Jakob rested his hand on my shoulder. "Faith, are you OK?"

"I don't know if I can do this. I can't watch some other girl put her hands on you or kiss you."

Jakob's hand stroked my shoulder. "I know. Believe me, I don't want to put you through this. It won't be easy for me either."

My vision cleared and I snapped my head around to face him. "Don't you dare make this about you. I'm the one that's being hurt by this."

Jakob let go of my shoulder and held his hands up. "You're right. I'm sorry. I can't imagine how hard this is. I wouldn't do it if we had another option. Just know that whatever happens, it's all an act. It's part of the mission."

Several tears flowed out of my eyes and dripped onto the floor. "Like you were with me when we met?" My lips quivered as I spoke.

Jakob was taken aback by my barb. "We've gone over this. Yes, I was only pretending to like you at first. But then I fell in love for real. Faith, I even risked my life for you."

The rage subsided. I still hurt, but I was finally coming to grips with this latest revelation. "I know. I probably shouldn't have said that. I just don't know what to think right now. Why didn't you ever tell me about this?"

"Well, I kinda thought it would take care of itself. As long as I never saw her again, she would just keep thinking I was dead, and I could just be with you. Please don't be mad."

I wiped the tears off my face with my dry sleeve. This shirt was definitely going to need a good cleaning after all this. I looked at Jakob with bleary eyes and took his hands in mine. "I don't know if I'm mad, or maybe I'm just shocked. I'm not mad at you for having a life before you met me. And I don't know if I should be mad at you for not telling me about her before. I kinda understand why you didn't, but this is a huge secret. And if you and I are gonna have a future together, we can't have huge secrets."

"No more secrets? OK, now that you mention it, there's this other girl..." Jakob's voice trailed off and he winked at me.

I slugged him in the shoulder and glared at him with a playful look in my eyes. "Not funny." My hand hurt, but it was worth it.

Once I had calmed myself down, Jakob and I went back to face the rest of the group. The looks on everyone's faces made it obvious that Paul had told them about Corinne while Jakob and I were in the hall.

Dad gave me a big hug. "You OK, Jellybean?"

"Uh-huh."

"I can't imagine how you're feeling right now. It's an impossible situation. But I know you, and I know you're strong enough to handle anything."

I leaned the side of my head against Dad's and whispered in his ear. "Daddy, I can't do this. This girl. She's gonna be all over Jakob, and there's nothing we can do about it."

"I know. Try not to think about that. Try to focus on all the people you'll be helping. Isn't that worth all this?"

I lifted my head off his shoulder and wiped my tears again. "I guess. This is almost worse than being executed. I felt a lot braver about that."

Dad lifted his eyebrows and smiled. "That shouldn't make sense, but it does."

Jakob and I rejoined the rest of the group at the table to figure out how to get Corinne to help us.

------- • ● • -------

We talked about our plan until nearly 2:00 AM before settling down for the night. Paul slept in the bunker's only bed because of his injury, which put Mom and Dad on the sofa and chair, while Jakob, Hope, Alex, and I spread out on the floor. Not the most ideal sleeping arrangement, but at least we were safe. Jakob either fell asleep quickly or acted like he was asleep, so he wouldn't have to talk about Corinne anymore. I desperately wanted to know more about her, but it would have been cruel to keep him awake for that. I tossed and turned for a couple of hours after bedtime, before finally falling asleep sometime around 4:00. The bunker must have had cameras because Charlie and Olivia walked in a few minutes after we woke up around 10:00.

Alex finally got his pancakes. They weren't as delicious as Dad's, but we certainly didn't complain. We told Oliva that we wouldn't need lunch because we had eaten breakfast so late, so she and Charlie put some snack foods in the kitchen before they left. Charlie stashed a couple of snack cakes in his pocket before closing the cabinet, but I didn't say anything. A shower and a fresh set of clothes made us feel human again. Paul was finally able to trim his beard with a set of clippers Charlie brought him, so he was in a much more agreeable mood.

Mia finally rejoined us around 2:00 that afternoon. She had told Duncan about our plan, and although he said it was risky, he didn't see a better option. What followed was a lengthy, and sometimes heated, discussion about the details of our mission. Jakob and I obviously had to go, but who would go with us? Dad didn't have any experience with this sort of thing, and Paul was too injured to be much help, so it would have to be just me and Jakob. At first, Jakob didn't want me to go with him to Corinne's house, but I refused to leave him alone with her. It's not that I didn't trust him. I didn't trust her. I had to hope she would behave herself around Jakob with another woman around. After much discussion, Jakob relented and said I could tag along, but I would have to pretend to be his partner. Corinne wouldn't be around when we did the video in Washington, so she wouldn't have to know the true nature of our mission. As far as she was concerned, we were only there to buy the equipment we needed.

Once we figured out *who* would go, we had to decide *when* we would go. Corinne lived in New Jersey, just outside of New York City, so it wouldn't be a very long trip. Paul argued it would be better to go during the day because there would be more cars and people for us to blend in with. Dad maintained it would be safer to travel at night when the traffic cameras would have a harder time spotting us. Plus, fewer cars on the road meant it would be less likely for us to have an accident. Mia was the tiebreaker, and she decided we should try to leave in the early evening. It would be darker, and there would still be enough cars to keep us hidden, without entangling us in the heavy traffic of rush hour.

We packed a few things in a duffle bag and ate an early supper of baked chicken, mashed potatoes, and green bean casserole. I was really craving one of Dad's grilled steaks, but that wasn't an option in the bunker. Maybe sometime soon though. After we ate, we discussed the details of the plan several more times, to make sure we had it down. This was only Phase 1 of our plan, but if it didn't go well, Phase 2 would be over before it began. After all this talking I was ready to get this over with. Strangely enough, I was more apprehensive about meeting Corinne than the rest of the plan. If I could get past the sight of her with Jakob, I could easily overcome any other obstacle that came my way.

Charlie and Olivia entered the room with two more rolling laundry bins, and we all looked at each other, knowing we would have to say goodbye soon. Olivia held up a plastic bag from a pharmacy. "Faith, this is for you."

Confused, I took the bag and set it on the table. I pulled out a hair coloring kit, a pair of scissors, and a pair of glasses. "What's this about?" We all knew the answer, but no one dared to say it out loud. I picked up the box of *Perfect Blonde* hair coloring and studied the picture of the beautiful woman. I put everything back in the bag and stared at it.

Dad walked up behind me. "Jellybean, you don't have to do this. We can find another way.

I turned around to look at the rest of the group and forced a smile across my face. "Ya know, I've been wanting a new hairstyle anyway. Let's do this." I grabbed the bag and marched toward the bathroom. Once inside, I shut the door behind me and looked at myself in the mirror. My hair had been brown my whole life, and I had kept it past my shoulders for years. I normally didn't do much to style it, just settling for a ponytail or messy bun most of the time. I ran my fingers through my long hair one last time. This was going to be several shades lighter than my natural color, so I had to be ready for a big change. I opened the box and steeled myself to take this gigantic step. Only one problem... I had no idea what I was doing, so I opened the door. "Mom, can you come in here and help me?"

About a half hour later, I looked at the new me in the mirror for the first time. I wasn't prepared for what I saw. I ran my fingers through what was left of my hair. It was blonde all right, but I wasn't sure if it was really perfect like the box said it would be. And now it barely reached the bottom of my neck. And I had bangs! I hadn't had bangs in years.

Mom removed her plastic gloves and threw them in the trash. "Do you like it?"

"I... I don't know. It's different."

"I think it makes you look older."

"Yeah. But at least I don't look as old as you."

Mom smacked me on the arm with the brush and left the bathroom. I stood and stared for another few minutes. It's funny how something like changing your hair can make you feel so completely different. I did look older. I didn't look like the eighteen-year-old girl that nearly got herself executed a few months ago. I looked like an eighteen-year-old woman who was about to change the world. I opened the door and stepped back into the room to reveal my new look to the rest of the group. Hope and Alex didn't seem to care, but everyone else stared in amazement. Jakob's and Dad's mouths both fell open.

I bobbed the bottom of my hair with my hand. "So, what do you think?"

Dad finally closed his mouth enough to speak. "You look great. It sure is different, but it looks great."

Jakob walked up and studied me for a moment. "New shoes?"

I smacked him on the arm, accidentally hitting him on the bruise I had left earlier. He deserved it again though.

Olivia and Charlie pushed the laundry bins closer to us to signal that it was time to leave. We prayed, we hugged, we cried, and we said goodbye several times before Jakob and I climbed into the piles of laundry. We rolled out of the bunker, into the elevator, out of the elevator, through the whooshing door, and up a ramp into a truck. The truck door closed, and we were off. A few bumpy minutes later, we arrived at our destination. The truck door opened, and Charlie told us it was safe to come out. We climbed out of our laundry bins and stepped out of the truck, and back into the garage we had been in the day before. Was Lenny here? I scanned the garage, but to my dismay, he was nowhere to be seen. He had probably already gone home for the day.

Charlie clicked a button on a key fob, and a small white van chirped. It looked kind of like the one that picked us up from the bunker, but with fewer bullet holes and the name *Dependable Plumbing* on the side. He opened the back doors and motioned for us to climb in. "You two have to ride back here so you're out of sight. I'll drop you off near Corinne's house and then you'll be on your own. Here's a phone. It's programmed with my number. You can call me when you get the equipment, and I'll take you to DC for the speech."

Jakob and I climbed into the back of the truck and looked around. Since this was supposed to be a work van, there were no actual seats; just a pair of jump seats along each wall. I wrinkled my nose and turned to Charlie, who narrowed his eyes at me. "It'll only take a couple hours to get there. You'll be fine." He slammed the van doors before we could say anything and made his way to the driver's seat. A few seconds later, we were off.

An awkward silence hung over the back of the van for the first hour or so. We both felt it, but it was easier to let it linger. I kept waiting for Jakob to speak first, but he just sat there. There were no windows in the back of the van, and the light coming in through the windshield was waning. A small overhead light illuminated the cargo area well enough that we could faintly see each other. Tired of waiting, I asked the question that had been burning inside me. "Is she pretty?"

"Is who pretty?" Jakob knew who I was talking about. He was obviously just stalling.

"You know who."

Jakob sighed. He had to know this question was coming, so he probably had concocted the perfect answer. "Faith, don't do this."

"I want the truth. Don't just tell me what you think I wanna hear."

"The truth? Okay, fine. Yes. Yes, she's pretty."

Not exactly the answer I wanted, but at least it seemed honest. "How pretty is she?"

"Faith, will you just..."

"Will I just what? Answer the question. How pretty is she?"

Jakob shifted his feet, causing some of the loose tools to slide around the floor of the van. "What do you want me to say? I told you she's pretty."

"How pretty?"

"Ugh, I don't know. Very pretty, I guess."

"Beautiful?"

"Faith..."

I mimicked the way Jakob said my name.

"Fine. Yes, I guess you could say she's beautiful."

The more I heard, the less I wanted to hear. But I had to find out what I was up against. "On a scale from one to ten, what is she?"

"Faith, that's not fair. You have nothing to worry about. I love *you*, not her."

A little trickle of relief settled in my heart. But not enough. "Jakob, I have one more question..."

Before I could say another word, Jakob's lips pressed against mine. Was he showing me how much he loved me, or just trying to get me to shut up? Either way, it felt good. Our lips released, and his hand found mine in the darkness. My mind was trying to tell me that he definitely loved me, but my heart was still nervous. We sat in the quiet darkness for a couple more minutes before I was compelled to speak again.

"Jakob?"

"Yes, Faith?"

"Is she prettier than me?"

"Faith?"

"Yes, Jakob?"

"It's not even close."

I squeezed Jakob's hand and leaned my head on his shoulder. I closed my eyes for a moment, then my head sprang back up. "Wait a minute, are you saying it's not even close because she's way prettier than me, or because I'm way prettier than her?"

Jakob grabbed my head and laid it back down on his shoulder. "It's you...by a mile."

I smiled in the darkness. "Only one mile?"

CHAPTER NINE

My exhaustion and anxiety battled the rest of the drive to New Jersey, with my anxiety winning the majority of the time. Jakob must have sensed my apprehension because, near the end of the drive, he squeezed my hand and kissed me on the nose.

"Oops, sorry. I was aiming for your forehead."

We both chuckled, then he actually found my forehead the next time.

Charlie called out from the front seat, "We got about ten minutes left. Get your things together."

Jakob turned on a small flashlight and looked through the duffle bag. We didn't have much stuff, and we hadn't taken anything out, but he still had to make sure everything was in order. He pulled out a set of binoculars and zipped the bag closed. "Charlie, there's a small shopping center with a grocery store near Corinne's place. We'll be able to see if she's home from there."

Even though our success depended on Corinne's help, part of me secretly hoped she wouldn't be home after all. A big part of me.

Charlie stopped the van and put it in park. "We're here." Why do people always say that? Obviously, we're here. You parked the car. My snarky side was trying its best to come out.

Jakob shuffled closer to the windshield and peered through his binoculars. "Her lights are on, but I don't see her car on the street."

I exhaled, but my relief was short-lived.

"No, wait. There it is. That truck's blocking the front of her car, but it's there." He scooted to the back of the van and rested his hand on my shoulder. "Are you sure you wanna do this? You can still back out and let me make the buy."

I glared at Jakob in the dark. "Are you trying to get me to stay here?"

"Well, sort of. I know what this is gonna do to you, and I'm trying to spare you."

"Jakob, seeing you with her is gonna be tough; but imagining what's going on and not being there would be worse. If she starts getting too frisky, I'll just hit her."

"I wouldn't do that, Faith. She's an expert in Silat."

"Big deal, I know Haiku."

"Ha ha ha!" Jakob's laugh was dripping with sarcasm. "Silat is one of the deadliest martial arts out there. It teaches you to take advantage of your opponent's weakness and neutralize them as quickly as possible."

"I thought you said she was an electronics expert."

"She is. Fighting is just a hobby."

I laughed an uneasy laugh. "At least you'll be there to protect me."

"Yeah right. She would destroy me without blinking."

"Sounds great. And why would you ever want to break up with a woman like this?"

Jakob wisely didn't answer that question. Instead, he put the binoculars back in the duffle back and zipped it up. "Thanks, Charlie. We'll let you know when we're done. It'll probably be late sometime tomorrow morning, but it all depends on how quickly she can get us what we need." He then turned his attention to me. "Last chance to back out. Nobody would blame you."

I opened the back door to the van and hopped out. "Let's go, slowpoke."

Jakob joined me outside the van and closed the doors. "Remember, from here on out, we're just partners on a mission. We can't let Corinne know we're in love. And I'm sure she has a ton of cameras outside, so our cover story has to start now. Ready?"

I put my fake glasses on, nodded my head, and off we went. This was a residential area, so we didn't have to worry about traffic cameras, and the minimal number of streetlights would provide enough cover for us to go unrecognized. Each side of the street featured row after row of small, similar-looking houses. Other than the various colors, it was difficult to tell one apart from another. Jakob pointed to a modest gray house not too far down the road.

That was hers. My heart pounded harder and harder, and my hands got sweatier and sweatier the closer we got. We were nearly there. I glanced at the number *13* on the side of the mailbox. I'm not superstitious, but that had to be a bad sign. We turned the corner and headed up the sidewalk toward her front porch. The number above the front door said *813*. Was she too lazy to fix the missing number on the mailbox, or did she like the message the number *13* conveyed?

We trudged up the steps of the front porch and Jakob knocked on the door. All the curtains were drawn, but we could see that some lights were on. Several agonizing seconds passed before the door unlocked and creaked open slowly. I was standing beside Jakob, so I couldn't see who answered the door.

Jakob waved his hand at the person in the doorway. "Hey, Corinne."

Then without a word, a fist emerged from the doorway, colliding with Jakob's face. I gasped and took several steps back as Jakob landed on his back. He rubbed his face and looked at his assailant. "I deserved that."

The voice in the doorway replied, "Yes, you did." She then reached out her hand to help him up.

Jakob moved his jaw around to make sure everything still worked and accepted Corinne's offer to help him up. Once he stood to his feet, this awful woman threw her arms around him and began to laugh. As if that wasn't bad enough, Jakob put his arms around her and squeezed her in return. I knew this was going to be bad, but I wasn't prepared for the anger building inside.

Jakob finally pulled away from the repulsive hug. "Are you gonna invite us in so I can explain?"

Corinne glanced around the front porch. "Us? Who's with you?" The front porch light was off, so she and I couldn't see each other very well.

The lump in my throat kept me from speaking, so Jakob took over. "Corinne, this is Riley. She's my partner."

Corinne tilted her head as she sized me up. Once she realized I posed no physical threat, she walked up to me and stuck out her hand. I gave her hand a good squeeze, but she showed me her grip was much stronger. "Riley? Is that your first name or last name?"

Jakob and I answered at the same time, but I said "First", while he said "Last". We stared at each other, worried that our cover was blown already.

Corinne cocked her head to the side. "Oh, you're a girl? And your name is Riley Riley? Did your parents not like you or something?"

Jakob and I both let out a nervous chuckle and paused to avoid another verbal misstep. I freed my hand from Corinne's death grip and replied. "They had a weird sense of humor. What can I say?"

Corinne shrugged and took Jakob by the hand. "Get inside, mister. I've gotta know what's going on." She dragged him into the house and closed the door behind them, leaving me alone on the porch. After a couple of seconds, the door popped back open, and Corinne stuck her head out. "Sorry, Riley Riley. I forgot you were out there. You can come in too."

"Thanks," I muttered as I walked past Corinne, and into the house. I took a deep, cleansing breath into my nostrils, and slowly turned around to get a good look at my new nemesis. Jakob had told me she was very pretty, but he had obviously lied. The woman standing in front of me wasn't *pretty*. She had to have been the most beautiful woman I had ever seen in my life. Flawless skin, perfect features, and naturally blonde hair that was stunning, even though it was pulled back in a simple ponytail. Her skintight workout pants and tank top accentuated a body that most men would find irresistible. She must really have a horrible personality if Jakob had even thought about breaking up with her.

While I tried to keep from throwing up in my mouth, Corinne strutted over to Jakob and pulled him with her to the couch. "Okay, spill it," she said as they both plopped down.

Jakob cleared his throat. "Well, as you can see, I'm not dead."

I shuffled into the living room and sat down in a chair on the opposite side of the room. Corinne didn't look at me, but she acknowledged my presence by grabbing Jakob's hands in hers and resting them on her knees. Just the way I liked to do it. He didn't fight it either.

As Jakob opened his mouth to speak, his voice cracked. He cleared his throat again and continued. "So, as you know, the first part of our mission was successful. That girl got what she deserved."

My heart stung at those words. *That girl*? Really?

Corinne's fingers stroked the top of Jakob's hand. "Good. She was trouble. I saw what she did on the Internet. What about her dad and his people? Did you catch them too?"

"Most of them. Their leader is still out there, but we put a dent in their network. That's why I'm here."

I raised a finger (no, not that one) and said, "That's why *we're* here."

Again, Corinne refused to look at me. Instead, she stood up and strutted to the kitchen, swinging her hips as she walked. "I'm fixing myself a drink. Jakob, you want the usual?"

I glared at Jakob and called into the kitchen. "Nah, we're good."

Not acknowledging my reply, Corinne called back. "Jakob, did you hear me?"

Jakob shrugged helplessly at me. "Nah, I'm good."

Corinne returned to the living room and set her drink down on the table, leaning down in Jakob's face with her low-cut tank top. He didn't even try to look away from the show. I wanted desperately to leave the room, but I wasn't about to leave Jakob alone with this depraved individual. I had to stay there and endure the agony.

Jakob cleared his throat for a third time. "So, Corinne, I... we're here for your help. There's some equipment we need, and you're the only person who can get it for us?"

Corinne let go of Jakob's hands and sat straight up. "Me? Why can't you get what you need from the office?"

She had a point. If Jakob was still working for the government, he would have access to all the resources he would need. Why would he go to Corinne?

Jakob leaned close to Corinne and spoke more softly than before. "We can't do that. We got word that REFUGE had infiltrated our office, and they're leaking information to them. This mission is off the books."

Corinne studied Jakob for a moment before answering. "But why me? I'm not in the game anymore, remember?"

Jakob cleared his throat yet again. That was getting almost as annoying as Corinne's advances. "That's exactly why we came to you. REFUGE doesn't know you exist." He laid his hand on her arm. "You're perfect."

The way he said that sent a shockwave throughout my body. My mind flashed back to when he and I first met, and he was flirting with me for his mission. The way he slipped into character was impressive and disturbing at the same time. I kept telling myself that all this would be worth it if we succeeded in our mission.

Corinne leaned over and planted her vile lips on Jakob's. I looked around for something to throw at her, but I had to show restraint. Once she backed off, she smiled her perfect teeth at Jakob and said, "You're not so bad yourself. What do you need?"

Jakob didn't look in my direction, which was smart, because the glare I was giving him would have melted him. Instead, he remained focused on the evil person sitting with him on the couch. "First, we need a leech. That shouldn't be too hard. But the second thing we need will be a little more difficult."

Corinne backed away from Jakob and sat up straight on the couch. "Hit me." That sounded like a great idea to me.

Jakob stood up and walked around the room to stretch his legs. "REFUGE is desperate. They know we're closing in, so they're making one last play. Our intelligence tells us that REFUGE is gonna hijack Chancellor Sloane's speech tomorrow night and broadcast a message of their own. We can't let that happen, so we need some way to stop them."

Corinne looked confused. "That's easy, just use a wide-spectrum jammer to block them."

"Not good enough. We need to know how they're planning on doing this. Do you know what equipment they would need to override his broadcast?"

Corinne looked up at the ceiling as she thought. "Well, Sloane likes to control his media, so I'm assuming the TV stations will carry the same feed from the White House. So, they would have to find a way to intercept the signal at the source."

If I were to continue the charade as Jakob's partner, I needed to participate in the conversation. "How would they do that?"

For the first time, Corinne looked me in the eyes. "A signal diverter should do the trick."

Jakob leaned forward on the couch. "Do you have one of those? We need to borrow it for a few hours so we can study how they work."

Corinne scoffed. "Yeah right. Like I would keep something that expensive around here. I know where to find one, though."

"How quickly can you get one?" I was dying to get this over with as quickly as possible.

Corinne grabbed her phone and started walking out of the room. "Let me make some calls."

Once she was safely out of earshot I glanced over at Jakob, but he refused to look at me. At first, it looked like he was ignoring me, but then I remembered his conversation about Corinne's cameras. We had to hide our true relationship at all times. "Jakob, have you ever heard of these things?"

Jakob looked at me, but his face was all business. "Nope. But Corinne's one of the best, so if she says this is what we need, I trust her."

I nodded. "Do you think these REFUGE people are really dumb enough to try something like this?"

Jakob raised an eyebrow but kept playing along. "I don't know. They're pretty desperate, so I think they'll try just about anything. We have to be ready, just in case."

Corinne paraded back into the room, which was probably a good thing since I had run out of ideas for small talk. I definitely wasn't as quick on my feet as Jakob.

She put her phone down on the coffee table and sat down on the couch way too close to Jakob. "Good news and better news."

I nearly tried to squeeze myself between them, but Corinne would probably tear my arms off. I had to keep playing nice. "What's the good news?"

Corinne kept her eyes locked on Jakob even though I was the one who asked the question. "I can get you a diverter in a few hours."

"A few hours? It's already late." My mouth spoke before my brain could stop it. Again.

Corinne locked her beautiful and terrifying eyes on me. "Yes. A few hours." She enunciated those words slowly to drive the point home. "I don't know what your background is, Riley Riley, but these things take time. You can't just go down to the store and pick one of these up." She looked me up and down again. "Why are you here, anyway? You don't look like a field agent."

My mouth froze. Jakob and I had rehearsed this, but the words wouldn't come out. After a few agonizing seconds, I remembered. "I'm good with computers. I hacked into REFUGE's mail server, and I've spent the last few months studying their operation."

Corinne squinted as she studied me for the first time. "Good with computers? I can see that. You look like you haven't been out of your basement in months."

If she only knew how right she was.

Jakob jumped in before the cattiness got too out of hand. "And what's the better news, Corinne?"

Corinne's demeanor completely changed when she looked back at Jakob. "Oh yeah. The better news. One thing about these diverters... they're short-range devices, so they'd have to be close to the White House to make it work."

"How close?"

Corinne shrugged. "I don't know. A couple hundred feet maybe."

"Why is that better news?" I said, trying to stay relevant.

Corinne rolled her eyes at my idiocy. "Don't you see? This is your chance to capture some of them. They can't get that close to the White House without being spotted."

My heart skipped a beat. Suddenly this mission just got a lot more dangerous. "What if they hide really well?"

Corinne shot me a look that was even less hospitable than before. "These diverters have to send out a signal strong enough to overpower the source, and you can't broadcast something that strong for very long without the White House locking on to it. Within a couple minutes, they'll know exactly where they are."

The wheels were turning in my mind, and judging by the look on Jakob's face, he was thinking the same thing I was. A couple of minutes probably wouldn't be enough time for us to overpower Sloane's broadcast, transmit our video, and get out without getting caught. Yes, my ultimate goal was to get invited to the White House, but it had to happen after we had come up with a plan for using the leech.

Corinne noticed the silence in the room. "I knew it!"

Jakob and I snapped back to reality, and said, "Knew what?" in unison.

Corinne stood to her feet and pointed her finger in Jakob's face. "You've turned. You're not here to stop REFUGE. You're here to help them. You need this diverter for them. Not for you."

I opened my mouth to protest her accusations, but Jakob held up his hand to stop me. Instead, he asked Corinne to sit back down.

Corinne ignored Jakob and paced the room as she continued to work things through in her mind. "I knew something seemed off about your story. Jakob, no offense, but sometimes you're a terrible liar." She stopped pacing and looked down at her phone on the table. "I should turn you in right now."

Jakob stood to his feet and grabbed Corinne by the arms as I swooped in and picked up her phone. She spun around, grabbed Jakob by the wrist, and flipped him to the ground with ease. I held her phone out toward her, to avoid the same fate. She snatched it from my hand and glared back at Jakob, who posed a much greater threat than I did.

Jakob called to her from the floor, "Corinne, wait. You're right. Sorta."

Corinne huffed back at Jakob. "You'd better tell me what's going on. And it better be the truth!"

"Fine. Can I at least get back on the couch first?"

Corinne didn't answer. She just gestured toward the couch with her head.

He slid onto the couch and shook his arm to relieve the pain. "Thank you. I'll start at the beginning. If you remember, my mission was to get close to that girl, Faith, so I could learn more about REFUGE through her and her dad. I pretended to like her, and I got her to fall for me. That part was easy since she'd never had a boyfriend before. She was so gullible, that I convinced her I was really in love with her, even after she caught my spying on them."

Corinne laughed out loud at that. "What? How stupid was this girl?"

Jakob continued. "I know, right? Anyway, long story short, we arrested her and her family, which was a great start, but we had an even bigger objective. Faith's dad was pretty high up in REFUGE but arresting him wouldn't stop anything. We needed to cut the head off the snake."

Corinne looked like she was buying what Jakob was selling. "You want the man in charge, don't you?"

"Exactly. That's why Agent Cross and I helped the Webbers escape before they were executed. By doing that, we earned their trust and eventually ended up at REFUGE headquarters. Our next step is to go along with their plan until we can meet Duncan. Once we get him, we can put an end to this thing once and for all."

"So, you need this diverter to keep making them think you're on their side?"

"Exactly. They gave me a video to broadcast for them. We just need the equipment."

I was speechless. Jakob's little monologue sure seemed believable. Maybe a little too believable. What if he was actually telling the truth?

Jakob avoided eye contact with me, as Corinne sat back down on the other end of the couch, continuing to think. She then locked her eyes on me. "So, who are you again?"

I pointed to myself. "Me?" I had to buy some time while I thought of a story. "I'm Jakob's partner. The computer expert."

Corinne shook her head and squinted at me. "Try again."

I looked at Jakob, my eyes pleading for him to help. He finally spoke up. "I told you, she's my..."

Corinne held up her hand to cut him off. "I need to hear it from Riley Riley."

My mouth went dry as my mind raced. "I work with Jakob."

"Who's your supervisor? Which field office are you from? What's your agent ID number?"

My stunned silence told Corinne everything she needed to know. "That's what I thought. I could tell you weren't an agent." She walked closer and stood right in front of me. "Are you ready to tell me the truth now?"

"The truth?" I looked at Jakob as if he could somehow transmit the words to me through telepathy. "Fine...I work for REFUGE. We're the ones trying to hijack Sloane's speech and broadcast a message of our own. Please don't turn us in."

Corinne returned to her seat on the couch and grabbed Jakob by the chin. "So, you really have turned, haven't you? All that talk about being a double agent, and trying to capture Duncan...those were lies, weren't they?"

Jakob nodded his head. "I'm sorry. I was trying to keep you from reporting us."

"Why shouldn't I? You're helping REFUGE overthrow Sloane. Isn't that the very thing you were trying to stop?"

Jakob flashed a charming smile, trying to ease Corinne's mind. "That's what Sloane thinks, but we just want freedom. We're no match for his military, so there's no way we could overthrow him. But if we broadcast this video, we can get people on our side again, and force his hand. You know as well as I do that we'd all be better off if we had more freedom. Besides, don't you want to get back at them?"

"Back at who?"

Jakob slid a little closer to her. "The government. You were one of their best agents, and they threw you out. This is your chance for revenge."

Corinne pondered Jakob's offer for a few moments, then spoke. "Okay, I'll help. But it'll cost you. Let me find out how much the equipment costs, then I'll give you my price. But I'm warning you. If things go south, I won't hesitate to roll over on you to protect myself."

Jakob sighed in relief. "Great. Just get us what we need, and Riley and I can be on our way."

Corinne's perfect smile reappeared. "Nope. I want in. I'll get you the equipment, but you'll need me to operate it. This has to work perfectly, and, no offense, but you and Riley Riley over here are just gonna mess it up."

I folded my arms across my chest. "I can do this. I really am good with computers."

"You may be good with computers, but this is my arena. The only way this works is if I come along."

She was right, but I couldn't let her come along. I had to try a different approach. "You said you were out of the game. We don't want you to put yourself in danger."

Corinne stood up and walked toward me again. "I can take care of myself. Care to find out for yourself, Riley Riley?" Although she was smiling, her intent was clear.

Jakob sprang to his feet and stepped between us. "As much fun as that would be, we need to think about the mission." He ushered Corinne back to the couch and sat down, putting his arm around her. Was he cuddling with her, or trying to restrain her so she didn't come after me? "Riley, I'm afraid Corinne is right. This has to go smoothly, so we need to accept her help."

I knew he was right, but how much more could I take of Corinne and her attitude? And what kind of name is Corinne, anyway? That's not even a real word. You couldn't say the word without sneering your nose and saying it all nasally. I threw my hands up in the air. "Fine. The more the merrier."

Corinne's toothy grin said, *See, I told you so,* but her mouth said, "Great. This is gonna be fun. We'll leave after my supplier calls me back. Jakob, will you be a dear and get my small travel bag out of our closet? I can't reach it."

Jakob released his grip on Corinne and strolled to the bedroom. Once he was out of the room, Corinne turned her eyes to me. The smile was gone. "You listen to me, Riley Riley. I know what you're up to."

"Me?"

She growled through clenched teeth. "Yeah. I see the way you look at Jakob. Just know this... he's mine. I lost him once and I'm not losing him again. If you so much as think about going after him, I'll break you. Got it?"

My eyes and mouth widened as I tried to come up with a response. She was so beautiful and menacing, I wasn't about to cross her. I squeaked out an "OK" and slumped in the chair. Mercifully, Jakob soon returned with a small suitcase.

He had to sense the tension in the room. "What's going on?"

I sat motionless, but Corinne chirped as if nothing was wrong. "Oh, nothing. Us gals were just getting to know each other. Right, Riley Riley?"

My first instinct was to correct her grammar, but my second instinct was to avoid getting pummeled. "Yup, we're gonna be great friends."

Jakob stared with a blank expression on his face and shrugged his shoulders. "Okay, whatever."

CHAPTER TEN

I spent the next several hours bouncing back and forth between disgust and despair. We had a solid plan, and now we had a new ally, but life had become infinitely more complicated by Corinne's presence. At one point, Jakob stepped outside to call Charlie and update him on our progress. Terrified of being left alone with Corinne, I hid in the bathroom while Jakob was on the phone. Terrified of leaving Jakob alone with Corinne, I returned to the living room as soon as I heard his voice inside the house. She was all over him the entire time. If we didn't need her for our mission, and if she couldn't kill me without thinking twice, I might have actually told her off.

Finally, around 3:00 AM, Corinne got a call from her supplier. He had the diverter and the leech and was ready to meet. Corinne hung up the phone and sat down next to Jakob. "His fee is fifty thousand."

Jakob reached for his phone so he could transfer the money. "Fifty thousand? I guess that's not too bad."

Corinne's beautiful smile reappeared. "*His* fee is fifty thousand. *My* fee is a million."

Jakob's head lurched forward. "Did you say *a million*?"

Corinne nodded; the smile refusing to leave her face.

Jakob continued to stare at Corinne with a blank expression on his face, while I held my hands up in protest. "That's crazy. He's only charging us fifty thousand for the devices."

"That's because he's an idiot. He doesn't know what he has here. I do."

"And what exactly do you have?" I was getting a little sassy, but I was beginning to stop caring.

"I have desperate people in a desperate situation. You need this equipment, and you need someone to work it. Unless you two know something I don't, it looks like you're gonna pay me the million, and we're gonna be spending a lot more time together. Otherwise, I turn you in. You have two minutes to talk it over while I fix myself a drink."

Once she left the room, I scurried over and sat next to Jakob on the couch, careful not to sit close enough that I risked the wrath of Corinne. "What are we gonna do? They only gave us a budget of two hundred and fifty thousand. Do you think she's bluffing?"

Jakob frowned at me as though I said the dumbest thing he'd ever heard. "Does she look like a bluffer?" He had a point.

"I don't know what to do. Sloane's speech is in like 15 hours. We aren't gonna find anyone else by then, will we?"

"Don't worry, Riley. I have a plan." I glared at Jakob for calling me that, but at least he only said it once.

Corinne strutted back into the living room and stopped when she saw me sitting next to Jakob. I scooted over to give her room to sit between us, but she just continued to stare at me. Not wanting to become a human pretzel, I returned to the chair I had become so attached to.

She took a long sip of whatever was in her glass, and sat down on the couch, practically on Jakob's lap. "Well, what did you decide?"

Jakob squirmed a little, but Corinne didn't flinch. "We don't have that kind of money... yet. How about I give you one-fifty now? Fifty thousand for the items, and one hundred as a down payment for your fee? Then, once you've held up your end of the bargain, I'll give you the rest."

Corinne studied Jakob. "Give me two hundred now, plus another million when we're done."

Jakob held out his hand toward Corinne to seal the deal. "Deal."

Corinne grabbed her phone and tapped on the screen a few times. "Send me the money. I know you still remember my number."

Jakob used the phone Charlie had given us and transferred the money to our new partner. Corinne watched her screen until she heard a ding and flashed a huge smile. She then stood up, grabbed Jakob by the hand, and pulled him off the couch. "Let's go."

I stood up and started gathering my things, but Corinne shot me a glare. "Jakob and I are going to make the buy. Alone."

"No, I wanna go too."

Corinne scoffed. "This is a job for an actual field agent. Tell you what, if he needs his computer worked on, we'll call you. Otherwise, you stay here, Riley Riley."

Jakob just stood there. Would it kill him to come to my defense? Maybe ask Corinne to go easy on me for once?

I held my hands out with my palms to the sky. "What am I supposed to do while you're gone?"

They headed toward the door, and Corinne spoke without looking back. "Oh, I don't know. I'm sure you'll think of something, Riley Riley. Just don't touch my stuff or I'll break your arm."

I passed the time while Jakob and Corinne were gone by lying down on the couch with my face buried in the pillows. I may have also been trying to conceal my tears from Corinne's cameras, but mostly I was trying to sleep. I must have dozed off a few times because the two hours they were gone passed relatively quickly. The sound of the unlocking deadbolt announced their return, and I stood to my feet. A little too quickly though because a head rush nearly caused me to black out. I fell back down on the couch as they entered.

Corinne looked around the room, probably trying to see if I had touched anything, then looked at me, squinting to look closer at my eyes. "What's wrong, Riley Riley? You look like you've been crying."

"No, I fell asleep for a little while, and I was rubbing my eyes. That's all."

"Uh-huh." She looked down at the couch pillows and saw wet smears on them. "Is that drool or snot? You'd better hope that washes out."

Jakob set a cardboard box down on the kitchen table and walked into the living room in time to hear the last part of that exchange. "Corinne, I'm sure it'll be fine. You'll soon be able to afford nice new pillows."

A smug grin stretched across Corinne's face as she picked up the wet pillow and hurled it at my face. "You're right. Here, Riley Riley, knock yourself out."

I caught the pillow right before it hit me and watched the two of them go to the kitchen. I then wiped my face all over the pillow and threw it back down on the couch. I didn't care if her cameras saw that or not. Jakob and that girl were looking through the items in the box when I caught up to them in the kitchen. "Did you get everything, Jakob?"

"Yeah. We're all set."

The box was filled with a smaller box and other assorted items that were foreign to me. I pointed to a tiny black object about the size of a large grape. "Is that the leech?"

Corinne rolled her eyes, but Jakob humored me with a response. "Yes. And all those other pieces go with the diverter."

The *other pieces* included a shiny, silver object that was about the size of a loaf of bread and a silver rod that appeared to be some sort of antenna. Part of me wanted to ask more questions, but that would have only brought more grief from Corinne. Instead, I watched as the two of them sorted through the box and set everything out on the kitchen table. Corinne walked into the bedroom and returned with a computer.

"We have to make sure we know how everything works," Jakob said as he plugged the shiny silver box into the computer.

I watched over Corinne's shoulder as she turned the computer on and launched the program that would access the diverter. A few clicks later, there was a window that said *Available Signals*, with a handful of options showing the frequency and strength of each signal. Below that were buttons marked *Live, Source, Broadcast,* and *Stop.*

I frowned at the screen. "What are those?"

Corinne replied without turning around. "Those are all the television signals in the air right now. We won't know what frequency the White House will be using, but we'll be able to find it. Hey Jakob, turn my TV on, switch it to the antenna input, then turn it to channel 9 for me."

Jakob did as he was told, and we were soon greeted with the morning news. Ironically, the anchors were discussing Sloane's upcoming speech. Corinne selected several different frequencies until the video in her *Live* window matched the video on her TV. She then hit the *Broadcast* button. The talking stopped, and the black screen from her *Source* window appeared on the television screen. Corinne clicked the *Stop* button, and the news broadcast returned.

"Did anyone else besides us see that?" asked Jakob.

Corinne shook her head. "Not unless they live within a few hundred feet of us and were watching channel 9 just now. And if they were, they probably just thought it was a glitch. No biggie. Well, at least we know this thing works. Now let's get outta here."

Charlie was waiting in the same parking lot when the three of us arrived. He had protested when he saw Corinne tagging along, but Jakob insisted that her presence was a necessity. A quick phone call to Mia settled the debate, and we began the journey. I was still repulsed by her presence, but the mission was bigger than my personal feelings. If all went well, we would be there around lunchtime. That would allow us enough time to eat, get some much-needed rest, and be in position in time for the big speech.

Our mission goal may have been to broadcast our video, but my own personal goal was to have Corinne back home and out of our lives by midnight. Jakob assured me that he would officially break up with her when we no longer needed her help, and I was counting down the minutes until that happened. We could then move on to the next phase of our plan, and our lives together.

Jakob and Corinne fell asleep shortly after we got on the road, but my mind wouldn't let me rest. I kept replaying Jakob's words after Corinne accused him of changing sides. He had told her that he was just pretending to work with REFUGE so they could get to Duncan and stop the rebellion before it could really begin. My heart was telling me that was just a tale he wove to convince Corinne that he hadn't really changed sides, but my head wasn't convinced. Even though he admitted he made it up, once I began to process everything, it made a lot of sense. The only way to really stop REFUGE would be to arrest Duncan, and the best way to get close to him would be to do exactly what Jakob and Paul were doing. I couldn't allow myself to think these thoughts about Jakob though. I was there when his chip was fried. I felt the power in the cabin when he prayed. He was just saying what he had to say to get Corinne to help us broadcast our video.

My heart skipped a beat when I thought about the video. I was supposed to broadcast a video saying that I was alive after all and that I wanted to meet with Chancellor Sloane to talk things over. This was a great plan, but now that Corinne was with us, it wouldn't work. I reached over and poked Jakob in the ribs to wake him up. After a few pokes and a couple of shoulder shakes, he finally awoke. Corinne was still sound asleep. She may have looked perfect on the outside, but she snored like an angry wildebeest.

"Jakob," I whispered.

"What do you want?"

I motioned for him to scoot closer to me. He rubbed his eyes and scooted over, leaving the wildebeest in her slumber.

I leaned over and whispered into Jakob's ear. "I just thought of something. Corinne thinks Faith's dead. What's she gonna think when I say my name on the video tonight?"

Jakob was either still groggy, or just wasn't comprehending what I was saying. "What are you talking about?"

"Think about it. Once we start the video, I'm gonna say my name, right?"

"Yeah."

"So, once she knows who I really am, is that gonna mess things up?"

Jakob's eyes finally opened fully as he pondered my question. He leaned over to whisper into my ear. "I don't think so. She's in it for the money, so it won't matter who you are. As long as we keep our relationship a secret."

I longed to take Jakob by the hand, but I had to show restraint. "How long do we have to do that? This is killing me."

"Hopefully just a few more hours. If we do this video, we can take her home, and go back to REFUGE."

I wasn't completely sold, but it was a little bit of hope to cling to. "Okay, I guess you're right."

"I'm always right. Now try to get some sleep."

CHAPTER ELEVEN

The drive to Washington took longer than usual because of traffic and the need to stay off the main highways. Before we got close to downtown, we went through a drive-thru and got some lunch, which we scarfed down in the back of the van during the last part of the trip. We finally arrived in DC two hours before the big speech. Just enough time to scout the area for a good broadcasting position, and get things set up.

Chancellor Sloane is very particular when it comes to the image he portrays. His suits are immaculate, and he always conducts himself with dignity and authority in person, and on camera. Part of his public image is the White House itself. Sloane does not allow antennas or satellite dishes that are visible to the public, maintaining the clean appearance of this symbol of power. A detail we planned to exploit later that night.

Before Jakob and I left Philadelphia, Paul had given us the scoop on Sloane's television broadcasts. The lighting, the makeup, the hair, everything is designed to make him look his best. The video originating from the Oval Office is completely controlled by members of Sloane's staff. That signal is then sent through a short-range transmitter across the street to the satellite trucks from the networks that would carry the speech. Technically each television network was independent, but they were all controlled by the White House, and loyally conveyed Sloane's carefully orchestrated messages. I asked Paul why they don't use the Internet, but that would risk compromising Sloane's precious picture quality. Radio waves and television satellites are much more reliable.

Our best chance would be to intercept and overpower the signal that traveled from the White House to the news trucks. That meant we would have to be close enough to hijack the signal at the source, but far enough away that we weren't easily spotted. We spent well over an hour driving up and down 17th St, trying to find the perfect spot to park. There were several parking garages in the area to choose from, but we settled on one that was on the northwest corner, across from the White House. Corinne suggested parking on the top level so our signal would be more powerful, but Charlie argued that would make us vulnerable to one of the government's satellite cameras. We couldn't risk being spotted from above, so we settled for the second level. We found an open parking spot on the side closest to the White House and parked the van. Charlie climbed into the back and closed the curtains that hung behind the front seats. Less than an hour to go.

Corinne took the diverter components out of the box and began to assemble it. The ride to DC was quite bumpy, so she had kept the sensitive electronics nestled in the packing foam for safe transit. We had successfully tested the diverter at her house, but there was no guarantee it would work in this environment and at this distance. We had no choice but to trust that Jakob's electronics expert lived up to the hype.

As Corinne worked, I rehearsed my speech in my mind. I would have to prove that this was a live broadcast, so I would mention things Sloane said during his speech. I would also have to be brief and to the point. Corinne had warned us that the White House would be able to locate us if we broadcast too long, so the longer I spoke, the greater the risk of getting ourselves caught. I glanced at the time. Only two minutes until showtime, but Corinne was still working. "Are you almost done?" I asked.

Corinne huffed. "This'll go a lot faster if you stop talking to me, Riley Riley."

"Can I help?"

"Not really." Her screen came to life with the window we had seen earlier. This time, however, there were several more signals to choose from.

Jakob pointed to the screen. "Find the strongest signal. That's probably it."

Corinne huffed again. "I know that Jakob."

The way she said Jakob's name almost made me snicker. She sounded like Hope when she's mad at me.

Corinne selected one signal after another but couldn't locate the one from the White House. I looked at the time. Sloane had been speaking for about twenty-five minutes. Finally, after an eternity, Corinne locked onto something.

"I think I got it."

We studied the computer screen carefully as the video of Sloane speaking from the Oval Office appeared in the *Input* window. Success!

We didn't know how long Sloane's speech would last, but the man loved to hear himself talk so we probably had some time left.

Corinne looked over at Jakob. "Where's your video?"

"No time to load it. We're just gonna do it live. Just use the camera on your computer and turn it toward Riley. She's gonna talk."

Corinne looked skeptical, but we didn't have time to play around. She turned the camera on, slid the computer to me, and got out of the way. I nearly jumped when I saw my image in the *Source* window on the screen. My new blonde hair and glasses really threw me for a loop.

Corinne pointed to the *Broadcast* button on the screen. "Click that when you're ready, then wait for your video to show up instead of Sloane's. Remember to keep it short."

I took a deep breath and cleared my throat. With a trembling finger, I clicked on the *Broadcast* button and stared at the screen. My image in the Input window was perfect, but Sloane's speech was still in the *Live* window. "What's going on?"

Corinne slid over so she could see the screen. "I don't know. Did you click the right thing?"

"I clicked the Broadcast button, but nothing happened. Are we on the right signal?"

Corinne growled. "Yeah. We can see the speech. Maybe our signal's too weak. Let me try something." She grabbed the antenna and took it to the front of the van, pointing it out the windshield toward the White House. "Anything?"

The video of Sloane got a little pixelated, but I could still see and hear him. "It did something, but I don't think this is gonna work."

Corinne crawled back to us and huffed. "Charlie, you gotta get us closer. Maybe if we broadcast while we're driving by, it'll work."

Charlie looked at Jakob, who gestured toward the driver's seat. He climbed back into his seat and backed us out of the parking spot. It started to sound like Sloane was wrapping things up, so Jakob told Charlie to hurry.

"I can't drive too fast or we'll get spotted!" Charlie didn't like taking orders from people half his age.

We descended to the ground level, Charlie paid the parking machine, and we were back out on the street. We turned left and headed toward the White House. The street in front of the White House was always closed to vehicle traffic, but maybe we could get close enough to hijack the signal to the trucks.

Corinne gave the computer back to me. "Here, keep clicking the Broadcast button. See if it works."

I did as I was told, but nothing happened to Sloane's signal. Another left turn and the picture quality on Sloane's speech got worse. Our diverter was starting to work. Once I saw my own face instead of his, I could start talking.

I called toward the front of the van, "Can you get us closer?"

Charlie replied. "I'm trying. There's a lot of traffic and the news trucks are blocking one of the lanes."

I rolled my eyes and turned my attention back to the speech. "I think he's almost done!"

Charlie didn't respond. Instead, he kept trying to navigate the van closer to the White House. My stomach turned as Sloane said a few more words, thanked the American people for their support, and the broadcast ended. I slammed the computer down in disgust. "We missed it!"

We turned right and traffic continued to crawl. My stomach churned, and my mouth began to water. I couldn't throw up in the van though. I opened the back door and hopped out of the van, walking down a sidewalk into a park across the street from the White House.

Jakob called to me from behind. "Riley! Riley, come back!"

I ignored Jakob's calls and kept on walking to clear my head. The nausea was beginning to subside, but the fresh air felt good and I had to enjoy it a little while longer. Jakob's hand grabbed my shoulder and spun me around. "Are you crazy?"

I shrugged his hand off of me. "Don't make a scene. Your so-called electronics expert failed us. Sloane's speech was our only shot."

"It'll be all right. We'll come up with something else. Just get back in the van before they see us."

I waved my arm around in a circle. "Who? That jogger over there? Or maybe that old lady with the chihuahua? Yeah, she looks dangerous."

Jakob stepped closer and turned me around to face the opposite direction. "Them."

Once my eyes focused, I saw a handful of news reporters standing in front of the White House fence, talking to their cameras. They must have been gushing about Sloane's speech, spewing the talking points the White House provided. A crazy thought popped into my mind as I watched them speak.

Jakob tapped me on the shoulder. "What are you doing? I don't like the look on your face."

I ignored him and glanced around the park to get an idea of my surroundings. The van was still parked on the side of the road, not too far away. If I ran my fastest, I could probably pull this off. I turned back to Jakob. "Go back to the van and have him meet me at that corner over there. Watch for me, so we can take off as soon as I get there."

"Do you mind telling me what you have planned?"

"There's no time. Just be there and be ready." I turned around and started walking toward the White House as casually as I could. I didn't turn around to see if Jakob went back to the van. I just had to trust him. I could blend in with the small crowd of onlookers that were lined up along the sidewalk, watching the reporters and taking pictures in front of the famous residence.

I had been studying the reporters for a few moments looking for the right opportunity, when someone tapped me on the shoulder and said, "Excuse me."

I ignored them, but they tapped again. "Excuse me."

I turned around to find a man with two small children, holding up his camera. "Do you mind taking our picture?"

I was trying to avoid being identified, but the kids reminded me of Hope and Alex, so I obliged. They stood together in front of the

White House fence, and I snapped several pictures. I returned their camera and turned my attention back to the television reporters. Most of them were packing up, but one woman was still talking to her camera. I could tell she was broadcasting live because she was answering questions from the people in the studio. This was my chance.

I glanced around one last time and walked up behind her camerawoman, pretending to take in the historic sights. I strolled up to the fence beside the reporter, just out of the camera's view, and took a deep breath. Now or never. I spun around and jumped into the spot right next to the reporter and snatched her microphone. "My name's Faith Webber. I'm the girl behind the Voice for Reason website. The girl Chancellor Sloane tried to kill. As you can see, I escaped, and I want everyone to join us again..."

The reporter tried to wrestle the microphone away, and some nearby tourists began to take video of the commotion I was causing.

"... join us as we unite to petition Chancellor Sloane for religious freedom. I'm asking the Chancellor to invite me to the White House so we can discuss this openly. Your move, Chancellor."

With that, I tossed the microphone back to the stunned reporter and sprinted toward the corner I had told Jakob about earlier. I had never run so fast in my life; it was almost as though my feet weren't even touching the pavement. I dared not turn around to see if anyone was following me. I would just have to keep running. I approached the corner, turning my head from side to side, scanning for my escape vehicle. There it was! The back door opened, and I hopped in. Jakob closed the door behind me, and we took off, away from the White House.

I laid down flat on the floor of the van, my body heaving as I gulped in as much air as I could. Jakob grabbed me by the arm. "Sit up and take long, deep breaths. You'll get more air that way."

I did as he said, and before long I felt better. I looked at Jakob and Corinne. They were staring back at me with the same expression my parents give me when they caught me doing something wrong. "Was anyone following me?"

Jakob frowned. "No. I'm scared to ask, but what did you do?"

I raised my eyebrows and shrugged my shoulders. "Plan B."

"Plan B," Corinne asked. "What's that? I didn't know we had a

Plan B."

I laughed. "I just made it up. Since we couldn't broadcast our video on our own, I jumped in front of a TV camera and said what I needed to say. It won't be quite the same, but hopefully, it'll get the job done." I was now aware that the van had stopped moving. "Charlie, what's going on?"

"More traffic. But don't worry, nobody's following us."

As soon as those words left his mouth, the sounds of sirens off in the distance behind us greeted our ears.

I looked at Jakob with widened eyes. "Think they're after us?"

"I don't know, but we have to assume they are. We gotta get off the road." Jakob climbed up to the front of the van and helped Charlie look for an escape route.

Charlie pointed at something off in the distance. "There. That parking garage."

The sirens were getting closer. Fortunately, they would have to deal with the same traffic that was slowing us down. We inched along, getting a little closer to the parking garage, but the sirens continued to grow louder.

Jakob looked over at Charlie. "We're not gonna make it there before the police get here." Charlie swerved the van to the left, sending Corinne sprawling across the floor of the van. I would have laughed if we weren't in such a tense situation. The sirens were almost on us now. I wished for windows on the back doors so I could see what was going on, but we would have to settle for reports from Jakob and Charlie. Just a few more feet until we were safe. The sirens sounded like they were right behind us. Jakob ducked down out of sight as the sirens passed by and continued down the road ahead of us.

I didn't realize I had been holding my breath until I let it out and looked around at everyone else. Nobody said a word as Charlie pulled the van into the parking garage and found a parking spot on the second level.

Jakob climbed back to the front. "We can't stay here forever, Charlie. What are we gonna do?"

Charlie smiled at the group. "I'm gonna change the van." He got out and shut the door behind him.

We all looked around at each other, then piled out of the back as Charlie reached toward the side of the van. "They're looking for a white plumbing van, so we need to be in a security van." He peeled the sign for the plumbing company off the side of the van and flipped it around, revealing the words *Safe & Sound Security* on the back. He stuck the sign back on the side of the van and walked to the other side.

"Are those magnetic?" I asked.

"Yep. But that's not all." He flipped the sign on the other side of the van and grabbed the key fob from his pocket. "For my next trick, I'm going to make this white van disappear." He clicked a button on the remote, and the white paint shifted to black. He got quite a kick out of his theatrics.

We hadn't heard any sirens since the police cars passed us on the street, so we began to relax. The four of us walked to the edge of the parking garage and peered down to the street below. Traffic was starting to clear up, so Charlie figured it was a good time to get Corinne back home. Not soon enough for me, though. Charlie clapped his hands, and said, "Welp, now all I have to do is change the plates, then we gotta go."

As he said those words, I became keenly aware of the fullness of my bladder. "I gotta go, too."

"Go? Go where?" Jakob was oblivious.

"You know...I gotta *go*." I started squirming in place to clarify what I was saying.

"Oh, okay."

The restrooms were on the opposite side of the parking garage, several hundred feet away. I walked quickly, but not so quickly that I would have an accident. It was a muggy evening, so Jakob and Charlie waited in the air-conditioned van. I was almost to the restroom when Corinne called from behind. "Wait up, Riley Riley! I gotta go too!" I turned around to see her trotting toward me. Ugh.

For some reason, I actually waited for her before walking into the restroom. She had been nothing but nasty to me, but the best way to get back at her was to be nice. Neither of us said a word as we took care of our business and washed our hands. We walked out of the restroom and began the long trek to the van. We had only taken a few steps when a black SUV skidded to a stop in front of us. The front doors opened, and four men in suits sprang out and surrounded us. Jakob and Charlie were too far away to help, so we were on our own. I looked at the men and looked at Corinne. She had the biggest smile I had ever seen.

"Hello, boys. Tell you what...you get back in your truck and forget you ever saw us, and you'll save yourselves a lot of pain."

What on earth was she doing? Was she stalling until Jakob and Charlie could get there? Or was she deranged enough to think she could actually take that many agents on her own? I would soon get my answer because the four men ignored her warning and began to walk closer to us.

Corinne tightened her ponytail and winked at me. "Watch this, Riley Riley." She lunged at the first agent, punching him in the throat and kicking him in the leg. The loud crack and subsequent scream told me she had broken it. I nearly threw up in my mouth. Two more agents came after her; one from the front, and one from behind. She squatted down and swept her leg in a circle, knocking them both to the ground, before springing back up and kicking one of them in the head, followed by the other. They were unconscious before they each hit the ground with a dull thud. Only one agent left. He took a more deliberate approach and waited for Corinne to make the first move. They circled each other like a couple of ravenous wolves, waiting for the right opportunity to pounce. A few seconds of circling was enough for Corinne. She took two steps toward the agent and lunged to her right. He moved to block her attack, and she spun around and clobbered him in the side of the head with the side of her fist. He collapsed to his knees, and she finished him off with a kick to the head. Corinne surveyed her handiwork and noticed the agent with the broken leg dragging himself to the SUV.

She skipped over to the last remaining conscious agent and squatted down in front of him. "Sorry, buddy. We can't leave any witnesses."

The agent looked at her with genuine fear in his eyes. "Just make it quick."

Corinne stood back up and kicked him on the side of the head, knocking him out cold. I stood in awe as I looked at the four grown, government-trained men she had just dispatched with ease. "Thank you, Corinne."

She reached into the SUV and pulled out one of their walkie-talkies. "I did it for me, not you. I wasn't about to let these losers bring me in."

Jakob and Charlie came sprinting around the SUV and stopped

in front of us. They saw the carnage and looked at Corinne with dumbstruck expressions on their faces. She smiled and waved them off. "Don't worry about it, I already took care of 'em. Let's go."

CHAPTER TWELVE

As we got back into the van and pulled out of the parking spot, Corinne turned the walkie-talkie up so we could hear the chatter. We couldn't tell exactly how many agents and how many SUVs were after us, but the number was large. They kept talking about a white plumbing van, so I was grateful for our new black security van. We descended to the ground level and made our way toward the exit. Charlie let out an "Ugh" from the front seat and we all craned our necks to see what was going on. There were three other cars in front of us, waiting to pay and exit. We settled back down on the van floor, patiently waiting our turn.

A voice on the radio called for unit 22 to report in. No response. "Unit 22, report in. Did you make contact?" Still no response.

Jakob chuckled. "Unit 22 must be the group Corinne took out."

Charlie moved forward a spot and waited for the next people to pay.

The radio spoke again. "Unit 22, this is 17. What's your twenty? Are you still in the parking garage?" Still no response.

Charlie snapped his fingers at us. "We got company. Stay down." The sound of squealing tires and a large vehicle flew past us into the garage. I looked up, and there was still one more car in front of us. It wouldn't be long before unit 17 saw what happened to unit 22 and came back looking for us. I climbed up to the front of the van and looked out the windshield just in time to see the driver in front of us drop their card. They opened their door, but they hit the concrete barrier in front of the booth. There wasn't enough room for them to get out.

The radio spoke again. "All units, be advised, Unit 22 is down.

Webber and a female accomplice attacked them. Agent Richards is in need of medical attention."

The idiot driver in front of us waved at us to back up so he could back up and open his door, but we were stuck. Charlie held up his hands in frustration, and the driver realized he would have to retrieve his card on his own. He reached down to the ground and felt around for his lost card. Charlie grew impatient and hopped out of the van, ran up to the car in front of us, picked up the card, and put it in the machine. Tires squealed on the level above us as Charlie then sprinted back to us. The gate opened, and the guy in front of us exited as the radio came to life again.

"All units, this is 17. We are about to exit the parking garage on New York and 17th. Suspects are in a white plumbing van. Consider them extremely dangerous."

Corinne giggled. "Extremely dangerous? Got that right."

Charlie lurched the van forward, paid our fee, and turned right.

Jakob sat up and looked out the front. "Charlie, what are you doing? You're going back toward the White House."

"They're looking for a white plumbing van going away from the white house. They won't even notice a black security van heading toward the White House."

Charlie had a point, but it was still an awfully big risk to go back toward the White House like this. At least we had the walkie-talkie so we could monitor the agents as they looked for us. The chatter continued for the next several minutes, but no one reported any signs of our plumbing van. I don't know exactly where we were, but I could tell the traffic was still heavy as the sun grew dim in the late evening sky.

After several excruciating minutes, we finally picked up some speed. Things were looking up, but we weren't out of the woods yet. Jakob had told us it was only a matter of time before the agents watched the traffic cameras near the parking garage and realized what we had done. Hopefully, we would be long gone from DC before they were able to put two and two together.

Corinne was surprisingly quiet. Perhaps the sudden adrenaline rush from her martial arts demonstration had left her fatigued. I wasn't complaining though. In fact, we were all quiet for an hour or so before Corinne had something to say.

"I got a question."

Neither Jakob nor I responded. We just waited for Corinne to speak again, which she would undoubtedly do.

"Back in town, when the agents were talking on the radio...they said, 'Webber and a female accomplice.' Why did they say, *Webber*?"

Jakob and I exchanged a glance, then I finally spoke. "I'm Faith Webber. I'm the one that Jakob was sent to get close to."

"I'm glad you finally decided to tell the truth, Riley Riley."

"You know, you really don't have to call me that anymore."

"Sorry, Riley Riley. Old habit."

I rolled my eyes and let out a sigh. If I pushed her out of the van at this speed, would it kill her or just hurt her? "Charlie, how much longer until we're back at Corinne's house?"

"Couple hours. As long as we don't have any setbacks along the way."

The inside of the van was dim, but there was just enough light for us to see each other. Corinne scooted even closer to Jakob and put her hand on his leg. "So, what's next?"

I cleared my throat before speaking. "Well, we're gonna take you home, then Jakob and I are gonna continue our mission."

"Which is?"

Neither Jakob nor I answered.

"What's the leech for?"

Again, no answer.

"Fine, don't tell me. I'll figure it out on my own." She paused for a few moments as she thought. "A leech lets you have access to a computer without being there. So, whose computer do you want to control? And why go through all this today? What exactly did you say on TV?"

"That's on a need-to-know basis. And you don't."

Corinne let out a huge belly laugh. "Oh, Riley Riley. You almost sound like you've convinced yourself that you're tougher than you really are. The leech is connected to your TV speech. But why?"

I began to fidget in my seat. She was getting way too close to the truth.

"It's Sloane. You want to get close to Sloane so you can plant the leech."

I shook my head with as much energy as I could summon. "Not

even close. I told you, you don't need to know. You did your part, now it's time for you to go home."

"Oh yeah?"

"Yeah. Just shut your mouth, Corinne."

"Or?"

"Or else."

Corinne scoffed, sending pieces of spit flying at me from across the van. "Cut the act. I know who you really are."

"Oh yeah? Who am I really?"

"You're just a child. You've never known tough times until now. You try to put on this *tough girl* act, but we all see right through it. Shall I go on?"

"Sure."

"You think you can help, but you don't have the courage or the brains to actually do it. You may have convinced yourself you're something special, but everyone else sees the truth. Even Jakob."

Jakob put his hand on Corinne's shoulder. "That's enough, you two. Drop it."

My breathing became faster and shallower as she continued.

"You're stupid. You try so hard to find the good in everyone, but you're too naive to realize that sometimes there is none. That's why Jakob was able to fool you so easily. You still secretly hope you'll be together somehow, but it's not gonna happen."

Jakob tried to calm the situation. "I said, that's enough. Calm down."

"I *am* calm. What about you, Riley Riley? I can feel the anger brewing inside you. You wanna jump across this van and hit me. But you know what'll happen, don't you?"

She was right. My fists were clenched, but she had disabled four agents back in the parking garage, so going after her would be stupid.

"Jakob never really loved you...and he never will."

I lunged across the van, swinging my fist at her perfect teeth. Without any effort, she grabbed my wrist and lifted my arm behind my back, forcing me to the floor. The pain in my shoulder was blinding as the muscles and ligaments began to stretch.

Jakob screamed out, "Corinne...Corinne, let go!"

"Shut up, Jakob! This is between me and her. What do you think now, Riley Riley?" She pushed my wrist up higher behind my back, causing my shoulder to nearly come out of its socket.

I had never felt pain like this. "I'm sorry! I'm sorry! Please let me go!"

Jakob tried to intervene again. "Corinne, let go or you won't get your money."

"You can't."

"Yes, I can. And all I have to do is make one phone call to the right agent, and they'll know you helped us."

Corinne gave my arm one last push before she finally released her grip and crawled back to her side. "Fine. I wouldn't want to get her blood all over me anyway. It's not worth it."

I lay on the floor with my face buried in my arms, whimpering for the next several minutes. I finally sat up and moved my arm around in a circle to assess the damage. My shoulder felt like a rubber band that had been stretched beyond its capacity and struggled to regain its original shape.

"Relax. I didn't break anything...yet."

A thousand sarcastic comments filled my head, but my body couldn't take the abuse, so I remained quiet."

Corinne sniffed. "You know, you can't get rid of me yet."

"Why not?" I muttered.

"You still need me to help with the leech. And besides, I know too much."

"You don't know everything," I spoke under my breath, but Corinne still heard me.

"I know enough. And now you're gonna tell me the rest so I can help."

— ● —

We had no choice but to tell Corinne the truth; well, most of it. She already knew enough to pose a problem for us, and we would need her electronics expertise if this mission were to be successful. For all her bravado, she seemed to harbor a good bit of resentment for the government that had dismissed her. Jakob wisely played into that angle, along with Corinne's love of money.

If you didn't know the truth, you would think the two of them were still as deeply in love as they were before he left. I knew all too well that Jakob could be very convincing when it came to things like this. I just had to hold it together so we could finish our mission, and she would be out of our lives once and for all.

We were still about twenty minutes away from Corinne's house when she got an alert on her phone. "That's weird. My cameras are offline."

Jakob's ears perked up. "Does that ever happen?"

"No. Either my power's out, or my Internet is down. Let me check something else."

Jakob glanced over at Corinne's phone to see what she was seeing. "What's going on?"

"Don't know yet. It's probably nothing."

"I don't know," Jakob said. "Someone may be on to us. Maybe one of those agents recognized you."

Corinne scoffed. "Nah. They would've said my name on the radio by now if they knew I was there."

"I don't know. But we can't take any chances. We have to go somewhere else."

"No way. All my stuff's there. And the leech. I'm sure it's nothing."

"But what if it isn't?"

Jakob was right. The chances that an agent recognized Corinne were slim, but even a slim chance had to be taken seriously.

Corinne bit her lip as she thought. "Make you a deal. We can go check things out, and if we see any signs of danger, we'll go somewhere else. Otherwise, I'm going in. Besides, even if someone *is* in my house, I can take care of them."

Jakob let out a forced chuckle. "Okay, fine."

After a few more minutes of driving, we parked the van in the same parking lot down the road from Corinne's house. It was nearly midnight, so traffic was light. Charlie got out of the van and pulled the magnetic signs off the sides. If any of the agents viewed the surveillance video from the parking garage, they would know how we camouflaged the van. Jakob grabbed the binoculars out of the duffle bag and fixed his gaze on Corinne's house. "I guess the power's out on the whole block. Corinne, check your phone to see if there's an update from the power company."

A moment later she had an answer. "Yeah. Their website says they're doing maintenance in the area and had to shut it off. Guess that explains it."

Jakob didn't seem convinced. "I don't know. Wouldn't this be the perfect cover story? If they only shut the power off to your house, it would look too suspicious."

It seemed plausible, but it also seemed a bit extreme. Then again, I knew first-hand what kind of lengths the government would go to in order to capture someone they really wanted.

Corinne reached for the binoculars and spied on her home. "I don't see anything out of place. No strange cars, no signs of anyone in the house. I think you're just being paranoid."

I spoke for the first time since nearly having my arm ripped off. "Corinne's right. They wouldn't shut the power off everywhere for this. It's just a coincidence."

Jakob threw his hands up in the air, knowing it was pointless to argue with the two of us. "Fine. But we've still got to be careful. We can't just walk in the front door. We have to act as though we expect someone to be in there waiting for us."

Corinne and I both nodded in agreement.

Charlie called out to the back of the van. "I called HQ to update them on our progress. They said Faith's little speech was generating quite a bit of buzz."

"I did? Did Sloane say anything yet?"

"Not yet. They think he's planning a response of some sort, but it won't come until tomorrow. Phase 1 appears to be a success."

Jakob reached out for a hug, but it wasn't toward me. He and Corinne embraced for a few moments, then she finally released her grip on him. He looked at me and held up his hand for a high-five. "You did it!"

I began to reach for his hand, but I held back. Corinne would probably rip my arm off and smack me in the head with it. Instead, I smiled a half-smile and nodded. "So, what's the plan?"

CHAPTER THIRTEEN

Charlie dropped Corinne off on the street behind her house. She was going to go in alone, get what she needed, and meet us back in the parking lot down the street. Once we were parked in the darkness, Jakob scooted over and put his arm around me in the dim light in the back of the van. "How you holding up?"

This was the first time he and I had been alone since Corinne entered our lives. I rested my head on his shoulder and relaxed in his embrace. I took a deep breath in through my nostrils, but all I could smell was her perfume on his shirt. The nausea was back again. I scooted away and sat on the opposite side. "I can't."

"You can't what?"

"I can't do this. I can't watch you with her anymore. We have to find another way."

Jakob pleaded with his hands. "I know this is hard for you. It's hard for me too. I don't like doing this."

"Then don't do it."

"We don't have a choice. We need her."

"For how much longer?"

Jakob shrugged. "I don't know. Maybe another day or two. I think we'll need her help to get the leech online."

"I can do that by myself. We just need to get the leech from her, then I'll handle the rest. Then we can get rid of her."

Jakob scooted closer and sat on the floor in front of me. "Not yet. We can't have her compromising the mission before you install the leech on Sloane's computer."

My skin began to crawl. It was getting harder to breathe. I tried to rub my hands and arms to make the feeling stop, but it didn't work. Jakob put his hand on my shoulder. "Faith, what's going on?"

"I don't know. I just...I don't know." I blinked my eyes, trying to clear my vision, but the walls continued to close in on me. "Jakob, I'm scared. I don't know what's happening."

He leaned forward and hugged me, so our heads rested on each other's shoulders. There was the perfume again. I could almost taste it now. I pushed Jakob away and started crawling around on the floor, my hands and knees moving around without my control. I curled up in a ball and began to sob uncontrollably. A million thoughts and doubts and fears flooded my mind. Jakob's hand touched the top of my head, and he began to stroke my hair. Another wave hit me as I remembered what I had done to my hair in the name of our mission. Just another sacrifice I've had to make. How many more would there be? And how long until it was all over? The hardest part of my mission still lay ahead. What if it didn't work out? What if Sloane arrested me after all? What if Jakob and Corinne ended up together? What if...What if...?

I opened my eyes and blinked them a few times to get my bearings. I was still lying on the van floor, but I could tell some time had passed. I sat up and looked at Jakob, who stared at me with wide eyes and an open mouth. "Jakob, what happened?"

"I was about to ask you the same thing. I think you blacked out."

I sat up and took a deep, controlled breath. "I think you're right. How long was I out?"

"I don't know. A couple minutes. Are you okay now?"

My heart rate and vision were normal. My skin no longer felt like it was crawling. "I think so. What was that?"

"It looked like a panic attack. I've never seen you do that before. You scared me."

"I scared me too. I've gotten a little anxious before, but never like that."

Jakob reached down and put his hand on mine. "You really need to get help. You're going through a lot, and you need to talk to someone."

I jerked my hand away. "I'm fine. Once all this is over, I'll be good."

"Faith, listen to me. Mental health is a big deal. You may think you're fine, but there's something going on. You gotta get some help."

"Fine. Once all this is over, I'll talk to someone."

"Promise?"

I leaned up and planted a passionate kiss on Jakob's lips to show him how fine I really was. "I promise."

Charlie leaned around from the front seat. "I hate to bring this up, but Corinne's been gone for about ten minutes."

Jakob grabbed the binoculars and focused on Corinne's house. I'm not sure what he thought he would see in the dark, but that didn't stop him from looking. "I don't see anything. I need to go check on her."

I grabbed his arm as he started toward the back doors. "Wait a minute. You sure that's a good idea?"

"Someone has to make sure she's okay."

"What if she's not? What if she got captured? If you go in, you'll just get captured too."

"You sure have a lot of faith in my skills, don't you?"

I let go of his arm. "It's not that. It's just that, if you stay here, you're safe. If you go in there, you're in danger."

He leaned forward and kissed me on the cheek. "I'll be fine. Trust me. If we're not back in five minutes, leave without us." With that, he hopped out of the van and closed the doors behind him.

I grabbed the binoculars and watched as Jakob ran down the street toward Corinne's house. I glanced over at her house but saw no signs of life. I turned my eyes back toward Jakob just in time to see him disappear behind some bushes. Still no signs of life inside Corinne's house. "What do we do if they don't make it back in five minutes, Charlie? Do we really leave?"

Charlie unwrapped a snack cake and stuffed it in his mouth. "I don't think we have a choice. We can't have all three of you getting captured. Right now, Corinne only knows part of the plan."

"Yeah, but she probably knows enough that it'll ruin it."

"But none of you know where our HQ really is, so if we go back there, we're safe. We just regroup and come up with something else."

I kept watching through the binoculars, looking for something that told me Corinne and Jakob were safe. Neither Charlie nor I said a word as we watched the time. The silence was interrupted by the sound of static and beeps coming from Jakob's duffle bag. I pulled the binoculars away from my eyes and turned toward the bag. Faint voices now joined the static and beeps. The walkie-talkie! I lunged forward, grabbed the radio, and turned the volume up.

"All units, this is 1206. We are nearing Maxwell's house. ETA is four minutes. We request backup. Keep the power turned off."

"1206, this is 1279. We are en route as well. ETA is 6 minutes. Stand down until we arrive."

I scrambled toward the front of the van. "Agents are coming. Lots of them. I gotta go." I jumped out of the van and ran toward Corinne's house, not bothering to shut the doors behind me. I didn't have to worry about being spotted since the first group of agents wouldn't be here for a couple more minutes. I followed the same path Jakob had taken, and toward Corinne's backyard. I took in a few deep, controlled breaths and checked my surroundings. No sights or sounds concerned me, so I made my way closer to her house. I made it to her backyard and sprinted toward the house. As I got closer, I could see some lights moving around, and heard some voices inside. They were too muffled to identify, but it had to be Jakob and Corinne.

I was finally to her house. Hopefully, they left the back door unlocked. I stormed up the back porch steps, but just as I reached for the doorknob, the deadbolt unlocked. No one came out, so I opened the door, whose loud creak announced my arrival. "Hey, it's me...Faith." Out of nowhere, something struck the side of my head, and everything went hazy. My face winced from the pain.

"Faith? Faith? You okay?"

I opened my eyes, but my vision was blurry. A battery-powered light provided enough light for me to tell I was lying on the kitchen floor while Jakob and Corinne stood above me. "What happened?"

"Corinne kicked you. She thought you were an intruder."

I rubbed the side of my head, trying to get the pain to leave. "I said my name when I came in."

Corinne laughed. "Sorry, Riley Riley. I must not have heard you."

Yeah right. She had to have done that on purpose. There's no way she didn't hear me.

I sat up and tried to shake the cobwebs out of my head. "Tell me you got the leech."

"Right here." Jakob patted the messenger bag he held over his shoulder. "What are you doing here? I told you to wait in the van."

"I heard some agents on the radio. They're on the way here."

Corinne ran to the front of the house and peeked around one of the curtains. "Are you sure?"

"Yes! They said they're almost to Maxwell's house. They're gonna be here any minute."

Corinne peered up and down the street. "I don't see anyone."

Jakob trotted over to Corinne and grabbed her shoulder. "Doesn't matter. We should go."

Corinne grabbed Jakob by the hand and dragged him past me without helping me up.

I crawled to a nearby stool and hoisted myself off the floor. "Never mind me. I can get up on my own."

The sound of car doors slamming out front was our signal to start running toward the back door. We turned around just in time to see four agents pour into the kitchen. Corinne took care of the first two, sending them crumpling to the ground in agony. Jakob began wrestling with the third agent, and the fourth agent, a man even taller than Lenny, grabbed Corinne from behind and lifted her off the ground. Her feet flailed in the air, as she was no match for his grip. I needed a weapon. I looked around the kitchen and saw a cast iron skillet sitting on the stove. I lunged for it and picked it up. Jakob was still wrestling on the ground with his agent, while Corinne still hung in the air, fighting to escape. Corinne and her agent were facing the opposite direction, so I was able to sneak up behind him. I lifted the skillet with both hands and struck him in the head with all the force I could muster. I expected it to make the comical sound I had heard in so many cartoons, but it was a much lower, sickening thud. He dropped Corinne, then fell to his knees where he was an easy target. I smacked him again, sending him face down on the ground. We both looked over at Jakob who continued to grapple with his new friend. "Need some help?" Corinne called out.

"No, I got this."

I was tired of waiting, so I walked over and struck the last agent on the head with the skillet. "What are you doing?" Jakob asked. "I was about to take him."

Corinne reached out her hand and helped Jakob to his feet.

"Yeah right," Corinne and I both said at the same time.

Jakob picked his messenger back up off the ground, and we

made our way toward the back door with Jakob leading the way. We were nearly outside when the front door and windows smashed open, allowing four more enemies in suits to enter. I screamed, and all three of us sprinted toward the woods behind Corinne's house. I turned around just in time to see the agents exit the house and run toward us through the backyard. The moon was full that night, which allowed us to see where we were stepping, but it also allowed the agents to see exactly where we were going. We had a good lead on them, but that lead wouldn't last long.

"You two go that way, I'll go this way!" Jakob called as we reached the edge of the woods. He went left, Corinne went right, and I went right with Corinne. She had already proven herself to be formidable in hand-to-hand combat, so I liked my chances of survival with her.

Corinne turned around and let out a groan when she saw me following her. "What are you doing?"

"Running."

"I see that. Why are you following me?"

"Jakob told me to."

Corinne stopped abruptly and grabbed my arm as I nearly ran past her. I braced myself for another blow to the head, but instead, she spoke. "We can't outrun them, so we need to hide. You hide behind this tree, and I'll hide over there."

We both got in position just in time to see three agents come tromping through the woods. I held my breath as they ran past without even noticing us. Once they were a safe distance away, Corinne walked over to my tree. "It worked."

I smiled at her for the first time ever. "Yeah. Good idea."

"Thanks. By the way, I want to say..."

Her speech was interrupted by the sound of another agent hitting her in the head, sending her to the ground. The agent turned and glared at me, then called to his partners. "I got Webber. Over here!" He walked closer to me; hands outstretched, ready to attack.

I didn't have the training Corinne had, but I had to try something. I faked to the right, causing him to shift his weight that way. In the process, he lost his footing and fell to his knees. I spun around toward my left and unleashed the hardest kick my leg could muster. I connected with the side of his head, sending him face down into the forest floor. Corinne picked herself up off the ground and studied the agent on the ground. "Did you do that?"

"Yeah. But I think the other guys are coming back." The voices began to get closer and closer, but this time they were coming from several directions at once. We were surrounded. Our eyes darted around, looking for sanctuary, but there was none to be found. We looked at each other, then both looked up. The tree next to us had branches that were low enough for us to reach if we worked together.

Corinne ran and stood underneath the lowest branch. "Boost me up so I can reach it."

"What about me?"

"I'll pull you up."

The voices were getting even closer now.

I looked at the branch and back at Corinne. "Why don't you boost me up?"

"I'm stronger than you. I can pull you up better than you can pull me up."

I didn't trust her, but I was out of other options. I clasped my hands together and held them out. Corinne stepped into my hands, and I lifted with all my might.

"Got it," she said as she pulled herself up.

The voices and footsteps were almost on us. I looked at Corinne and held up my hands, hoping she would make good on her promise. To my surprise, she reached down for me. I took her hands and pulled, but I was too weak to pull myself up.

Corinne crawled closer to the trunk of the tree. "Down here. Grab my hands and try to walk up the tree."

I took her hands once more and used my feet to push myself higher. My right foot found a knot that provided some leverage, and soon I was next to Corinne on the branch. We scrambled up a couple more branches and sat on opposite sides of the trunk, waiting for our visitors to arrive. We didn't have to wait long as several agents converged on the spot where we just stood. The agent I had kicked was with them. They looked all around as Corinne and I clung close to the tree trunk, trying to stay hidden. I wiped the sweat off my face with my sleeve so it wouldn't drip off me and land on one of the agents. The leader of the group barked out some commands, and they went along their way, continuing their search through the woods.

Corinne looked at me with relief in her eyes, but I wasn't ready to relax yet. "Don't get too comfortable. We're not out of the woods yet." I wasn't trying to be funny, but it still struck Corinne that way. She covered her mouth to contain her laughter.

"You're so goofy, Riley Riley." The way she said it actually had a slightly friendly tone.

We stayed in place for several minutes as the voices grew fainter and eventually disappeared. We sat in awkward silence, trying to figure out when it would be safe to climb down from our perch.

I broke the silence. "So, what were you gonna say?"

"What do you mean?"

"A few minutes ago. It sounded like you were going to thank me for taking out that agent."

Corinne snorted. "Oh, that? Yeah, you did good. Although he probably just slipped and hit his head and you took the credit."

"No way. I used your move and kicked him in the head. Although I think it hurt me as much as it hurt him. My foot's really starting to kill now."

Corinne let out a tiny laugh, then the awkward silence returned.

"Corinne?"

"What?"

"I...uh...well, I just..."

"Stop."

I wrinkled my forehead. "Stop what?"

"Stop trying to be nice. You don't like me, and I can't stand you. Don't even pretend you don't know that. I have a job to do, and I'm gonna do it. Then I'm going to take my money, take Jakob, and live a nice, happy life."

That stung, but I refused to sink to her level. "You know how you said that you know who I really am? Well, you were right. I'm not cut out for this."

"No kidding."

"I don't have the experience and skill you and Jakob do. But you're stuck with me, and if you wanna get your money, you're gonna have to live with me for a while longer."

"Fine. Just as long as we understand each other. Now let's get going. I haven't heard any sounds besides your annoying voice in a long time."

Satisfied that we were in the clear, we crawled down to the

lowest branch, hung on by our arms, and let go. Corinne landed with much more grace than I did, but at least we both made it. We took off and ran back in the direction of the van.

It's amazing what your body is capable of in times of stress. I've never been very athletic, but I've learned that when my life is in danger, I can run really far, really fast. Corinne and I made it back to the parking lot without any agents or any snarky remarks. It took a moment to find the van though. The security signs were gone, and it was light gray now. The van's back doors opened, and Jakob popped his head out. "Took you long enough."

We hopped into the back, and Charlie pulled out of the parking lot, and out onto the highway.

I reached over to hug Jakob, but Corinne beat me to it. She even threw in a kiss for good measure. She never missed an opportunity to make my life miserable.

122

CHAPTER FOURTEEN

Corinne finally let go of Jakob and stroked his hair a few times. "What happened to you?"

Jakob laughed. "It's funny. All the agents chased you two, so all I did was jog back to the van and wait. What happened to you?"

I opened my mouth to answer, but again, Corinne beat me to it. "You wouldn't believe it. One of the agents caught up to us, and Riley Riley over there said she knocked him out cold. Although I think he probably tripped and hit his head."

I objected to that accusation, but Corinne kept talking anyway.

"Anyway, we were surrounded, so we climbed up a tree and waited for them to leave."

Jakob looked at me and chuckled. "Another tree?"

I shrugged my shoulders. "What can I say? I'm a regular lumberjack."

Corinne smiled. "Yeah, you already dress like one."

I was wearing shorts and a t-shirt, but whatever. She was just saying that to embarrass me in front of Jakob. I turned the volume on the walkie-talkie up so we could hear the agents. There was a little bit of yelling, and a lot of swearing as they searched the woods and Corinne's house. Luckily, there was no mention of our van, so it looked like we were in the clear for now.

Corinne's face grew angrier and angrier as she heard them searching her house. "They'd better not mess with any of my stuff." She tried to access her cameras again, but they were still offline.

Jakob reached over and put his arm around Corinne. "I'm sure it'll be okay. We have the leech, and soon you'll have your money."

That brought a smile to Corinne's face. "Yeah, but still. I don't like people messing with anything that's mine." She squeezed Jakob and glared at me when she said that last part. Message received.

I crawled toward the front of the van to get away from Corinne and talk to Charlie. "Where are we going?"

"Somewhere that's not here.

"Okay, but that doesn't help. Are we going back to HQ?"

Charlie shook his head. "Can't do that. Not as long as Corinne's with us."

She was becoming quite a nuisance. "So, where do we go then?"

"There's another safehouse about an hour away. We'll go there so we can rest and regroup."

Rest. That concept had been foreign to me for a while. I don't know how much sleep I had gotten the last several days, but it wasn't enough. I crawled back to my seat in the back of the van and closed my eyes. Partly to rest, but mostly so I wouldn't have to look at Corinne who was resting her head on Jakob's shoulder. There was no chatter in the back of the van, which was fine with me because I didn't want to hear anything Corinne had to say.

It was nearly 2:00 AM when we finally arrived at the safehouse. The van came to a stop and jolted us awake.

"We're here," Charlie said as he opened his door and climbed out of his seat. The rest of us gathered our belongings and made our way to the back of the van. We stepped out into the night air and took in our surroundings. I frowned at the sight of another cabin, but at least it was someplace for us to get cleaned up and get some sleep.

We followed Charlie up the front steps and waited as he placed his finger on the doorknob. A green light above the doorknob told us his fingerprint was accepted, and the deadbolt whirred open. Once we are all inside, Charlie closed and locked the front door, and walked over toward the fireplace. "Sorry, there's no magic basement here. But we're safe. There's a shower and some cots for you to sleep on. I'll get you some robes so we can wash your clothes."

That sounded amazing. After my sprints in DC and in the woods, I was overdue for a shower and some clean clothes. Jakob told Corinne she could shower first. While she was getting cleaned up, Jakob sat on the couch next to me, taking my hand in his. Neither of us said a word for a few moments. It was nice just to have contact with him again. I squeezed his hand and smiled. "I hate this."

"I know. So do I."

"Every time she puts her hands on you, I want to scream, or throw up, or throw something at her."

Jakob wrapped his arm around me and pulled me close to him. "Trust me, I don't like it any more than you do. I feel like I'm betraying you, and worst of all, you have to watch the whole thing."

"It'll be over soon. Just don't let things get out of hand. I don't want you alone with her."

"What does that mean? Don't you trust me?"

I sat up and scooted back a few inches. "Well yeah, I just don't trust her."

"Don't be silly. Nothing's gonna happen."

"Nothing's gonna happen? How can you say that? Stuff *is* happening. And sometimes it seems like..."

Jakob stared at me, waiting for me to finish the sentence. "Seems like what?"

I looked down at my hands. "Nothing."

"No, go ahead and say it. No secrets, right?"

I looked back up at Jakob, my vision blurred by the tears in my eyes. "It seems like you like it when she's all over you." My head sank back down again.

Jakob placed his fingers under my chin and lifted my head. "I hate it. But I can't act like I hate it, because then she'll know something's up. I wish I could make you believe that."

"So do I."

The bathroom door opened, and I sprang to my feet. I walked toward the bathroom, covering my face as I passed Corinne in the hall. She couldn't know I had been crying.

I turned on the shower and stepped inside, letting the soothing water cascade down from my head to my feet. Now that I was alone, the emotions that had been bottled inside came out in waves of tears and spit and snot. My legs buckled, and I fell to my knees, weeping even harder into my hands. "God, I need you. I need you to help me. I know you have a plan, but right now, I'm not seeing it. Please make this be over soon. I wanna follow your will, but please don't make me suffer more. I just...I just need to know you're still with me. Please show me you're still there."

I stayed on the shower floor, waiting for some sort of answer from God, but I didn't hear or sense anything noticeable. After a few more minutes, I felt a little more peace than I had before, so I stood up and began scrubbing. It took a long time, and several applications of body wash before my skin finally felt clean. Washing my hair was easy though, after my recent haircut. I dried myself off, put my robe on, and walked back toward the living room where Jakob and Charlie had set up our cots. Two of them were on one side of the living room, while the other was about fifteen feet away. Of course, Corinne put her cot close to Jakob's. Whatever.

After Jakob's shower, we threw our nasty clothes into the washing machine and started it up. Charlie half-joked that we should probably just burn our clothes since they were so disgusting. We would have considered that if we had some spare clothes lying around, so doing laundry was the best option. We had some time to kill, so we convened in the living room to map out our next steps.

Charlie started things off by telling us that he had spoken with the folks at HQ. "They're thrilled with the results of your speech, Faith. They wanted me to tell you that you did a great job of improvising when the original plan failed."

I wanted to stick my tongue out at Corinne, but I simply said, "Thanks. So, we just wait here and see what Sloane does next?"

"Pretty much. They want us all to talk more tomorrow...I mean today. There's nothing we can do right now, so we'll take some time to rest. Why don't you all go to bed? I'll put the clothes in the dryer when they're ready."

Charlie turned the lights off and walked out of the living room toward his bedroom. None of us said a word, and before long, I was fast asleep.

I normally don't remember my dreams, but that night, I had one of the most vivid dreams of my life. I saw a herd of sheep in a beautiful pasture, with a shepherd and his gray dog sitting under a nearby tree. The dog's eyes were busy, watching for any signs of danger while the shepherd relaxed, and the sheep grazed and drank from a brook. A fence surrounded the pasture, but it was designed more to keep the sheep in, rather than to keep the danger out. The green of the pasture and the sound of the brook were soothing. This was a place I would love to visit at some point after things settled down. The bliss was interrupted by the sight of a black wolf creeping toward the pasture fence. I tried to scream at the shepherd, but my mouth wouldn't make a sound. The wolf crept closer. It jumped through the openings in the fence and took off toward one of the sheep. I screamed again for the shepherd, but again, no sound came out of my mouth. I wanted desperately to do something, but I was frozen.

The wolf was nearly to the sheep when out of nowhere, a gray blur plowed into the wolf and sent it rolling across the pasture. I looked back to the shepherd, and he was standing up, watching his dog take on the wolf. I looked back toward the action and saw that the shepherd's dog wasn't a dog at all. It was another wolf, but it was a much bigger wolf than the one that attacked the sheep. The black wolf attacked again, but the gray wolf sank its teeth into the black wolf's neck and flipped him over. Rattled, the black wolf stood again and stared at the gray wolf, who stood his ground. Not willing to risk another attack, the black wolf retreated. The gray wolf took a few steps to make sure the intruder was gone, then ushered the sheep closer to the shepherd. The victor trotted up to the shepherd and sat in front of him, eager to receive praise for a job well done. The shepherd stroked the wolf's head and said, "I needed you to save my sheep, and you did. Well done, my good and faithful helper." The two of them then sat back down under the tree.

The sound of a slamming cabinet door woke me from my sleep. Jakob was still in his cot, but Corinne was in the kitchen making all sorts of noise. If she was awake, everyone else should be also. I lay there for a moment, thinking about my dream. It felt weird like it was supposed to symbolize something. Then it hit me. Maybe I was the wolf, and God had sent me to save his sheep. It's funny how God doesn't always answer when and how we expect him to, but He still answers.

We had slept through breakfast and ate a delicious lunch

consisting of macaroni and cheese with tuna, baked beans, and fruit cocktail. It was almost as though we were back in our underground bunker, but this time I had to deal with Corinne. Every word she said to me was like a tiny hammer, chipping away at my resolve. She knew I had feelings for Jakob, but we couldn't let her know he also had feelings for me. I almost slipped up a couple of times, but my brain actually stopped my mouth for once in my life.

After lunch and a brief nap, we gathered in the living room for a strategy meeting. Charlie had spoken with Mia, and now he was going to share that information with the three of us. "First of all, Faith, your dad says hello. They're doing fine. And Paul is getting stronger each day. Second, Corinne, I'm afraid you need to leave the room."

A look of shock appeared on Corinne's face while a slight smirk appeared on mine.

"Why do I have to leave?"

Charlie unwrapped a snack cake and studied it as he spoke. "We're going to be discussing sensitive information, and while we appreciate your help so far, we can't let you hear what we'll be saying. I'm sorry."

Corinne looked at Jakob, but he didn't step in to vouch for her. "Fine. I'll go lay down in the bedroom."

Once she was out of earshot, Charlie continued. "Sloane gave a press release to address Faith's little speech from last night."

"Oh yeah? What did he say about me?"

"Basically, he said that he welcomed a meeting with you and that the invitation was open. He said to come to the front gate of the White House any time."

Jakob didn't seem to like the open invitation. "How do we know he won't try to kill her again?"

Charlie swallowed the last bite of his snack cake. "That was the whole point of her making the broadcast last night. Now that everyone knows Faith's still alive, he can't kill her."

Jakob furrowed his brows. "I still don't like it. I feel like she's walking into a trap."

"Wasn't that the point of this whole thing? We didn't go through everything yesterday just to give up now. She can do this."

I stood to my feet and walked over toward the fireplace. "Will you two stop talking about me like I'm some sort of child? This is my choice, stop trying to make it for me."

Jakob and Charlie both looked at me, but neither said a word.

I turned to face the two of them. "Charlie's right. The whole reason we risked our lives yesterday was to tell the world I'm still alive so I could get to Sloane. Now's our chance, so I'm gonna take it."

Jakob stood and walked closer to me. "I know what you said, but now that it's happening, I don't have a great feeling about the whole thing. Are you sure about this?"

I glared at him for a moment. "Yeah. What's the worst that can happen?"

Jakob smirked. "Ummm...you could be arrested...or killed."

I waved my hand to dismiss Jakob's rebuttal. "He already killed me once, remember? He can't do it again. That's double jeopardy."

Jakob began to open his mouth, but the smile on my face let him know that I knew what double jeopardy really was. "If you say so. But we need to figure out how you're gonna plant the leech. I guess we need Corinne for this part."

I rolled my eyes, but Jakob was right. She was the only one of us who knew how that thing worked. Jakob walked down the hall and retrieved Corinne from her "time out". She dragged Jakob by the hand and sat them both on the couch.

"What did I miss?"

Charlie looked over at Corinne. "Our plan worked. The Chancellor invited Faith to the White House to talk. Now we need you to help us with the leech. How does it work?"

Corinne took in a long breath and sighed as if she were trying to figure out how to explain something complicated to a room full of idiots. "Well, it needs to be close to the host computer."

"How close?" Charlie asked.

"Close close. Like stuck to it if possible. Maybe it'll work if you stick it on his desk somewhere."

I closed my eyes and shook my head. This wasn't going to be easy. "But how do we communicate with it?"

"It has a tiny cellular antenna, and once the leech connects with the Internet, you can control Sloane's computer through the Internet."

Jakob smiled. "That's awesome. Then what?"

Corinne shrugged her shoulders. "Beats me. Riley Riley's the computer expert."

Everyone turned and stared at me for an answer, but I had nothing. "I don't know how that leech works."

Charlie gave us a long look before speaking. "Ladies, it looks like you need to work together on this. Corinne, you know the hardware, and Faith you know the software."

Corinne smiled her biggest smile yet and held out her hand. "Sounds fun. Whaddya say, Riley Riley?"

Unfortunately, Charlie was right. I needed her help, and she needed my help if we wanted this to work. I reached out and shook Corinne's hand. "Okay, fine. But Charlie, we're gonna need some supplies."

CHAPTER FIFTEEN

Charlie wouldn't return for several more hours, so Jakob, Corinne, and I passed the time by watching TV and discussing how we would get the leech to work. We spoke with Paul on a video chat, and he gave us more insight about Sloane's computer and the software he used to control Project Oversight. The news was less than promising. Not only was this computer in the White House, but it was on Sloane's desk in the Oval Office. Paul said that Sloane conducts most of his business in the Oval Office, so there was a decent chance he would meet with me in there; however, there are some things Sloane prefers to keep off the record. Those meetings are held elsewhere in the White House. We would have to hope and pray that I somehow ended up in the Oval Office.

Charlie finally returned with the equipment we requested, and Corinne and I sat down at the table to get to work. Corinne attached the leech to one of the computers Charlie had brought us and handed me a folded sheet of paper and a microdrive. "Here's your instructions, Riley Riley."

I hooked the microdrive to the other computer Charlie brought. "You know, you really don't have to call me that anymore."

"I know. So, what's your plan?"

"Well, I need to figure out how your leech communicates with the Internet. Then I need to write a program for REFUGE that'll allow them to connect to it so their AI software can do its thing."

I launched the program that ran the leech and saw a blank screen. "Now what?"

"You should be able to see what's on my screen."

"I got nothing."

Corinne sighed. "Are you sure you're doing it right? You're supposed to be the computer expert here." At least she didn't call me *Riley Riley* this time.

"I've never used this program before. Gimme a minute."

"This isn't gonna work if you don't know your stuff, Riley Riley."

I rolled my eyes at her and my computer. Finally, after several frantic clicks, I saw a word-processing program on my computer. The words on the screen said, "It's about time, Riley Riley!" I frowned and squinted my eyes at Corinne, who was howling with laughter. I deleted her words and typed "Very funny."

Jakob walked up to see what all the ruckus was about.

I smiled at Jakob. "Good news..."

Corinne jumped in before I could finish. "The leech works. Watch. I can still control my computer even though she's using the leech." She began typing a special message for me, but once I saw what she was typing I deleted it, sending Corinne howling again.

I cleared my throat to get Jakob's attention. "Now we need to test the leech to see what kind of range it has."

Corinne stood up, holding the leech a few inches away from her computer. "Still working?"

"So far so good."

She moved it a few more inches away. "How about now?" I nodded my head, so she moved so the leech was about a foot from her computer. My screen flashed a couple of times, and the word-processing program went in and out of focus.

"I think that's about as far as we can go. This thing isn't very strong, is it?"

Corinne put the leech on the table and plopped herself back in her chair. "They make leeches with more range, but those are too big. This one works fine. You'll just have to put it really close to his computer."

Jakob walked over and stood behind me, looking at my screen. "What's next, Faith?"

"Now I need to test a few more things to make sure the leech works right away. I don't want to leave anything to chance."

Corinne must not have liked Jakob standing closer to me than her, so she grabbed Jakob by the hand and led him away from the table. "C'mon, let's leave Riley Riley alone to do her work."

I don't know where she thought they were going. It's not like we were staying in a mansion or anything. Some peace and quiet made it easier to work my magic. All I needed to do was to install the leech on or near Sloane's computer. If all went well, it would connect to the Internet and allow someone at REFUGE to reposition the Oversight satellite so one of REFUGE's dishes could communicate with it. Once that happened, neither the White House nor the Pentagon could communicate with it anymore, and we would be able to free all the people under Sloane's control. We just had to hope all that could happen before someone discovered the leech.

I finished testing everything, then e-mailed the ID information on the leech to REFUGE, along with instructions for logging into it. I needed a break from staring at the computer screen for so long, so I stood up and stretched. I looked around the living room, but I was alone. Charlie was back in the bedroom, probably taking another nap, but where were Jakob and Corinne? I walked to the back door and saw the two of them cuddling on the back porch swing, talking and laughing. I opened the back door and stepped out into the fresh air. The sun had set, and the last remnants of orange clung to the western sky, resisting the call toward the horizon. It was unseasonably cool, which was welcome after all the sweating I had done the day before.

Jakob looked up at me, but Corinne continued to stare off into the woods. "Hey, Faith. Did you get it all done?"

I sat down on a wicker seat, next to the swing. "Yeah, I think so."

Corinne sneered at me. "You think so? You'd better be more sure than that."

"Well, it works here. But a lot could go wrong once I get there. You know a little something about that, don't you?"

Corinne ignored my jab and nestled her cheek on Jakob's shoulder. "Fine by me. I'm getting paid no matter what happens to you."

"I guess you're right. But you'd better hope I don't tell them all about you if I get caught."

Corinne sat up and shot a cold stare at me. "Is that a threat, Riley Riley?"

I laughed an uneasy laugh. "Not at all. I was just trying to have some fun."

Corinne scowled at me and laid her head back on Jakob's shoulder. "Whatever."

I chuckled to myself. It was nice to give a little grief back to Corinne considering how much she had given me. It was still sickening to see the two of them so close, but the jealousy was beginning to wear off. I was becoming more desensitized to it over time, but the biggest factor was my relationship with Jakob. He and I had exchanged some tense words, and I couldn't help but feel a void beginning to form between us. A void that Corinne was all too eager to fill. Right on cue, Corinne kissed Jakob on the cheek and whispered, "I love you." She may have whispered it, but she did it loudly enough for me to hear.

Jakob leaned over and kissed her on the head, then whispered into her ear. At least he had the decency to do it in such a way that I couldn't hear him.

I stood up and stomped toward the door, but before I could escape, Corinne called out to me. "Where are you going, Riley Riley? You're more than welcome to stay out here and enjoy the fresh air with us."

"I'm good. The fresh air is making me sick." The door was much lighter than I anticipated, so I ended up slamming it on my way in. Oh well. It was an appropriate punctuation mark on the evening. While Jakob and Corinne cuddled outside, I talked to some IT people at REFUGE and showed them what they would need to do on their end to take control of Sloane's computer. Once we discussed everything, there was a real sense of optimism. As long as I could hold up my end of the bargain.

— • ● • —

After another gourmet meal from boxes and cans, we sat down for our last strategy meeting before my trip to the White House the next day.

"I'll drive Faith to DC," Charlie said. "Jakob, you and Corinne can stay here."

My heart sank at the thought of the two of them alone in the cabin. "Why don't they come with us in case something goes wrong?"

Charlie shook his head. "That's precisely why they can't come with us. The fewer of us that are out in the field, the lower the risk."

"Can't Corinne come with me? What if we need her Kung Fu skills?"

Corinne bristled at my backhanded compliment. "It's Silat. I can show you some moves if that helps you remember."

"Nah, I'm good."

Charlie continued. "That's another reason I don't want her on the trip. It's no secret the two of you don't get along, and I don't need that extra stress."

"Fine. What if I take Jakob with me? He can protect me too."

Now it was Jakob's turn to get defensive. "Wait, I was your second choice for protection?"

Corinne laughed. "You know it's true."

Jakob shrugged his shoulders. "Maybe."

Corinne patted him on the hand. "It's okay. You're good at other things."

An awkward silence fell on the room, and everyone refused to make eye contact.

Charlie nearly choked on his water. "I'm gonna see if we have any dessert around here." He foraged through the pantry and sat back down with a couple of snack cakes of some kind. "Now, where were we?"

Corinne grabbed Jakob's arm and rubbed it. "We were talking about Jakob and me staying here while you took Faith to Washington."

Charlie unwrapped his dessert and took a bite. "Right. Faith, I know you don't want to hear this, but it's best if you and I go alone."

He was right, but I still didn't like it. I refused to look at Corinne, but I could feel the warmth of her smile anyway. At least we would be rid of her in a day or two.

"It's okay Riley Riley. I can take care of Jakob if any bad guys pay us a visit."

Jakob squirmed in his seat but refused to say anything.

Charlie swallowed his last bite of dessert. "There's one more thing. When I talked to HQ, they told me they want Corinne to come back with me and Jakob."

My eyes widened at Charlie. "What for?"

"She's the one that knows the most about this leech. If anything goes sideways, they want her around to take care of it."

This day just got better and better. "I set it up so you won't have to do anything but click a few buttons. It'll all be automatic."

"Better to be safe than sorry. We won't take her to HQ, but she'll be with an IT team at another REFUGE location."

I nearly asked if Jakob was going to be on that team, but I decided against it. "Okay. How are we gonna do this?"

Charlie opened the second snack cake. "Well, you and I will leave tomorrow after lunch and get there late afternoon. I'll drop you off a couple blocks from the White House, and you'll just stroll up to the front gate and introduce yourself."

"I just walk up and introduce myself? That's it?"

Charlie inhaled the snack cake in one bite, then spoke. "Well...yeah."

Corinne stood to her feet. "I'm gonna go take a shower. Try not to have too much fun without me."

Once she was gone, Charlie slid a sheet of paper across the table. I picked it up and read the phone number written on it. "What's this?"

"It's one of our REFUGE hotlines. Call that number night or day and someone will answer. You need to memorize it before you go tomorrow." He slid a phone across the table. "You can take this, but I can't program any phone numbers in it. Any questions?"

I shook my head and Charlie excused himself in search of more snack cakes. Once we were alone, Jakob scooted his seat closer and put his lips on mine.

I closed my eyes to enjoy the kiss, but all I could see was Corinne kissing him. I pulled away and put my head down. "I can't do this."

"Sure, you can. We have a good plan, and you'll pull it off."

I tried to blink away the tears forming in my eyes. "No. I can't do *this*. I can't pretend that I'm not in love with you. We've gone far enough now. You need to tell Corinne the truth tonight."

"Faith, I can't do that."

"Why not?"

"It's not the right time. Maybe once you get done in DC, we won't need her anymore. But we can't risk the mission when we're this close."

I looked at Jakob and sighed. "That's not the real reason."

"Sure, it is."

I shook my head and looked down at the table. "No, it's not. You're falling back in love with her. Not that I can blame you. She's everything I'm not. She's beautiful, confident, smart, and strong."

"Faith, listen to me. You're all those things, whether you think you are or not. You gotta believe me. You're the only woman I want."

"Look...I just...Can we just not talk about this right now?"

We sat in silence for a few moments as I ran through our plan in my head. I could get to the White House, but how would I get the leech on Sloane's computer? I was imagining myself in the Oval Office when Jakob grabbed my arm.

"Uhh, Faith? We've spent so much time figuring out what to do once you put the leech in place...but how are you gonna get it into the Oval Office in the first place?"

"What do you mean? I'll just hide it in my pocket or something."

"What if they search you?"

My heart sank even lower than it already was, and my stomach began to churn. "I don't know. I never thought about that."

Jakob rubbed my arm. "I think I have an idea, but you're probably not gonna like it."

That wave of nausea came back with a vengeance. "I think I'm gonna be sick."

A mischievous grin spread across Jakob's face. "Perfect. We can work with that."

CHAPTER SIXTEEN

Despite all the anxiety and tension of the week, I slept surprisingly well that night. We ate a decent breakfast, hashed out the plan a few more times, then ate lunch. I hadn't spoken to my family in a few days, so Charlie offered to arrange a video chat for us. Soon my whole family was on the screen staring at me. Mom and Dad sat on chairs while Hope and Alex sat on their laps.

They all spoke in unison. "Hi, Faith!"

"Hey. How is everyone?"

Alex waved his hands back and forth to get my attention. "Faith, where are you?"

"Hey, Alex. I'm in a cabin somewhere. But I'm about to go to the White House.

Alex looked confused. "Why? Didn't you just go there a few months ago?"

I laughed. "Yes, Alex. I'm going to have an important meeting with Chancellor Sloane."

Hope made a face like she had just smelled something rotten. "Bleh. We don't like him."

"I know. But this is gonna be a good meeting."

Alex pushed Hope's face aside so he could see me better. "Make sure he doesn't try to kill you again."

You had to admire Alex's bluntness. "I'll try."

Dad put Alex down and said, "Kids, why don't you go watch TV while we talk to Faith?"

Hope and Alex said goodbye and scurried off my screen, leaving me and my parents to stare at each other, waiting for someone to speak.

Dad gave me a look like he wanted to say something he knew I wouldn't want to hear. "Faith, are you still sure about this? There's still time to do something else."

"Dad, I know you're nervous. So am I. But this is gonna work. I really believe that."

"I know you do. But as your father, I still don't like any plan that puts you in danger."

"I won't be in danger, remember? He invited me publicly. He can't do anything to me."

Dad opened his mouth to speak, but Mom cut him off. "We have faith that you'll be okay, but we're your parents, so we'll always be protective of you."

"I know, Mom. I'll always appreciate you two."

Charlie waved at me from across the room, telling me it was time to sign off.

"I gotta go. I'll talk to you in a few days when this is all over."

They both waved and said they loved me.

"I love you too."

I signed off the computer and joined Charlie by the front door. "Let's do this."

The two of us walked out the front door and stepped out to the front porch where Jakob and Corinne stood. Charlie looked at Jakob and Corinne. "I'll be back in a few hours. Just sit tight until I get back." They both nodded, and Charlie walked down the steps, leaving the three of us on the porch.

Corinne held out her hand. "Good luck, Riley Riley...don't screw this up."

I wanted to shake her neck, but her hand would have to do. She gave my hand a good squeeze and said, "Don't worry, I'll take care of Jakob while you're gone."

A fire began burning inside me. "You know what Corinne, there's something you need to know about me and Jakob."

Her eyebrows lifted. "Yeah?"

"Yeah." I looked over at Jakob, who held his eyes wide open at me, begging me not to speak my mind. "We...we..."

Corinne glared at me. "You what?"

My shoulders slumped and my confidence disappeared. "You were right about my feelings for Jakob."

A huge smile appeared on Corinne's face. "I knew it."

"I used to be in love with him, but now I don't think I am anymore. So, you have nothing to worry about." I turned and walked down the porch steps; head held high. It was good to leave on my own terms. I marched to the back of the van and yanked the handle, which was still locked, causing my hand to slip off. I winced as the door handle tore the nail on my middle finger. So much for the shred of dignity I thought I had. The door finally clicked, and I opened it with my other hand. I climbed inside and shut the door without looking back toward Jakob and Corinne. Did they believe what I had said about my feelings for Jakob? More importantly, did I believe it?

It was around 3:30 when Charlie and I reached the capital city. The nervousness in my stomach had grown the whole journey, and now that we were almost at our destination, it had reached a crescendo. Even though I put on a brave front, deep inside I was quite nervous about this little plan of ours. In theory, it was sound, but real life doesn't always go according to theory. I spent much of the drive contemplating, planning, and most importantly, praying. I pictured the wolf in my dream and used that to reassure myself that I was on the right path.

We came to a stop, and Charlie put the van in park. "Do you have your phone and charger?"

"They're in my backpack along with everything else."

"Good. Try to keep your phone on you at all times in case we need to reach you."

"What if they take it from me?"

"You're not under arrest, so we don't think they will. If they do, we'll figure something else out."

Everyone at REFUGE shared the same sense of optimism. When a challenge arose, the response was always "We'll figure something out." It was inspiring at first, but as time wore on, it began to sound somewhat delusional.

Charlie looked at me with intensity in his eyes. "This is it. You know what you're supposed to do?"

"Yeah"

"Good. Remember, the phone is for emergencies only. Don't call us until you've planted the leech and you're ready for us to get you. Remember your exit plan. I'll be in the cabin for the next few days, so I can pick you up at a moment's notice."

"Got it."

"And Faith, be careful."

I nodded my head. "I'll do my best." I crawled to the back of the van, opened the door, and stepped out onto the curb. Once I shut the door, the van sped off and I was on my own. I tossed the backpack over my right shoulder and began the trek to the White House. On the way, I passed by several official-looking buildings and pedestrians, none of whom took note of me. Instead of hiding in the cramped bunker for the last couple of months, we could have just hidden in plain sight on the streets of a big city. Except for the traffic cameras and facial recognition software, of course. I turned a corner and found myself in the park I had run across the night of Sloane's speech. It really was beautiful now that I had a chance to slow down and admire it. I walked past statues of famous people I didn't recognize and watched as people walked around, living their normal lives. Being in the presence of so many other people was soothing, but truth be told, I was stalling a little. I had a mission, but I wasn't all that eager to take the next steps.

I found an empty bench near a statue of some guy I didn't recognize and let out a deep sigh. So many questions entered my mind. What if I couldn't get into the Oval Office? What if I couldn't get near his computer? What if the leech didn't work? What if Sloane refused to meet with me? What if he had me arrested? Would I ever see my family again? Would I ever see Jakob again? Were he and I really supposed to end up together? This whole crazy plan depended on a great number of situations playing out exactly right. I was going to need a lot of help, yet I was all alone...except for the little girl who was tapping on my arm.

"Have you seen my daddy?" She couldn't have been more than five or six years old.

"I'm sorry, I don't know who your daddy is. But I'll help you look for him." I stood up and looked around the park, even though I wasn't sure exactly who I was looking for. I took the little girl by the hand, and we walked toward the center of the park, hoping she would see her father or her father would see her.

A minute or so later the little girl reached her arms out and yelled, "Daddy!"

A man in a navy-blue sweater vest and khaki pants came running up to us and hugged the little girl. "There you are!"

The girl wiped the tears from her eyes. "I thought you left me."

"No baby, you walked away from me. You should know I'd never leave you alone." The man looked over at me with relief in his eyes. "Thank you."

I nodded at them both, then they walked away, hand in hand. Although this wasn't the same man in the sweater vest I had encountered in the woods, he was dressed the same way. More importantly, his words seemed to be meant for me as much as they were meant for his daughter. I walked back to the bench and sat down. With my head resting in my hands, I began to pray silently. "Thank you for those words, God. I have all these questions, and I don't know the answers, but I know you do. Please give me strength as I take the next steps and help everything to work out. It may not go the way I think it will, but it will go according to your plan."

I lifted my head and opened my eyes to find a small crowd forming in front of me. Some of the people were pointing, some were whispering, but all stood in amazement. I stood up and tucked the sides of my hair over my ears.

Several people gasped, and one woman said, "It's her."

I had been in hiding so long, my first instinct was to run, but my mission called for me to be taken into government custody anyway. The longer I stood there, the larger the crowd got. I glanced around, trying to make sense of everything when a little girl tugged on my arm.

"Are you her?" she asked.

"Am I who?"

"Are you Faith? The girl from the TV?"

I smiled at her and nodded.

The little girl was missing her front teeth, but her smile was still adorable. "I knew it. My parents were talking about you. They said you're gonna save the country."

I blushed and stroked her hair. "Well, I don't know about that, but I'm gonna do my best to help."

One by one, people came up to me. Some wanted to shake my

hand, the little girls wanted a hug, but everyone offered words of encouragement. My confidence swelled as I greeted all my new fans. More and more people grew curious about the growing crowd, so they came over to see what the fuss was about. Before I knew it, a couple hundred people were standing with me.

One of the women hugged me with all her might. "Where did you all come from?" I asked her.

"We've been waiting for you. We saw you on TV and we knew you'd be coming here eventually. This is our chance."

"Your chance for what?"

"Freedom. We've been running a secret church for the last few years, and living in fear the whole time. Some of our members have been arrested, and we've tried to keep going, but we were about to shut the whole thing down. Then you came along and we found the courage to keep going."

I looked around at the other people in the crowd. "Have you all been waiting here for me?"

Some of the people looked puzzled, but many of them said "Yes."

Wow. It's one thing to know you have a following of anonymous people online, but to see an army of real people supporting me was humbling and empowering at the same time. Inspired by their encouragement, I stood up on the bench and waved at the crowd. "Thank you for coming out here! I can't believe so many people care about me and what we're trying to do! I'm going to visit the Chancellor and demand that he gives us back our freedom!"

Every sentence was met with thunderous applause and shouting.

I hopped down from the bench and pointed to the White House. My new friends and I marched together across the park, and across the street toward the White House fence. I didn't have to worry about being seen, because my legions of followers were giving me all the attention I needed. I motioned for the crowd to stay back, and I walked up to one of the gates, where several armed guards waited. "I'm Faith Webber. I believe the Chancellor is expecting me."

The tallest of the guards spoke to his radio. "Base? She's here."

In a flash, several men in dark suits were at the gate to greet me. One of them opened the gate, and three men surrounded me. I braced myself for a physical altercation, but I was pleasantly surprised when they politely gestured for me to walk with them. One of them even said, "Right this way, Ms. Webber."

The gate shut behind us, and we made our way toward the White House. The crowd cheered behind me and began chanting my name. "Faith! Faith! Faith!" I threw up a quick wave, and before I knew it, we were inside the building.

CHAPTER SEVENTEEN

It had been nearly three months since I was last inside the White House, but it seemed like I was just there, having dinner with Sloane. The architecture, decorations, and busy people in dark suits brought back a wave of memories and a flood of emotions. Our plan was a good one, but it was still risky. We were all confident that Sloane wouldn't have me killed, but he could still make life miserable for all of us. Agents had searched my backpack when they brought me in, and much to my surprise, they didn't confiscate it. They even let me keep my phone. Maybe this was going to work after all.

As my new agent friends and I walked down the labyrinth of halls, my breathing became shallow, and my pulse quickened in a familiar manner. I tried to slow my breathing and hold off another panic attack, but I was losing. My hands took on a life of their own, squeezing and wringing each other. One of the agents who had introduced himself as Berkley noticed my agitation and stopped the procession. "Ms. Webber, are you all right?"

I stopped in my tracks and looked up into his eyes. Mustering all the strength I had, I stiffened my lips and replied, "Never better. Can we continue please?"

Seemingly satisfied, Berkley turned around and continued toward our destination.

Somehow fighting off the panic attack, I followed along, taking in the sights and sounds of the White House. All the halls looked alike, so I had no idea whether I had been in this part of the building during my last visit. No matter where we were, I had to find a way to get into the Oval Office so I could plant the leech near Sloane's computer. Subtlety and coolness had to be my approach though. I couldn't appear too eager to go into that famous room. "Where are we going, anyway?"

Berkley stopped at an elevator and pressed the button. "You'll use one of our guestrooms during your stay."

My *stay*? How long did they plan on keeping me? I cleared my throat. "That sounds nice. Will I get a tour of the White House while I'm here? I only saw a couple rooms last time."

The elevator door opened, and Berkley ushered me inside. "The Chancellor has plans for you. I don't know if you'll have time for a tour."

"Plans? What kind of plans?" My breathing became shallow again.

Berkley led us out of the elevator, around another corner, and down another hall. "The Chancellor didn't say, and we know better than to ask."

My stomach churned, and a wave of nausea spread throughout my body. "Not yet," I muttered to myself. We turned one last corner and approached a door with agents on each side.

"You'll wait in here," my guide said. "Please give us an hour or so to get some clothes and prepare your room." He pointed to a beautiful African American woman in another dark suit. "Agent Jackson is here to keep you company." With that, Berkley turned on his heels and exited the room.

Agent Jackson held out her slender hand to greet me. "Welcome, Faith. I've heard a lot about you."

I took her hand, not knowing whether she was being polite or sarcastic. "I'm sure you have." We both chuckled as we shook hands. The tone in the building was definitely much lighter this time around. Perhaps I would survive after all. I set my backpack on the bed and walked toward a window to see if I could figure out which way I was facing. "Where am I?"

Agent Jackson followed behind me, but she seemed like she was just keeping me company rather than hovering over my every move. "This is one of our guest bedrooms. You're on the third floor, which used to be attic space. You know, this was not part of the original White House. They added all these rooms later."

I peered out the window and located the Washington Monument stretching toward the sky. If I squinted my eyes enough,

I could make out a building that looked like the Lincoln Memorial, but at that distance, it was hard to tell.

"It's quite a view, isn't it? Maybe we can take you out to the solarium while you're here. The view's even better there."

"Sounds nice." I turned around and looked at Agent Jackson. "How long do you think I'll be here, anyway?"

"Hard to say. The Chancellor was pretty upset with your little stunt the other night."

My face turned warm as I blushed. "Yeah, I bet he was. He's lucky though. Our original plan was to interrupt his speech, but that didn't work. I'm sure he would've gotten really mad if we did that."

Jackson chuckled. "For your sake, I think you're also lucky that didn't happen. It would not have ended well."

I walked over and sat down on the bed. "Does that mean it's gonna end well now?"

Jackson's expression dropped. "That's not up to me. It's up to him."

"Is he still mad?"

Jackson sat on a chair across from me. "Hard to tell. He was...irate last night, but he seemed a little calmer this morning. I'm not that close to him, so I don't know what he and his advisors are planning."

I took in a deep breath and let it out. "So, what happens next?"

"All I know is that you are our guest, and our instructions are to take good care of you until the Chancellor is ready to meet with you."

I nodded my head. "Do you know when that'll be?"

"The Chancellor has some other matters to attend to this evening, so my guess is tomorrow morning after breakfast."

My heart sank. "There's no time today? I really wanted to get this over with."

"I'm sorry, sweetheart. The Chancellor is a busy man."

I sighed again. "What am I gonna do until then?"

Jackson's eyes scanned the room as if she were trying to find something that would occupy the mind of a teenager. "Well, aside from eating supper in a little while, I don't know."

"Do you think I could get a tour or something before we eat? I'm not real hungry yet."

Jackson thought for a moment. "I think we can arrange that.

Give me a few minutes to take care of some things, and then I'll show you around."

"Sounds good. I'd like to freshen up anyway. It's been a long day. May I please have a bottle of water?"

"Sure." Jackson left the room, and I went into the restroom to wash my face. I had lied when I told Jackson I wasn't hungry. In all honesty, I was starving. But I had to get into the Oval Office and plant the leech before I ate anything. Before I left Jakob behind at the cabin, he taught me an old trick he learned during his training. He told me that with a little bit of practice, a person could "recall" something they had ingested in the last few hours. I had no clue what that meant so he clarified things by saying, "You can puke up something you had swallowed before." The safest way to smuggle the leech into the White House, and eventually the Oval Office would be to swallow it, then "recall" it when I was near Sloane's computer.

At first, I thought he was joking, but when he demonstrated it for me, I was disgusted and impressed at the same time. He had me practice a few times, and although it felt really strange, it was pretty easy. I just needed to drink some water ahead of time to make the process easier.

By the time I finished in the restroom, Agent Jackson had returned.

"Ready to go?" she asked.

I nodded my head. "Do I need to bring anything?"

"No, just leave your backpack in here. It'll be safe."

We left the room and made our way down the hall to the elevator. Jackson pushed the button and looked at me while we waited. "Any requests?"

"Uhhh...I don't know. What am I allowed to see?"

The elevator door opened, and we stepped inside. "I'll show you a few of the highlights, then it'll be time to eat. The second floor houses the Chancellor's residence, but we can go downstairs."

The elevator dinged, and the door opened on the first floor. Jackson held out her hand, and I stepped out into the hallway. "The only room I've ever heard of is the Oval Office. But if Chancellor Sloane's busy, we probably can't go there, can we?" I held my breath as I awaited the answer.

"You're in luck. He's in the Situation Room this evening, so I think we can go to the Oval Office if you want."

We walked down a couple of halls, and through a door that led outside. Based on the view of the Washington Monument, I knew we were on the south side of the White House. I took a sip of water from my bottle. "Where are we going first?"

"I don't know how long we'll have, so we'll start in the Oval Office. That way we'll be sure to see it even if our tour gets cut short."

Those words sent a chill through my body as the reality of the situation hit me. As I took another gulp of water, my hand trembled so much I nearly poured water down my chin.

Jackson led the way as we walked down a covered sidewalk. "This is the West Colonnade. It's how the Chancellor goes to work every day. They used to call it the 45-second commute, but Chancellor Sloane likes to say that he has it down to about 40 seconds."

I took another sip of water and put the lid back on the bottle. "I guess he wants to outdo everyone else, doesn't he?"

Jackson smiled at me, then opened a door that led back inside. "This is the West Wing, where the Chancellor and his staff work."

"Is anyone still here?" It was late on a Friday afternoon so maybe people had already left for the weekend.

"Yes. Some of the staff are with the Chancellor, but people always work late around here. Working at the White House is not a nine-to-five job."

We walked in and were immediately greeted with the sounds of a thousand important conversations. A few agents noticed our arrival, but quickly went back to their tasks. The rest of the people in dark suits were so busy with their work that they didn't notice Agent Jackson and her special visitor.

I had to walk carefully to keep from running into anyone. "Who are all these people?"

Jackson navigated the mass of humanity with ease, not at all like my teenage klutziness. "Clerks, secretaries, attorneys, advisors, and the like. A few hundred people work in here full time, but a lot of other people come and go."

"Wow. I guess I just assumed it was only the Chancellor and a few other people."

A few turns later we met the Chancellor's personal secretary.

She and Agent Jackson exchanged a smile and a few polite words, and the secretary opened the door for us. The room looked just like I had seen on TV shows and movies, although it was a little smaller than I thought it would be. It was still quite a sight. Two sofas and several chairs sat on one end of the room while the Chancellor's desk sat at the other. My heart pounded as I looked around the room, making sure my plan would work. I couldn't go straight for the desk though. I would have to find a way to get to the desk and plant the leech without raising any suspicion. Easier said than done.

Agent Jackson circled the room with me, never drifting more than a few feet away. "What do you think?"

"Not bad. I thought it would be bigger though."

Jackson laughed, but I was being serious. We walked around the sofas and I imagined how many famous people had sat there throughout the years. Maybe Sloane and his advisors had even discussed me in this office a few times. I traced my fingers on the back of one of the sofas. "This is really cool. Thanks for bringing me in here."

Jackson smiled. "You're welcome."

I walked over toward the desk and peered out the windows that provided the backdrop for many of Sloane's speeches that we had seen on TV. Fortunately, Jackson stayed on the other side of the room. This was my chance. I walked to Sloane's desk, flung his chair out of the way, and collapsed to the floor. Just as Paul had said, there was a small trash can under his desk. I grabbed it and used my new skill to empty the contents of my stomach into the trash can, hoping the leech came out with the water.

"Faith, are you okay?" Jackson's voice called from across the room, but she would undoubtedly be coming to my aid quickly.

"I don't know. Just give me a sec." My hands scrambled through the disgusting concoction in the trash can, searching for the leech. On Jakob's advice, I had avoided eating any food that day, so I wouldn't have any solid chunks to sort through. Fumbling through the bile water was bad enough though.

"Faith?" Jackson's voice was getting way too close.

"Hang on. I'm sorry. You probably don't want to see this." Where was that stupid thing? My fingers finally locked on to something small and solid. I made another retching sound as I pulled the leech out of the trash can, wiped it off, and pulled the adhesive backing off. I glanced up to find a place to stick it, bashing my head in the process.

Jackson's hand tapped me on my lower back, the only part of me that was sticking out from under the desk. "Faith?"

I pushed the power button and stuck the leech to the underneath side of Sloane's desk, pressing it for a few seconds. It held.

I scooted my way out from underneath the desk, bringing the trash can with me. "I'm so sorry. I don't know what happened. I just got dizzy all of a sudden. I knew I was gonna puke so I hoped he had a trash can down there. I didn't get anything on the floor."

Jackson glanced down at the floor, then patted my shoulder. "It's okay. Why don't we just go back to your room so you can lie down?"

"Sounds good." I set the trash can on the floor beside the desk so it would keep people from snooping near the leech.

We walked out the door, and Jackson told the secretary what had happened. She said she would get a cleaning crew in there. Hopefully, they wouldn't inspect too closely.

Agent Jackson and I got back to my room, and I laid down on the bed. She told me a doctor would check on me in a little while, but I should just rest until then. Once she had been gone for several minutes, I rolled over and got my phone. Jakob had warned me, saying if the White House didn't confiscate my phone, that meant they would be monitoring my calls and texts. I would have to operate under that assumption. I texted Charlie's number and said, "Things are going well so far. I can't talk to Sloane until tomorrow. I got a quick tour of the White House. I actually got to see the Oval Office. Things were good until I threw up in the trash can. How embarrassing LOL! Just nervous, I guess. I'm okay now though. I'll let you know how things go. Love you!"

Charlie wouldn't be able to respond, because sending a transmission from his phone could give away his location. I would have to trust that everyone would be able to do their part. I had just sent the message when someone knocked on my door. "Come in," I called.

Agent Jackson and a woman with a small bag entered the room and shut the door. "Faith, this is Nurse Kelly. She wants to check you out and make sure you're all right."

I sat up on the bed and leaned against the headboard. "Thank you. I feel pretty good now."

Nurse Kelly pulled a chair up next to the bed and sat down. She checked my pulse and temperature and looked into my throat. "What happened, Faith?"

"I don't know. I just got dizzy, and the room started spinning like I was on a wild amusement park ride. I saw the trash can and...well...you know the rest."

"What have you eaten today?"

"Nothing. Honestly, I've been nervous about coming here so I couldn't eat."

Nurse Kelly nodded and frowned at me. "Any chance you're pregnant?"

I nearly threw up again. "No way!"

Kelly smiled. "Looks like your blood sugar just got too low. We'll get you some electrolytes, and something light to eat."

"Thank you."

Jackson walked to the door with Kelly but stayed behind after Kelly walked out. She turned and looked at me with a strange look on her face. "Are you sure you're okay?"

"Yeah. Now that I've sat down I feel pretty normal again."

Jackson sat down in the chair next to the bed. "Good. By the way, we found something that belongs to you."

My heart skipped several beats. "You did? Where?"

"In the Oval Office. The cleaning crew found it under the Chancellor's desk. I'm hoping you can explain it to me."

Jackson could probably see my heart pounding through my shirt. "Uhh, sure. What is it?" I knew exactly what it was, but I had to play stupid.

"This." She reached into her pocket and moved her closed hand toward mine.

She opened her hand to reveal a small, metallic object. I nearly fainted when I saw it. "Oh, that? It's a funny story."

Jackson smiled a broad smile. "I'd love to hear about it. I've never seen a charm like that before."

"Oh, I got that from my dad a few years ago. He knows how much I like butterflies. I guess it fell off my bracelet when I was sick."

"It's beautiful. They cleaned it up for you. If you give me the bracelet, I'll have someone repair it for you."

I unhooked the bracelet from my wrist and handed it to her. "Aww, tell them thanks for me."

Jackson nodded and stood to her feet. "I'll leave you alone for a while. Just open the door and ask someone if you need anything. Your supper will be here shortly if you feel like eating."

"Thank you. Some food sounds amazing."

Jackson walked to the door and opened it. "You're welcome."

I waited until the door closed before I collapsed onto the bed and let out a huge sigh of relief. Now I would just have to wait for the leech to get a signal, and let the REFUGE technicians do their thing. One step closer to our goal.

156

CHAPTER EIGHTEEN

I tossed and turned pretty much all night, catching only a few minutes of sleep at a time. The bed was one of the most comfortable I had ever slept in, but it didn't matter. My body was exhausted, but the stress of the week and the anticipation of my meeting with Sloane kept my mind racing. Jackson thought I would be able to meet with Sloane sometime after breakfast, but she wasn't sure exactly when. It was a Saturday morning, so his schedule was more flexible than it was during the week. There was still no guarantee he would have time for me anytime soon. Whatever crisis had him in the Situation Room the day before may still be occupying his attention.

Breakfast was delicious. I had my share of scrambled eggs, bacon, sausage, and pancakes. Dad's pancakes will always be my favorite, but these were a close second. I ate in my room and spent most of the morning watching TV. Agent Jackson stopped in to check on me every once in a while, but for the most part, she left me alone. I was beginning to think she had forgotten about me when she came in and said Sloane was ready to see me. The knots in my stomach returned, and it took all my power to get my mind to tell my legs to move. As we walked down the hall, several questions ran through my mind. What was Sloane going to say? What was I going to say? Was REFUGE able to move the Oversight satellite? I didn't have much time to think very long, because, after a couple of turns, we walked into a room with wall-to-wall windows and a beautiful view of Washington.

I turned away from the windows and looked at Agent Jackson. "What is this?"

"The Solarium. It's kind of a retreat within the White House. It's the Chancellor's favorite room. He asked you to meet him in here."

I studied the room as I walked. The mix of sofas, loveseats, and soft chairs made this look quite casual compared to the other White House rooms I had been in. And the view. I could tell why Sloane loved it so much.

"Welcome back, Faith." The Chancellor's voice boomed from behind me.

Startled, I spun around to see Sloane standing in the kitchen area. "Uh, hello. How's it going?"

How's it going? Where did that come from? I don't think I've ever said that to anyone in my life, so why did I say it now? And who says that to the most powerful person in the world? We were not off to a good start. I glanced around the room, expecting to get scolded by one of Sloane's agents, but we were alone.

Sloane was taken aback by my strange greeting. He stared at me with squinted eyes for a moment before shaking his head and walking toward the back door. "Well, it has been a long, very interesting week to say the least. I thought I would come up here to clear my head this morning."

I stood in place, not sure whether to follow Sloane or just keep standing there like an awkward teenager. "I like the view. This is a beautiful room."

Sloane simply nodded as he faced away from me and out the windows.

One of Sloane's butlers entered the room, carrying a silver tray with two coffee cups and a glass of orange juice. "Your coffee, Chancellor."

Sloane turned around and removed the coffee cup from the tray. "Thank you, Sanford."

Sanford brought the tray toward me. "Orange juice or coffee, Miss Webber?"

I wasn't very thirsty, but it would be rude to refuse, so I took the glass of orange juice. "Thank you."

Sloane took a sip of his coffee and smiled. "Sanford, please tell the others we are not to be disturbed. And make sure there is no recording."

"Certainly, sir." Sanford nodded and left the room.

I took a deep breath in through my nose, savoring the smell of Sloane's coffee. I love the smell of good coffee even though I never drink it. No doubt his was a very expensive, very sophisticated brand, and I could tell he was drinking it black. I took a sip of the orange juice, nearly gagging on the pulp in the juice. I quickly swallowed it to avoid causing a scene. I've never been a huge fan of orange juice, but aside from the pulp, this was delicious. I wasn't surprised though. Sloane had impeccable taste.

Sloane walked toward a couch and motioned toward me. "Faith, please join me." Something about Sloane's demeanor was much different from the last time I saw him. He was not hostile or threatening. He was civil and cordial, and it actually seemed genuine.

I sat down on a couch facing Sloane and set my orange juice down on the coffee table, taking care to place it on a coaster. We both sat in silence for a few moments, waiting to see if the other person would make the first move. I couldn't stand the silence anymore, so I spoke. "So, I guess you saw me on TV the other night, huh?"

Sloane cracked a smile. "I certainly did. Not live though. My advisors showed it to me a short while later. They also told me you had managed to escape...again. You have proven to be quite evasive."

"Yeah, I get that a lot. Running for your life has a funny way of making a person capable of things they never knew they could do."

Sloane took a sip of coffee and set the cup back down. "It took me a few moments to recognize you because of the hair. It's quite a change, but it suits you. You look more like a woman than the teenage girl I met before. I can also tell the last few months have been trying. I suppose living underground for that long has been difficult."

"Yeah, well, it's not like we had a choice. We knew if we peeked our heads out, we would end up dead."

Sloane nodded. "Yes, you certainly would have."

I was a little disturbed by the way Sloane said that so matter-of-factly. "How did you know we were down there anyway?"

"I normally prefer not to give away my secrets, but I'll indulge you this once. We knew Jakob had gone to that cabin because it was the last place his chip was operational. After his chip malfunctioned, we lost the ability to track him. I sent agents to the cabin on several occasions, hoping to see signs of life, but they saw nothing. We just assumed you had moved to another location. Until we read your story."

I blinked my eyes and shook my head. "My story? What story?"

Sloane smiled and crossed his legs. "The story you sent to your friend Audrey."

There was no use playing dumb anymore. "How?"

"I have my ways. I must say, I am impressed with your ingenuity. Hacking into that agent's phone in order to e-mail your document? That was brilliant. I wasn't sure whether to kill you or hire you for my IT department."

"I know which one I would have preferred."

"Yes, I suppose I do. At any rate, it took a while to decode your encryption, but once we knew about the secret bunker underneath the cabin, we knew you would be hiding there. My agents breached the cabin and the bunker, but it was too late. Our drones tracked you for a while, but as you know, they were destroyed. We had lost you again."

I let out an uneasy chuckle. "Yeah, sorry about the drone. I hope it wasn't expensive."

"It was."

"Oh. Well, it's not like we had a choice."

Sloane's lips wrinkled and he paused for a few moments before speaking again. "Faith, may I be completely candid with you?"

That question caught me off guard, but I nodded my head. "Sure."

Sloane stood and walked toward the back door, gazing off into the distance. "After you escaped again, I was livid. I thought we had eliminated you, only to find out you had survived. And to make matters worse, I was betrayed by one of my most trusted colleagues." Sloane turned and faced me. "I'm assuming he and Jakob are still with your family somewhere?"

"I'd rather not say."

"I thought so." Sloane turned back toward the window. "I have been filled with anger and hatred for you, Paul, Jakob, and your father for the past few months. It has consumed me. I spend most of my time and energy focusing on you and working toward your apprehension. I haven't slept well, and when I do, all I see in my dreams is the face of the young lady I have worked so hard to kill."

My mind wanted to respond to that, but my mouth wouldn't move.

"And then Thursday night, when I saw the video of you asking to meet with me, I was perplexed. Why would you risk your life by coming here and making that speech? And why would you want to meet with me after everything that has transpired? My desire to capture you and put an end to your interloping was stoked into a white-hot flame of hatred. It was almost as if you were toying with me. Mocking me publicly. The only time I have ever been more irate was after my wife and daughter died."

I looked around the room, trying to figure out a way to escape before something really bad happened.

Sloane turned back around and walked toward me. He sat back down on the sofa and look into my eyes with a piercing intensity and surprising sincerity. "That night, when I finally drifted off to sleep, I had a dream. A dream so vivid, I can still see every moment of it."

I leaned forward in my chair, dying to hear what Sloane had to say.

He closed his eyes as if he were picturing himself somewhere else. "In my dream, I saw a picturesque landscape full of rolling pastures, covered in the greenest grass. There was a stream nearby, and the sound of the flowing water and cheerful birds created a symphony that would rival those of Mozart and Beethoven. It was almost as though I were gliding over this scene, taking in all the sites, smells, and sounds. I never dream in this much detail, so this was a new experience for me."

I was mesmerized by his description of his dream. I closed my eyes, and I was transported there with him. I could picture everything as he described it. His tone changed, and I opened my eyes in time to see his eyebrows furrow.

"Then I saw a shepherd, walking with his flock to graze in one of the fields. The sun shone down upon them as the sheep wandered around, getting their fill of the lush grass. As I watched, a slight breeze turned into a gust of chilling wind. The sun disappeared, and dark clouds formed in the sky. Something was wrong, but I didn't know what. Then I saw it. A wolf emerged from the woods and made its way through the tall grass at the edge of the pasture; but the sheep and the shepherd were blissfully unaware of the danger close by, ready to strike. The wolf waited patiently for an unfortunate sheep to wander too far from the others, and too close to him. It wasn't long before he got his wish. One sheep ventured out on its own, and in a flash, the wolf pounced. Before the sheep had a chance to evade its predator, the wolf sank its teeth into the sheep's throat. The sheep tried to scream, but the struggle proved to be short-lived. The wolf feasted for several minutes before the shepherd saw what was happening and chased it away. The shepherd knelt next to his lost sheep and watched as the wolf ran away satisfied."

I was mildly disgusted but fascinated by the way Sloane told his story. "That's awful. What happened next?"

Sloane drew in a deep breath and continued. "Well, I found myself back at the start of the dream, gliding over the pasture and watching the sheep grazing. The shepherd watched over his flock with more diligence this time, scouring the nearby grass for any signs of the wolf. Several minutes later, the wolf appeared again, but the shepherd couldn't see it. As quickly as the last time, the wolf attacked and grabbed a sheep by the throat, killing it with a few violent shakes of its head. The shepherd saw the commotion and sprinted toward the wolf and sheep. The wolf was able to devour several bites before the shepherd got close enough to scare it away. Similar scenes played out a multitude of times over the course of my dream, and each time, the wolf was the victor."

I shook my head in disbelief. "Did the shepherd ever get the wolf?"

Sloane smiled. "Finally, after losing several sheep, the shepherd set out a trap to capture the wolf. He set it on the ground in the tall grass, safely away from the pasture, and waited for the wolf to take one wrong step. The next day, it happened. The shepherd heard whimpering and howling from the area of his trap, and he knew his plan had worked. He walked toward the area of the noise with his rifle at the ready. He closed in on the wolf, whose front left leg was caught in the metal trap, broken and bleeding." Sloane paused for dramatic effect.

"What happened next?"

"Well, the shepherd closed to a distance at which he knew he wouldn't miss with his rifle. The wolf was too busy licking its leg and trying to extricate himself from the trap to notice the shepherd. As the shepherd neared the wolf, he raised his rifle to his shoulder and looked down the barrel at the wild animal. Finally, the wolf looked up, and the two locked eyes for a few intense moments. The shepherd drew his breath in, finger on the trigger, ready to fire, but something held him back. The wolf's eyes, which had been so full of evil, were now filled with fear. The two enemies stared each other in the eyes, almost as if they were somehow communicating with each other. Then the shepherd did something completely unexpected."

"What did he do?"

The shepherd lowered his rifle and draped it back over his shoulder. He then approached the wolf, slowly and methodically, taking care not to threaten the wounded animal. The wolf pulled his head back away from his ensnared leg, and the shepherd pried the trap open, freeing the wolf's leg. The wolf jumped on its three good legs, away from the trap and the shepherd. It was unable to put any weight on the injured leg though. It hobbled a few steps toward the woods, then stopped. It turned around and faced the shepherd, who was still kneeling on the ground, but now his arms were stretched out wide, inviting the wolf to come to him. In that moment, an unspoken bond formed between the two, and the wolf hobbled to the shepherd."

I blinked my eyes and shook my head. "Wow. I've never heard anything like this."

"It gets better. The shepherd opened his canteen and poured water on the wound. The wolf growled but refrained from biting his new friend. The shepherd examined the wolf's leg and realized it was broken. He could set it, but he needed to get back to his home to fix it the right way. He held his hand out to let the wolf sniff it and show that he meant no harm. The wolf sniffed a few times, then looked the shepherd in the eyes again, as if to say he was ready to accept assistance. The shepherd slowly reached his hand out and stroked the wolf on the top of the head. He then ran his hand down the wolf's back, letting the wolf know he meant no harm. The wolf laid down and lowered its head, and the shepherd scooped him up and carried him back to his home, where he tended to his wounds. The next thing I saw in my dream was the shepherd walking out of his home and toward the sheep with the wolf alongside him. Some time had passed, and the wolf was completely healed. The two of them had formed a strong bond, and the wolf never left the shepherd's side. The pair made it to the pasture with the sheep, and the shepherd relaxed under a tree while the wolf stood guard."

My eyes widened as Sloane told this part of the story. It was starting to sound eerily familiar. "Let me guess what happened next. A black wolf came out of the woods to attack one of the sheep, but the shepherd's wolf ran out and stopped it. He bit the black wolf a couple times in the neck, and then the black wolf ran away."

Sloane's face froze. "How did you know that?"

"The night I interrupted your speech, I had a dream that started with a big, gray wolf stopping a black wolf from attacking the sheep. My dream didn't have the part before that though. Did the shepherd say something to the gray wolf when he came back?"

Sloane nodded his head, and at the same time, we both said, "I needed you to save my sheep, and you did. Well done, my good and faithful helper."

Tears began to form in both of our eyes. Something powerful was happening, but I had yet to fully grasp the magnitude of it. Sloane had seemed like a different person that morning, and once he told me of his dream, I began to understand what was going on. "Chancellor, when I had that dream, I thought God was showing me that I was the wolf. Now I realize I'm not the gray wolf..."

Sloane finished my sentence for me. "I am." He gathered himself and cleared his throat. "Faith, I'm about to tell you something I've not told a soul. Not even my chief of staff. I believe God was talking to me through that dream. For years I have persecuted Christians, killing thousands of them because of my personal vendetta against God. Then when I thought you were dead, I began to second-guess my actions. Something about our dinner together had a profound impact on me. It was guilt. You see, when we spoke that night at dinner, I didn't see you. I saw the daughter I never got to raise. Then when you somehow knew the names of my wife and daughter, it shook me to my core. There was no way for you to know both of those names, yet you did. I nearly pardoned you, but my pride would not allow me to. When I discovered you were still alive, a small part of me was relieved. I refused to give in to my emotions though, so I suppressed my feelings and continued to hunt you and your family because that's how Chancellor Sloane would respond. All the while, the conflict grew inside me. Part of me wanted to spare your lives, but that would have required me to undo everything I had done and change my entire image. I just could not allow that to happen. My wife always told me I was too headstrong for my own good."

"I think she was right." The words escaped before I could stop them.

Sloane actually laughed at my comment. "Yes. It's true. When I saw your face on television Thursday night, the part of me that wanted to spare you overtook the part of me that wanted you dead; but I could not allow myself to give in. I retired to my bedroom and wrestled with feelings of guilt and inadequacy. Even if I wanted to change, how could I? I had killed so many innocent people. God could never forgive me for that. Then I had the wolf dream."

I walked over and sat next to Sloane on the couch. "Don't you see what God was telling you? The gray wolf had killed several of the sheep, but the shepherd chose to show him mercy. Then what happened?"

"The wolf repaid the shepherd by protecting his sheep."

We sat in silence for a few moments, letting that last sentence have its impact. I patted Sloane on the arm. "So, what happens now?"

Sloane sighed. "Well, I'm not exactly sure, but I have been contemplating my next moves. As I said, you are the only person who knows about any of this, and I need to keep it that way for the time being. No need to cause a stir until I have a concrete plan in place. I have an idea though."

"What are you thinking?"

"I would like to create an initiative called 'Faith in America' and grant people the freedom to practice religion again."

My eyes lit up. "Wow. You even named it after me." I chuckled at my lame attempt at humor.

"Actually, I did. If I do this, I want you to be my spokesperson. Who better to be the face of this program? If you endorse my idea, and you act as my ambassador, the people will be more likely to accept it."

My mouth fell open. "I... I don't know what to say. I mean, this is exactly what we've been working for. It's hard to believe it's actually happening. What's the catch?"

Sloane smiled a genuine smile that was a little strange to see. "Catch? No catch. Work with me, and I'll give you the freedom you all so desperately want. You have all risked your lives to accomplish this, so take advantage of the opportunity. The only question is, do you believe me?"

I studied Sloane as he spoke. He seemed genuine, but then again, I had been fooled by him before. Why admit to all this? What angle could he possibly have? Was he just trying to get us to comply so we would stop going after him? Then I thought of the dream. We both had the same exact dream on the same exact night. That couldn't have been a coincidence. And the symbolism of the dream. That couldn't have been a coincidence either. There was only one explanation for all of it. Playing along was my best option. If he were up to something, hopefully, I would figure it out before it was too late. If he were being sincere, everything would be great.

I nodded my head in agreement. "I believe you. Let's do this."

The Chancellor and I spent the next couple of hours planning and talking about his "Faith in America" initiative. The more he spoke, the more he sounded like a man on a mission. After everything he had done, it wouldn't be enough to just make a formal declaration; he wanted a grand spectacle to convince people he was doing the right thing. Working with me and REFUGE would be a huge step in that direction. After a lunch featuring a juicy cheeseburger, crispy fries, and a caramel sundae (The Chancellor had a steak and baked potato), we had the basic framework of a plan in place. We were still sitting at the table when it hit me.

"Chancellor Sloane? What about your mind-control chips?"

"What about them?"

I wiped my mouth to make sure I didn't have any embarrassing food smudges on my face. "Well, this plan of yours..."

"Ours"

"Sorry, this plan of ours. It goes against everything you've done for the last several years. Do you need to use mind control to convince everyone in the government to go along with it?"

Sloane stroked his chin for a moment as he thought. "Hmm. You raise a good point. This is a momentous turning point for my administration. If I follow through with this, it would signal a departure from tricks and manipulation to get my way. I would like to think I can refrain from using mind control in the future. Why do you ask?"

I definitely couldn't say, "No reason. It's just that I planted a device near your computer that would allow REFUGE to take control of your Project Oversight satellite, move it to another location so you couldn't communicate with it anymore, and take away your ability to impose your will on everyone."

"Faith? Are you still with me?"

I took a drink of lemonade to stall. "Oh, I was just thinking about it. I know it's been a huge part of how you run the country. I was hoping you wouldn't need it anymore." Would he buy it?

The Chancellor studied me for a moment before speaking. "Very well. My apologies, but I must cut our meeting short. I have a briefing in approximately twenty minutes. I do not want you to feel like my prisoner, but I implore you to stay here for another few days until we make our formal announcement."

I shrugged my shoulders. "Uh, sure. But can I call someone and tell them what's going on?"

Sloane frowned. "Let me think. If I allow it, I would ask you to refrain from speaking about our plans. We must keep this a secret until the time is right."

I nodded my head. "Sure. I can just hang out until you need me again."

Sloane stood and reached his hand toward me. "Faith, I sincerely appreciate your cooperation. I know it's a leap of faith to trust me, but I hope our identical dreams convince you of my sincerity." His verbosity would give Mia a run for her money.

I stood and shook his hand. "It's my pleasure. I can't wait."

Sloane nodded and walked out the door, leaving me alone in the solarium. I walked to the back wall that was full of windows and scanned the horizon. The Washington Monument dominated the view, but to my left, I could see the Capitol building. My eyes were taking in the sites, but my brain was everywhere but Washington. REFUGE was probably able to relocate the satellite by now. Otherwise, I would have heard from them. Sloane would soon realize what happened. When he did, how would he react? Would he back out of our plan if he knew I had planted the leech? Keeping this a secret would jeopardize Faith in America before it even started. But how would he react if I told him about the leech? If I knew about his plan a day earlier, I would never have planted it in the first place. Would he understand that, or would he be so angry he wouldn't care? Like many situations over the last several months, there was no easy answer. I was so focused on these questions; I didn't hear Agent Jackson enter the room behind me.

"Faith, are you ready?"

My body jolted and I turned around. "Oh, you scared me. Yeah, where are we going?"

"That's up to you. The Chancellor's orders are to treat you as a distinguished guest, so what would you like to do?"

"I didn't get a lot of sleep last night, and it's been a big day today, so could I go back to my room and take a nap? Maybe I'll be up for something later."

"Whatever you say, my dear. I'll take you back to your room now."

Once Agent Jackson left my room I went straight for my phone and dialed Charlie's number. He probably wouldn't answer, but I could at least leave him a voicemail to tell him how things were going. I listened to the generic voicemail greeting, then spoke. "Hey, it's Faith. Things are going well here. The situation may be changing, so you should just sit tight until you hear from me again. I need to stay here a few more days, but I promise, I'm safe and they're treating me nice. I'm staying in a nice bedroom in the White House, and the food is great. I'll call you again when I know more, but remember, just hang out until I call back. Love you all. Bye."

I set the phone down and exhaled. I couldn't come out and tell them not to hijack the satellite, but hopefully they understood what I was trying to say.

CHAPTER NINETEEN

Dad hung up the phone and stared at the group in disbelief. "You're not going to believe this, but Faith left a message for Charlie, and it sounded like she was telling us to abort."

Paul squinted his eyes. "Abort? Abort what? The satellite mission?"

"It sounded like it. Here, let me play the message." Paul and Mom listened to every word but Hope and Alex were too busy playing and arguing to care. "Hear that? She said, 'just hang out until you hear from me.' She's telling us to stand down."

Paul shook his head as if he didn't agree with Dad's assessment of the message. "I don't know, Andrew. That's quite a leap."

"Well, what else could she be saying?"

Paul stroked his beard as he thought. "I don't know. But what could have happened that would cause her to say that? What would have changed her mind? Perhaps she's saying it under duress."

It was Dad's turn to shake his head. "No, she said everything was good. She wouldn't have said that unless everything was truly good."

"It doesn't matter, Andrew. It's too late anyway. The people at REFUGE already moved the satellite, and now they are trying to program it so we can free all the people under the Chancellor's control."

Dad stood up and began looking for a phone. "I have to call Duncan, or Mia, or someone. We need to pause and see what Faith tells us next."

Right on cue, Mia strode into the room. "Gentlemen. I bring good news. Our technicians have nearly finished cracking the code and achieving our goal of freeing the American people. Faith's mission was successful."

Dad stopped his search. "Great, but I have something to share with you first." Paul let out an audible groan, but Dad was undeterred. "Faith left a voicemail for Charlie and I think she was telling us to abort our mission."

Mia put her hand on her hip and stared. "Abort our mission? Why would she say such a thing after risking her life for this mission?"

"I don't know."

"What did her message say? I'm sure she would not have just come right out and said to abort."

Dad played the message again and everyone stood in silence. Dad and Paul looked to Mia for direction. "This changes nothing. We proceed as planned."

Paul shot Dad an *I told you so* look, but Dad either didn't see it or chose to ignore it. He held his hands up to plead with Mia. "Can't you see what she's saying? She knew someone would be monitoring her phone calls, so she had to speak in code. Something has changed, and we need to wait until we know what it was."

Mia scoffed. For the first time, she was showing signs of frustration. "Mr. Webber, I sympathize with your plight, and I understand why you would think such a thing; however, we cannot jeopardize our entire plan on some wild leap of logic. For all we know, the Chancellor could have discovered her plan and forced her to leave that message."

Dad closed his eyes and rubbed his head. "I know my daughter. She's trying to tell us something. Can we please just talk to Duncan?"

Mia's eyes told Dad everything he needed to know. "Mr. Webber, as I stated before, Duncan and I are of the same mind when it comes to matters of importance. I know him well enough to know how he would want this situation to carry out."

Dad pleaded with his eyes. "But..."

Mia stopped him dead in his tracks. "This conversation is over. I came in here to share news of our success, and now you have soured my mood. Please excuse me." Without another word, Mia turned and left the room."

Mom smirked. "Way to go, Andrew. You soured her mood.

You're always doing that to people." The fact no one laughed at her attempt to bring levity to the situation soured Mom's mood too.

Paul stood up and walked into the restroom, leaving the Webbers alone in the room. Mom walked over and wrapped her arms around Dad, who was still standing where he was when he was souring Mia's mood. "For the record, I want to believe you. But why would she tell us to wait? I can only think of two things that would cause her to say that."

"What's that?"

"If Sloane agreed to step down or legalize religion."

Dad laughed. "Yeah, right. Neither of those things is happening without a fight. Maybe everyone else is right. It would take an extraordinary circumstance to make Faith change her mind about the satellite. I find it hard to believe something like that would happen. But at least we know she's okay."

Paul emerged from the restroom in time to interrupt the embrace. "Oh, my apologies."

Mom and Dad let go of each other and Dad smiled at Paul. "The more I think about it, the more I think I'm putting two and two together to get five."

Alex, who had just come in to get a drink, tugged Dad on the pant leg. "Daddy, two plus two is four." Alex then walked away to keep playing with Hope.

Dad laughed and shook his head. "Kids. Speaking of kids, Paul have you heard from Jakob?"

"Yes. He and Corinne are still with Charlie in the safehouse."

Mom bit her lip. "I heard things didn't go well between Faith and Corinne. Evidently, she's quite a handful."

Paul nodded. "I'm afraid you're right. Faith and Jakob are in an impossible situation. Because Jakob never broke up with Corinne, he must carry on the way things were before he left. That means he and Faith cannot show their true feelings for each other."

Mom grabbed Dad's hand and squeezed it. "I can't imagine how difficult that must be. And it must be tearing Faith apart to imagine what the two of them are doing without her. I just hope Jakob holds up."

"I don't understand why we have to stay here." Corinne's voice carried a hefty amount of frustration.

Charlie closed his eyes and wrinkled his forehead. This was not the first time they had had this conversation. "It's not safe. I have my orders, and we are to stay here until I'm told otherwise."

Corinne paced the floor, clenching her fists over and over. "Are we prisoners or something?"

Jakob stood and tried to soothe the raging beast. "Look, Corinne. I don't like this either, but it's not like we have any other options. Where are we gonna go? We're both wanted, so if we went back out in public, there's no telling what'll happen."

Corinne huffed and stormed outside, slamming the back door in her wake. Jakob and Charlie looked at each other, trying to figure out who would go after her. Jakob rolled his eyes and walked out the back door, closing it softly behind him. The door had taken enough abuse already. Charlie shook his head, then went to the kitchen for another snack cake.

Jakob walked up to Corinne, who was running her finger across the balcony railing. "Are you okay?"

Corinne shook her head. "What's going on, Jakob? You know these people better than I do. Why can't we leave?"

"Look, these people are super paranoid and careful. They don't want anyone at their headquarters who could potentially snitch on them."

Corinne frowned and locked eyes with Jakob. "You went there. Why do they trust you? Don't they know who you are?"

Jakob smiled. "They know me. They don't know anything about you, and what kind of person you are."

Corinne leaned a little closer to Jakob and smiled. "And what kind of person am I?"

Jakob gulped. He knew he was heading for trouble, so he patted Corinne on the shoulder like one of his guy friends. "You're a good person."

"Wow. That really means a lot."

"That's not what I meant."

Corinne cocked her head. "So, I'm not a good person?"

Jakob stammered for a moment before he managed to produce a sentence. "No, I mean, yes. I just...like I said, they're very paranoid." He looked at Corinne just in time to see her put her hand on his arm.

"Do you still love me?"

Jakob's eyes widened. "What?" He heard what she said, he was just trying to buy some time.

"Do...you...still...love...me? It's a very simple question."

"You know the answer to that question."

Corinne slid even closer, pressing her body against his. "Say it then."

Jakob quivered as her breath landed on his ear. "I did."

Corinne leaned toward Jakob, their noses nearly touching. "I want you to say the words."

Jakob leaned back far enough to create some distance, but not far enough to upset Corinne. "I already said I do. What more do you want?"

In a flash, Corinne's leg swept Jakob's legs out from underneath him and she pinned him to the balcony floor. "It's her, isn't it?"

Jakob groaned as he hit the ground. "Who?"

"Riley Riley. You have a thing for her, don't you?"

"First of all, ouch. Second, her name is Faith."

Corinne pushed Jakob's arms into the floor with all her strength. "And third?"

"Okay, fine. Maybe I thought I caught some feelings for her for a while, but that was just part of the act. That all went away when I saw you again."

Corinne studied Jakob to see if there was any dishonesty in his words. "I don't know if I believe that."

Jakob leaned up and kissed Corinne, catching her off guard in the process. Their lips finally separated, and Jakob smiled wildly. "Do you believe me now?"

Corinne smiled her perfect smile in return. "I don't know. I might need more convincing."

CHAPTER TWENTY

Chancellor Sloane sent word that I was to meet him after dinner that night. My heart skipped a beat at first but given the nature of our meeting earlier in the day, I had no reason to be suspicious. Besides, I wasn't really in a position to refuse since I didn't know if my REFUGE friends had been able to hijack Sloane's satellite. Being unable to communicate with them really put me in a tough position. If I told Sloane what was going on, there was no telling how he would react. I came to the conclusion that I had no choice but to let things continue. If Sloane followed through on his Faith in America plan, REFUGE could just give control of the satellite back, and all would be good.

Agent Jackson walked me from my bedroom to the dining room, where the smell of Italian seasonings greeted my nose. The last time I was in this room I was wearing that beautiful Lizzy Sebastian dress and receiving my death sentence. I blinked my eyes to drive that memory from my mind and sat down at the table. Agent Jackson made sure I was comfortable, then turned toward the door. I called her name before she could leave the room. "Agent Jackson?"

She stopped in her tracks. "Yes?"

"Umm, I don't really wanna eat by myself. Can you stay in here with me? Please?"

Jackson looked down at her watch before answering. "I go off duty in a few minutes, but I can stick around for a little while."

"I'm sorry. If you need to go, it's okay."

Jackson walked back toward me and waved her hands. "No, don't worry about it. I don't mind."

I lifted the silver cover from my plate to reveal a platter full of spaghetti and meatballs. It smelled amazing. "Do you want some?"

Jackson laughed. "That's okay. I'll have supper waiting on me when I get home. My husband is grilling steak tonight."

"I love steak. So, you don't care if I start eating?" Once I smelled the spaghetti, I was hungrier than I thought. She shook her head and I dug in, twirling a bunch of noodles around my fork, and stuffing them into my mouth. Since it was just us girls, manners didn't matter. I didn't bother wiping my face as I inhaled several mouthfuls of spaghetti. It was probably a good thing that I wasn't wearing the fancy dress after all. The sauce was a million times better than the stuff we had been eating in the bunker. I finally wiped my face, sat back, and picked up a piece of garlic bread.

Agent Jackson smiled as I stuffed my face. "Looks like you're enjoying your spaghetti."

"I'm sorry. It's so delicious, and I haven't had many real meals lately." Mom would yell at me if she saw me talking with my mouth full of bread, but what she didn't know wouldn't hurt me.

"I saw pictures of the safehouse you were hiding in. I imagine that was tough."

I nodded my head and wolfed down a second piece of garlic bread. "Yeah, but it's better than being dead."

Jackson nodded. "Very true. It's amazing what we are capable of when their lives are in danger. I admire your bravery."

I stopped chewing and stared at her for a moment. "Huh?"

"You've been through so much at such a young age. It's quite a story. When it's all said and done, you should write a book."

I swallowed the bread that was in my mouth and took a sip of water. "Yeah, but I doubt anybody would actually believe it."

We sat in silence for the next several minutes as I ate my body weight in spaghetti and garlic bread. I was taking one last drink of water when another agent entered the room.

"Ms. Webber, the Chancellor is ready for you now."

Agent Jackson stood to her feet and held out her hand. "Faith, I've enjoyed our time together. I'm off tomorrow, but perhaps our paths will cross again while you're here."

I wiped my face and shook her hand without standing up, even though I probably should have. I never know how to handle situations like that. "Thanks for everything. Enjoy your steak."

My agent companion led me to the solarium, and I walked in to find the Chancellor sitting at the table, finishing his meal.

He motioned for me to sit across from him. "Please be seated. Would you care for some coffee?"

I needed to stay on his good side, so I accepted his offer. "Yeah, sure."

He poured some coffee from a pitcher into the empty cup in front of me. "How do you take it?"

I squinted my eyes. "How do I take what?"

"Your coffee. How do you take it? Cream, sugar?"

My face turned flush. "Oh, that. Uh, I just like it normal."

Sloane smiled and set the pitcher back on the table. "Very well. I appreciate your patience today. I am eager to introduce my new...*our* new initiative, but you and I must iron out some of the important details before I meet with my staff about it."

I took a sip of the coffee. It smelled good, but once it hit my tastebuds the bitterness caused an involuntary facial reaction that amused the Chancellor. "Ya know, I forgot that I like cream and sugar after all."

Sloane slid a platter across the table, and I poured in so much cream and sugar that my cup nearly overflowed. I stirred as the dark black liquid turned a milky beige. I took another sip. It wasn't nearly as gross as before, but it still wasn't all that great. I drank it anyway, so I wouldn't look awkward...well, even more awkward than I already looked. I wiped my lips with my napkin. "So, what kind of details do we need to talk about?"

Sloane slid his chair back and crossed his legs. "Well, I could simply sign an executive order permitting religious freedom, but I feel such a decision requires more fanfare. In order to convince the populace of my sincerity, I want to make this announcement with you by my side. You can help me champion this cause, and usher in a new era."

I stared at this man as he spoke. His whole demeanor was completely different than it was when I met him. The anger and bitterness were gone, and he seemed much more at peace. Then I remembered his news conference that responded to the protests I inspired with my execution. "Mr. Chancellor, sir? Am I allowed to ask you a question and not get in trouble?"

Sloane studied me for a moment before responding. "Of course."

I wrestled for several long moments, trying to find the right approach. "Well, when all those people started protesting a few months ago, you said you were gonna give them what they wanted." I paused for a moment as my heart pounded harder and harder. The next sentence would tell me how serious Sloane was about this program. "Well, you didn't really do anything though. I think maybe you just said what you needed to say so everyone would go home."

Sloane frowned as he studied me in return. "Faith, no one dares confront me like that. It seems as though you are calling me a liar."

My heart sprang up into my throat. "No no no, that's not what I meant. I just...I mean..."

Sloane's frown melted into a smile. "I admire your honesty and bravery. If you had confronted me like this a few months ago I would have had you arrested. Or worse."

My heart settled a little, but I wasn't out of the woods.

"But you are correct. I was lying. I knew I had to suppress those protests by any means necessary, so I made an empty promise. My hope was that people would eventually forget about you and your story, and return to their normal lives. And they did."

I nodded my head. His apparent honesty was refreshing and gave me confidence that he was sincere about this whole thing. "I gotta say, this is almost too hard to believe. How do I know you aren't just making another empty promise?"

"What would I have to gain by these actions? What would I have to gain by lying to you?"

He had a point. "I don't know. Maybe you're scared of REFUGE. Maybe you know how strong they are, and you're afraid they'll get enough people to agree with them and..."

Sloane smirked. "And what? Force me out of office so they can take over?"

"What? No. I told you, that's not what they want. They just want freedom."

Sloane uncrossed his legs and scooted closer to the table,

resting his forearms on the table. His intense stare had returned. "Faith, I want you to listen carefully. I know what REFUGE is doing. My intelligence is not wrong. Everything we have tells us they want to overthrow me and take over. This Duncan Yodesica is only after one thing. My power."

"You're wrong. They're peaceful, Christian people."

"Think about it, Faith. Most Americans support me, so it would be impossible to convince them to support a revolution. What group of people would support them then? The Christians. By appealing to them, and feeding them the false story about religious freedom, they gain the financial support and manpower to achieve their goal. It's a brilliant strategy."

I scoffed. "But..."

"Stop. Don't just speak out of reaction. I asked you to think about it, so please do me the courtesy of thinking before you speak. Take a moment and really digest what I'm saying. Please."

I gave myself some time to think about his claims. There was no way he was right. Why would they want power? It didn't make sense.

Sloane watched me for a moment as I thought. "Can you at least admit that there is a possibility that I am right?"

"Everything they've done has just been to put pressure on you. Not take your job."

Sloane took a deep breath in through his nose. "What do you really know about them? Have you ever met Duncan?"

I shook my head.

"So, what do you really know about them?"

I knew quite a bit, but I also knew I couldn't tell him everything I knew. "Everyone I've met at REFUGE seems nice."

"They seem *nice*? That's why you believe them? No offense, but you can't trust everyone who seems nice."

I cocked my head to the side. "Well, you seem nice. Does that mean I can't trust you?"

Sloane chuckled. "Well played. But we were talking about REFUGE. Why do you suppose they have so much money and such modern technology? Why do they have so many safehouses and bunkers?"

I shrugged. "I don't know. Just being careful, I guess."

Sloane leaned back and crossed his legs again. "We could argue about this endlessly. I see that you will not be easily convinced, so we will table this discussion for now. Just keep an open mind, and really analyze what you know about REFUGE."

"Sure. I'll do that."

•━●━•

The Chancellor and I spent the next couple of hours discussing the best way to implement Faith in America. He would discuss it with his advisors sometime in the coming days, and schedule a press conference for the middle of the week. Around 11:30, we ended our meeting, and two agents walked me back to my room so I could settle in for the night. I immediately checked my phone for a reply from Charlie but saw nothing. What was taking them so long? Things were going well with the Chancellor, but that would change quickly if he found out about the leech. I had to get back into the Oval Office and unhook it. Maybe it wasn't too late.

I opened the door and looked around for an agent. "Excuse me? Is anyone out there?"

A man in a dark suit peeked around the corner. "I'm here. What do you need?"

I stepped out into the hallway. "Sir, could you please come here for a second? I need a favor."

He sighed and walked toward me as if I had asked him to stroll across the Sahara Desert. "What is it?"

"Agent..."

"Lewis. Agent Lewis."

I smiled as big as I could. "Agent Lewis, thanks for coming over here. I just realized I left something in the Oval Office. Can you take me down there so I can get it?"

"The Oval Office? What were you doing in there?"

"Oh, just looking around. I always saw it in movies and wanted to see what it looked like in real life."

Judging by the look on Agent Lewis' face, he didn't like what I said. "Who took you down there?"

I let out an uneasy chuckle. "Oh, I'm bad with names. It began with a D or J or something. Anyway, I'm missing one of the charms from my bracelet and I think it fell off when I threw up into the garbage can under the desk."

Lewis frowned and shook his head. "I heard someone threw up in there earlier. Didn't know it was you. I can have the cleaning crew look for it."

"Oh, don't bother them this late. I can find it real fast. Please? Just take me down there. I promise I'll be done quickly."

Lewis sighed again. "Fine. I'll give you two minutes. But we have to go now."

I smiled and patted him on the shoulder. "Great. Let's go."

We made it to the Oval Office, and I sprinted straight to the desk. I hit my hands and knees, nearly knocking the chair over in my haste. My goal was to get down there and grab the leech before Lewis could see what I was up to. I felt around the desk for a few moments before finding the leech. I finally located it and pulled it off the desk.

"Find yet it?" The sound of Agent Lewis' voice grew closer.

I couldn't reach my pants pocket, and my top didn't have any pockets, so I did the only thing I could think of. I swallowed the leech again. I didn't allow myself to think about what was still on that thing from before.

Agent Lewis nudged my foot with his foot. "Find it?"

I scooted out from under the desk. "No, I guess it must have fallen off somewhere else. I'm sorry."

Lewis rolled his eyes in much the same way I always rolled my eyes at my parents. "Fine. Let's go."

We walked toward the door, but as Lewis reached for the knob, the door swung open. In walked the Chancellor with another man in a suit. The tension in their conversation was palpable. They both stopped dead in their tracks, and the Chancellor stared at me with wide eyes. "Faith? What are you doing here?"

"I thought I lost something, but it wasn't here. I'm sorry. I'm going to bed now."

Sloane furrowed his brow at me. "What did you lose?"

I shrugged and smiled. "It's just a charm from my bracelet. I thought maybe it fell off, but I couldn't find it. It must be somewhere else. Good night."

"Fine. Lewis, escort Ms. Webber back to her room. Something's come up and I must deal with it right away."

Lewis nodded and gently nudged me on the back. "Yes, sir."

We made it about halfway down the breezeway when the man who walked in with Sloane chased us down. "Wait! Agent Lewis!"

We both stopped and my heart sank to my feet. I looked around, trying to find an escape route but there was no way I could outrun these men.

"Agent Lewis, escort Ms. Webber back to the Oval Office. The Chancellor needs to see her."

CHAPTER TWENTY-ONE

I walked back into the Oval Office, palms sweating and stomach churning. It was unlikely that Sloane knew about the leech, but it was likely that he knew about the lost satellite, and when he heard that I had been in the Oval Office earlier he put two and two together. Sloane was sitting at his desk with the other gentleman standing behind him. They were both staring at the computer screen and shaking their heads in unison.

Sloane looked up and shot a glare at me, not unlike the look I had seen on his face during my last trip to the White House. "What did you do?"

I pointed to my chest. "Me? What do you mean?"

Sloane pounded his fist on the desk, causing everyone in the room to jump. "Enough games! What did you do?"

Tears formed in my eyes, and I collapsed to the ground. "I'm so sorry. I did it Friday before we talked."

Sloane removed his glasses and stood to his feet. "I want you to tell me everything. You owe that to me."

I brushed my sleeve across my face, wiping the tears and mucus off. "Okay."

He walked to the two sofas across from his desk and sat down, motioning for me to sit on the sofa across from his. "This is my chief of staff, John Collins. I'm going to tell you about a problem we have, and you're going to tell us how you created this problem for us. Then I'll decide what to do with you. Deal?"

I nodded and sat on the sofa with my head down. "Yes, sir."

"A short while ago, Mr. Collins informed me that one of our communications satellites had disappeared. I asked if had been destroyed, but he told me it had simply disappeared, and no one could locate it."

I nodded my head as he spoke. None of this was news to me.

"This was obviously concerning, given the nature of this particular satellite, which is controlled by the computer at the Resolute Desk."

My face wrinkled. I had no idea what the Resolute Desk was.

Sloane noticed my confusion. "The computer at my desk over there. We were trying to figure out how this satellite could disappear, then I found you here in the Oval Office, claiming to be searching for something you lost in here earlier. Faith, I don't believe in coincidences. I believe your presence in this office..." his face went blank. "This whole thing...your little speech in front of the news camera asking to meet with me; that's why you wanted to get invited here." He stood to his feet and paced back and forth in front of his desk.

I sat speechless, unsure whether I should spill my guts or try to deny it. After all, he had no proof...yet.

Sloane continued to pace, his mind churning to put the facts together. Collins cleared his throat, but the Chancellor didn't respond. Collins turned to me. "So how did you do this?"

Honesty was going to be my best option at this point. Maybe the new, softer Sloane would understand why I did this and grant mercy upon me. "I used a leech."

Collins stared at me. "A leech? What's that?"

Sloane emerged from his catatonic state. "It's a device used to control a computer from a remote location." He walked back over and sat across from me, leaning forward on the sofa. "You pretended to be sick and reached for the trashcan under my desk, then you planted that thing. Then once your mission had been accomplished, you returned to retrieve it. Does that sound right?"

My speechless expression told Sloane everything he needed to know.

"Why don't you tell me your side of the story? And don't omit anything."

I took a moment to gather my thoughts, then spilled my guts. "You're right. We knew that your microchips are your biggest weakness, so we had to figure out a way to hijack them. Paul told us that your computers in the White House and Pentagon were the only ways to reach them. If we could plant a leech on one of those computers, we could control the satellite long enough to move it somewhere else. There was no way we were getting into the Pentagon, but if I could get myself invited to the White House, I could try to find a way to plant the leech in here. I asked Agent Jackson if I could take a tour of the Oval Office, then I umm...produced the leech and planted it under your desk."

Sloane squinted at me. "Produced the leech? Produced it from where?"

"I swallowed it right before I got dropped off across the street, then puked it up later." That was probably the first time anyone had ever said the word "puked" in the Oval Office.

Collins cringed, but Sloane was unfazed. "So do you have the leech now?"

"Yes, sir."

"May I have it, please?"

"Sure. Can I have some water?"

Sloane signaled to Collins, who retrieved a bottle of water from a nearby refrigerator. I walked over and got the trash can from under Sloane's desk, took a few gulps of water, and yacked the leech into the garbage can. "You'll probably wanna clean that off before you touch it."

Collins took the trash can, gagging in the process, and left the room. I sat back down across from Sloane, bracing myself for his wrath, but hoping for his mercy.

"Faith, I am not often caught speechless, but this story is beyond anything I have ever heard in my life. Where did you get this leech? And how did REFUGE know how to interface with the satellite?"

"We got the leech from Corinne Maxwell. She used to be an agent, but she got fired or something. Once the leech connected itself to the Internet, someone at REFUGE linked up with it so REFUGE could move the satellite. I don't know exactly how they did it though."

Sloane sat back and crossed his legs. "Tell me again why REFUGE wanted control of this satellite."

"Well, they knew that they could use the satellite to free all the people under your control. Without that satellite, you would be forced to give in to their demand for religious freedom."

"Or?"

I shook my head. "Or what?"

Sloane sighed. "Surely you see this now."

"See what?"

Sloane uncrossed his legs and leaned forward again. "Faith. They don't want that satellite to free everyone. They want that satellite to control my military."

My heart skipped a beat as I realized there may be an ounce of truth in Sloane's statement. The feeling quickly faded though. "There's no way. I keep telling you, that's not what they're doing."

Sloane closed his eyes and sighed. "I refuse to argue about this with you. Eventually, you'll realize the truth for yourself."

At that time, Collins returned with the leech in his hand. "All clean, Chancellor. It's safe to handle."

Sloane took the leech and studied it. I wasn't sure what he hoped to discover, but I was in no position to question his actions.

I couldn't take the silence anymore. "You gotta believe me. I did this before you and I talked yesterday. If I knew about your Faith in America plan, I wouldn't have done it."

Collins' ears perked up. "Faith in America? What's that?"

My hands flew to cover my mouth as Sloane glared at me. "Well, I suppose the cat is out of the proverbial bag now." He turned to Collins. "I intended to tell you about this after Faith and I ironed out some of the details, but here it is. Faith in America is the name I came up with for a new religious initiative."

Collins cocked his head to the side. "Religious? I don't understand. You already banned religion."

Sloane nodded. "You are correct. But I have given the matter much thought over the last few months, and I would like to change course."

Collins shook his head. "I can't believe this. Sir, are you sure you know what you're doing?"

"I was, but frankly I am too agitated to think about it right now." He turned his gaze to me. "Faith, I think it would be best if you retired for the evening. I am struggling to maintain my composure, and I would rather think this over alone. One of the agents out in the hall will take you back to your room until further notice."

I stood to my feet and walked toward the door. "I understand." I had nearly reached the door when the Chancellor spoke again, causing me to stop.

"Oh, Faith? One more thing about your plan does not make sense. I must give you credit for your creativity in placing that thing on my computer, but what was your exit strategy?"

I turned to face the Chancellor. "Exit strategy? What's that?"

"How did you plan on getting out of the White House when you planted the leech?"

I shrugged my shoulders. "Beats me. Guess we hadn't gotten that far. Planting that leech was so important, we figured we would just come up with something. We're just flying by the seat of our pants."

Mia's face was flush with anger as she hung up the phone. "We've lost the leech!"

Dad sprang to his feet. "You lost it? What do you mean?"

Mia's expression conveyed anger at the situation, and at my father's seemingly unnecessary question. "We can no longer communicate with it. It appears as though it has been discovered."

Concern spread across Dad's face. "Paul, what's that going to mean for Faith?"

Paul shook his head. "I don't know, Andrew. But it's probably not going to be good."

Dad grabbed Paul by the shoulder. "We need to go get her before something happens. If she's in danger, we can't just leave her there."

"Out of the question." The two men stared at Mia as she spoke. "We cannot risk everything for one person who may or may not be in danger."

Dad's eyes widened. "Excuse me? That one person is my daughter, and she's risking her life for your organization. She deserves more respect than that."

Mia took a step back. She was not in physical danger, but she needed to regroup. "My apologies, Mr. Webber. I should have phrased that more carefully. REFUGE is indebted to Faith, and her bravery. If we can surmise a way to facilitate her escape without endangering the rest of our cause, I will wholeheartedly endorse it."

The three of them stood motionless for a few moments before Dad broke the silence. "What if it's just a glitch? What if they didn't discover the leech after all?"

Paul stroked his chin as he thought. "I suppose that's possible. Perhaps we should hold off on any plans for a rescue attempt until we see if the leech comes back online. If it does, we'll have our answer."

My dad pondered Paul's offer. "I suppose you're right. It's going to take us a while to come up with a rescue plan anyway, so we can hold off on any action until we see what happens. Maybe we should try calling Faith to see what's going on. Charlie has the number to her phone, doesn't he?" Dad's suggestion drew a sharp glare from Mia.

Mia strode toward the door. "Gentlemen, it's getting late. I suggest we all wait until morning before deciding what, if any, action is the most prudent. By then we will know whether the leech is offline because it was discovered, or because of a technical malfunction."

After Mia left the room, the two men stood silent, just staring at each other. Dad closed his eyes and rubbed his temples. "I don't know. I'm still worried that it's not a glitch. We knew someone could discover the leech the longer it sat there."

Paul nodded his head slowly. "I was hesitant to say anything, but I'm afraid you're probably right. I have a feeling this wasn't a glitch."

"What do we do now?" Dad asked.

As the men thought, Olivia entered the room. "Do you need anything before I leave for the night?"

Dad's eyes sprang open. "Yes. We need you to call Charlie. We think someone discovered the leech, and we need to warn Faith."

Olivia stopped walking and looked at my father. "Call Charlie? I'm afraid I can't do that. I don't think Mia would approve. Besides, he wouldn't be allowed to call Faith anyway. Too risky."

Paul walked up to Olivia with a strange look in his eyes. Olivia took a step back and eyed him closely. "Mr. Cross, what are you doing?"

"We won't do anything as long as you help us by calling Charlie so he can warn Faith."

Olivia continued to walk backward. "Mr. Cross, I will not be bullied."

Paul closed in on Olivia, so they were close enough to touch. She tried to take a step back, but she was up against the wall.

The two of them stood right up against each other for a few tense moments before Paul retreated. "You're right. Please accept my apologies. I suppose the tension of the moment got the better of me."

Olivia took a few uneasy steps away from him and made her way toward the door. "Very well. Now if you're all squared away, I'll be leaving you alone for the night."

Dad stared at Paul with confusion in his eyes. "What was that all about? You weren't really going to hurt her, were you?"

Paul shrugged his shoulders. "If it came down to it, I would have done what I had to do to protect Faith. Fortunately, it didn't come down to it." He reached into his pocket and pulled out a phone. "I got what we needed."

"Is that Olivia's?"

Paul nodded his head as he began scrolling through the phone. "We may not have much time before she realizes it's gone, so we need to hurry and call Charlie." He initiated the call and waited for an answer. "Hello, Charlie? This is Paul Cross. Olivia let me borrow her phone. We have a problem."

"What's wrong, Mr. Cross?"

"It looks like someone discovered the leech, so I need you to call Faith and warn her. We need to come up with an extraction strategy."

"How do you know they found it?"

"Charlie, I'm not trying to be rude, but time is of the essence. The longer we wait to act, the more danger Faith will be facing. Can you please call her? I would, but I don't have her number."

"Sure thing, Mr. Cross. We are only a couple hours away. You and Mia come up with a plan, and I'll go get her."

"Thank you, Charlie. Mia and Olivia are working on the exit strategy as we speak, so don't call us until we call you with further instructions."

"Yes, sir." Charlie hung up the phone and set it on the table where he sat with Jakob and Corinne. "I need to call Faith."

A look of concern appeared on Jakob's face. "What's wrong?"

"It looks like someone discovered the leech, so we need to warn her."

Corinne busted out laughing and poked Jakob in the ribs with her boney finger. "Poor Riley Riley. I knew she couldn't handle it."

Jakob ignored Corinne's jab and turned his attention to Charlie. "What's the plan?"

Charlie stood up and retrieved his computer from his messenger bag. "I just talked to Paul. They're going to come up with an exit strategy, but I need to get a message to Faith to warn her." He set the computer on the table and turned it on as he sat back down. "Corinne, can you help me with this call? I hate having to do this, but we don't have a choice. My computer should mask our location for a while, so keep an eye on the screen to make sure we aren't being tracked."

"Sure thing." Corinne scooted her chair over, so she was practically sitting on Jakob's lap.

Charlie connected his phone to the computer and dialed the number. They all waited for what seemed like an eternity as the call was routed through countless intermediaries to conceal their location. They had to assume every call placed to and from my phone would be monitored by the Secret Service, but Charlie's computer should buy them enough time to make a quick call. There was no answer, so Charlie hung up.

Jakob held up his hands in frustration. "Why did you hang up?"

"She didn't answer."

"I noticed. But why didn't you leave a message?"

Charlie opened the wrapper of the snack cake that had been tempting him for the last several minutes. "Too dangerous to leave a message."

Jakob grabbed Charlie's arm, causing him to drop the unwrapped snack cake on the ground. "Can you at least send her a text to let her know she's in danger?"

Charlie huffed at the site of his snack cake staring at him from the floor. "Why did you do that?"

Corinne howled again as Jakob apologized. "I'm sorry. I didn't mean to knock it out of your hand."

Charlie picked the snack cake up, blew on it a couple of times, picked a few pieces of dirt off it, and stuffed the whole thing in his mouth at once.

Corinne nearly gagged while Jakob just shook his head. "Nice. Now can you please text Faith?"

Charlie finished chewing his snack cake and picked his phone up again. He typed the words of the text message and sent them. "Now, we wait."

Back in the White House, the words *Call me when you can* appeared on my phone. Agent Belford smiled as he read the message. "Carlton, let's go pay Ms. Webber a visit. She has work to do."

192

CHAPTER TWENTY-TWO

This room was a lot less comfortable than the bedroom I had enjoyed the previous night. If I didn't know I was still in the White House, I would have thought I was back in the government compound I was in after my arrest in the spring. I had grown tired of sitting on one of the four metal chairs and putting my head down on the table, so I walked around, trying to figure out what was going to happen next. There were no windows, and there was no clock, so I had no idea what time it was or how long I had been there. It felt like late evening, but there was no way to know for sure. Maybe once Chancellor Sloane calmed down, he would realize I only planted that leech before I knew he had changed his mind about religion. I hoped with all my heart that he would see the truth sooner rather than later.

I traced my fingers along the textured wall as my mind wandered. It went right to Jakob and Corinne, and what mischief they were up to. The discomfort in my stomach grew as the worst-case scenario played in my mind. Jakob had assured me that he was only acting, but he was also "only acting" when he first met me. What if those old feelings came back? They obviously had a strong history together. Corinne was everything I'm not. Beautiful, confident, and strong with perfect skin, perfect teeth, and perfect hair. I ran my fingers through my imperfect, dyed-blonde hair and sighed. A couple of lonely tears trickled down my cheek as I slid down the wall and collapsed to the floor. As I sat there hugging my knees, the lonely tears soon turned into a steady stream. My breathing became rapid and shallow, and I started rocking back and forth against the wall. The harder I tried to calm down, the harder I cried. No doubt some agents were watching me on camera, but I was beyond the point of caring. I just lost it. It didn't matter who heard me blubbering; I had to let it all go. The sadness. The pain. The anxiety. The stress of the last several months. After several intense minutes, I had no more tears to give. My head hurt like crazy, but strangely, I actually felt better. Releasing my emotions had a soothing effect on me. I wiped my tears and nose on my sleeve, stood to my feet, and sat back down in the chair to await my fate.

Turns out, I didn't have to wait long. A man in a dark suit entered the room and sat down. Did these guys all shop at the same store or something? He introduced himself as Agent Belford and said he needed my help.

"My help? I'm kinda surprised. Seems like I've done enough already."

Belford chuckled. "That you have. You certainly have a penchant for finding trouble, don t you?"

"Is the Chancellor still mad at me?"

"Well, he certainly isn't happy. For the moment, we are not focused on the past as much as the future, and how to reclaim our lost satellite."

"You gotta believe me, I did that before I even met with the Chancellor, and he told me he'd changed."

Belford squinted at me. "Changed? What does that mean?"

"He told me he was gonna make some changes about religion. I didn't know about that when I planted the leech, or else I wouldn't've done it. I swear."

"Faith, I don't know what changes you're talking about, but I assure you, whatever you think you heard, is not what the Chancellor said."

"Yes, he did. He just hadn't told anyone yet."

Belford closed his eyes tightly. "We are wasting valuable time. The point is, you planted that device and gave REFUGE control of our satellite. Now they have relocated it, and we cannot control it anymore. You created this mess, and now you can redeem yourself by helping us fix it."

My head dropped. "I don't know if I can."

"Do you know what may happen if you refuse?"

I shrugged my shoulders as I mumbled. "I've already been arrested and threatened with death. I don't really care about myself anymore."

"You don't care if you go to jail for the rest of your life?"

"Not really." Deep down, I didn't believe that, but it felt like the right thing to say.

Belford pulled his phone out of his pocket and unlocked it. "I believe you. That's why I have an insurance policy." He held his phone so I could see the screen. My heart skipped a beat as I looked. It was a picture of Audrey sitting on a cot in the cell I had occupied a few months before. My brain told my mouth to speak, but no words came out.

Belford smiled. "I take it by the look on your face that you recognize that young lady. Don't worry, she's safe...for now."

I looked at Belford with wide eyes. "What's she doing in there?"

"You know, you're pretty clever when it comes to computers, but your skills couldn't protect you forever. Once we traced your e-mail to her, we learned quite a bit. About you, REFUGE, and your best friend. We paid her a visit the other day and convinced her to help us. All you had to do was reply to her e-mails, and all this could have been avoided."

"You made her send those? My dad knew something was going on, so he wouldn't let me answer."

Belford nodded. "Your father is a smart man. For the record, we only asked her to send one e-mail. We embedded a tracking program in that last message. If you had replied, we would have been on you before you could blink."

"Okay, but how can you keep her like that? She didn't do anything wrong."

Belford held up a finger. "On the contrary, she is guilty of treason."

"Treason? How?"

"By assisting a known traitor. She read your story, so she knew exactly what you were up to. By failing to come forward, she committed treason herself. By sending that story to her you put her in danger. Not the way I would treat my best friend."

I held my hands out in protest. "Wait a minute. She thought I was dead. Why would she need to report anything?"

"She still had a duty to report what she knew about REFUGE and their plans."

I threw my hands in the air. "That's stupid! You can't arrest her for that, and you know it."

"Faith, I suggest you calm down and think rationally. Your anger will not help Audrey. Only your cooperation can do that."

I closed my eyes and grumbled under my breath.

Belford leaned in toward me. "Did you say something?"

"I said, how can I be of service?"

Belford overlooked my sarcastic tone. "Well, you can get back in the Chancellor's good graces if you help us locate the REFUGE traitors. Do that, and Audrey will go free."

"Joke's on you because I don't know where they are. They blindfolded us when they took us to their headquarters, so I couldn't tell you where they are even if I wanted to."

"I understand. So, you would help us if you could?"

I shrugged my shoulders. "Sure. Why not?" There was nothing I could do to help them anyway, so why not appease them?

Belford smiled and slid my phone across the table. "So glad to hear you say that. Turns out, you got a phone call and a text a little while ago. Looks like someone is quite eager to hear from you. Why don't you give them a shout?"

I picked up the phone and saw the text from Charlie. "What do you want me to do? It's not like he's gonna tell me where they are. Besides, last I heard they had people all over the place."

"We don't need you to ask them anything. Just tell them everything is all right and keep them on the phone long enough for us to find their location."

I spoke without looking up. "You know their phones are encrypted. You won't be able to track them."

Belford snatched the phone out of my hands and stood up. "I wouldn't be too sure about that. Just keep them on the phone and we'll do the rest. Come with me."

I sighed and followed Agent Belford down the hall and into another room full of computers, screens, and other assorted electronic equipment. It looked like the kind of room my dad would love to have for his football games. He always talked about having a room full of TVs so he could watch all the games at once, but Mom shot that idea down every time. A few tears formed in my eyes as that thought entered my mind. Whatever Charlie had to say must have been important to risk making a call.

Belford motioned for me to sit in a chair next to another man in a dark suit, who was sitting at a computer. The monitor in front of him displayed a map of the world. Belford held out my phone but didn't let go even though I had grabbed it. "Try anything stupid, and Audrey will pay. Don't follow my instructions, and Audrey will pay. Try to warn them..."

"Let me guess, Audrey will pay?" I lowered my voice and made a sarcastic face as I spoke. Belford didn't enjoy my impression, but I was amused that I actually sounded a little like him.

"You're on thin ice, Webber."

The smirk left my face as I nodded and took the phone and dialed Charlie's number. It barely rang once before Jakob's voice greeted my ears. "Faith? Is that you?" The computer screen in front of us sprang to life, and a dotted line began to zoom back and forth between different places all around the world. The hunt was on.

"Yeah, it's me. I saw that you called but I was in the shower. The showers are really beautiful here, but it's the White House so I guess you would expect that."

"I'm sure they are, but I need you to listen. Remember that ring you lost? Well, it looks like someone found it."

"Ring? I don't have a ring. Well, I did, but that was a long time ago. Unless you proposed and I forgot about it. He he he."

Jakob paused to give me time to decipher his code. "Faith, are you okay? You sound weird."

The line on the screen continued to bounce around the world. Belford whispered to the nearby agent. "How much longer?"

"Not sure. There are a lot of hops. Someone knows what they're doing."

Belford waved his hand at me in a signal to keep talking.

"Yeah, I'm fine. Just kinda distracted. What've you been up to, Jakob?"

"Faith, did you hear what I said? Your ring was found. Do you know what that means?"

"I heard you, but I don't have a clue what you're talking about. I don't remember losing a ring."

Jakob let out a loud groan, and I could almost hear Corinne making a sarcastic remark in the background. "Listen to me. They found your ring...by...the...computer. The one from Riley Riley?"

Belford and the other agent looked at each other and whispered the words "Riley Riley?"

"Jakob, I didn't lose a ring, and why would they have found it by the...oh, *that* ring."

Belford and the other agent both rolled their eyes. They had cracked Jakob's code long before I did.

"Yeah. You're going to be in big trouble when your dad finds out."

I already knew that my leech had been discovered, but now that REFUGE knew, there was no telling how they would respond. I had to tell them about the Chancellor's change of heart without giving anything away to the agents in the room with me. "You know, that was an old ring anyway. I don't think Dad's gonna be as mad as you think he will. I'm sure he'll understand."

The map on the screen zoomed in on the United States as the dotted line continued to bounce around. They were getting closer.

The frustration in Jakob's voice was evident. "Faith, you're not making any sense. I think it's time you come home."

"Come home? Why? Things are good here. I met with the Chancellor, and it was good."

Jakob paused, then spoke with hesitance in his voice. "You did?"

"Yeah. I'm telling you; things are good here. You have nothing to worry about."

The screen zoomed in on the northeast United States. "Almost there," Belford whispered.

"Jakob, trust me on this. I'm fine. Speaking of lost things, remember that lost dog you just found? You really should give it to the rightful owner. I'm sure they really miss the dog and everything will be fine if the dog goes back because the owner has promised to be nice to the dog and take care of the dog."

"What? Why are you being so annoying? I don't understand what's..."

The screen zoomed in even closer.

"Jakob? Jakob, are you there?"

Jakob sighed into the phone. "How could you do this to me?"

The line went dead, and the dotted line stopped moving. Belford pounded his fist on the desk. "How close are we?"

The other agent tilted his head to the side and frowned. "We narrowed it down to a radius of around 100 miles, but not close enough to go after them. That was one of the most sophisticated algorithms I've ever seen. I don't know who was masking their call, but they sure knew what they were doing."

I closed my eyes as some bile rose to the back of my throat. I knew exactly who was masking that call.

***

Corinne turned the computer off and smacked Jakob on the arm. "That was too close. I told you to hurry, but you almost stayed on the line too long."

Jakob shook his head. "I know. She's helping them. I can't believe she'd do that."

Corinne rubbed Jakob's arm to soothe it. "I told you that girl's trouble. She almost got you caught. What are you gonna do now?"

"I don't know. I just can't believe she would help them. After what they did to her. It doesn't make sense."

Corinne stood up and kissed him on the forehead. "Who knows? I could tell she's unstable and weak. It was probably easy for them to manipulate her. Why don't we go for a walk so you can clear your head?"

Jakob waved her off. "Not right now. I need to talk to Charlie and come up with a plan."

"Yeah, you're right. We need a plan."

The two of them went to the kitchen, where Charlie was looking through every cupboard, hunting for a snack. He really had quite the sweet tooth.

Jakob tapped Charlie on the shoulder, nearly sending him through the ceiling. "Dude, you can't sneak up on a man like that when he's looking for food."

"I'm sorry. But you need to know what's going on. Faith just called back. I tried to warn her that they found the leech, but she said everything was okay there. Then she kept trying to stall so they could trace the call."

Charlie's eyes widened. "They didn't find us, did they?"

"No. Corinne set the computer up to hide our location, then when they got within a couple hundred miles we hung up."

"It was easy," Corinne chirped. "But Riley Riley almost got us caught. She's helping them now."

Jakob stepped in to stop the Faith-bashing. "There's something else. Faith told me to return the lost dog we found. Think she was talking about the satellite?"

Charlie closed the cupboard and stared at Jakob. "Return the lost dog? I suppose she could've been talking about the satellite, but why would she want us to give it back after all this? Unless she really is helping them track us. Why would she do that?"

Jakob shrugged, but Corinne spoke up. "She probably did it to save herself. She got caught and sold us out." She moved closer and took his hand in hers. "Do you think she's telling them any important secrets?"

Jakob didn't pull his hand away as he thought. "I don't think so. I don't think she knows much."

Corinne scoffed. "You can say that again."

"No, I mean she doesn't know much about REFUGE and their plans. She couldn't help them even if she wanted to. Could she, Charlie?"

"I don't think so. Duncan plays things very close to the vest. He and Mia are about the only people that know everything that's going on. Everyone else is on a need-to-know basis."

Jakob paced across the kitchen floor, causing Corinne to free him from her grip. "So, what do we do now, Charlie? Faith either doesn't realize she's in danger, or she's really working with them now."

"I don't know. I'll call Mia and brief her. She'll want to know what happened with our phone call. Corinne, how confident are you that they couldn't trace us?"

Corinne rolled her eyes and sighed. "I know what I'm doing. They know the call came from somewhere in the northeast U.S., but there's no way they can tell exactly where we are. They were at least a hundred miles from locating us."

Charlie nodded and turned his attention back to the cabinet. "Okay, good. I think we're safe for the time being. I guess we just sit tight until..." The sound of Charlie's phone ringing stopped him mid-sentence. "Hey, Olivia...Yeah, we talked to her. It was strange though...Jakob tried to warn her that she was in danger, but she either didn't care or didn't know what he was talking about...No, he was speaking in code. That's why we think she may not have understood...Okay...Okay...We can do that...Sure...Just let me know what to do next...Okay, bye."

Jakob and Corinne both held out their hands as a signal for Charlie to fill them in.

"That was Olivia. She said to stand down."

Jakob took a step forward. "Stand down? Why did she say that?"

"Turns out, we started getting a signal from the leech again. Looks like it was a glitch after all. I guess it's a good thing you didn't just come right out and warn Faith."

Jakob looked at Corinne, who had a slightly disappointed look on her face. "That's great. But what does that mean for us?"

Charlie dug around in the cupboard again, pushing aside various boxes and cans. "That means we stay put for the time being. Olivia said they're meeting tomorrow morning to plan our next steps. They'll call me when they...yes! There was one more after all!"

Charlie tore open the last remaining snack cake wrapper and stuffed the whole thing in his mouth in one bite.

CHAPTER TWENTY-THREE

I didn't get much sleep that night. It was nice that they allowed me to go back to my bedroom, but a member of the endless army of agents sat in my room all night to make sure I stayed out of trouble. I tried to talk to her a couple of times, but she had the personality of a box of linguini. As I tossed and turned, my mind kept racing; wondering what the Chancellor was going to do to me. I prayed that he would understand my side of the story. If he had truly changed, surely, he would be able to see why I did what I did. It was out of my control, so all I could do was wait and pray.

I wasn't hungry, so all I ate for breakfast was a couple of slices of toast. I decided against the coffee. There wasn't enough sugar and creamer in the world to make it taste appetizing. Around 8:00, Agent Jackson entered the room and told me the Chancellor wanted to see me in the Oval Office.

I followed her out the door and into the hall. "Is he still mad?"

"Honestly, I'm not sure. I haven't spoken with him today. I heard what happened, so it wouldn't surprise me if he was still angry."

I sighed. "Yeah, I was afraid of that."

We walked in silence the rest of the way. Once we made it to the Oval Office, the secretary pressed a button on her phone. "Chancellor, they're here."

"Send Ms. Webber in...Alone."

I took a deep breath and followed Agent Jackson to the door. She opened it and stood aside, allowing me to enter. The Chancellor was standing at his desk, and Chief of Staff Collins was standing near the sofas. Sloane waved me in and motioned for me to sit on one of the sofas. "Hello, Faith. Have a seat." I sat down, and the Chancellor and Collins sat across from me. The Chancellor studied me for a moment without speaking.

I couldn't stand the silence, so I spoke first. "Look, I know you're probably still mad at me, but I promise, I did it before I knew what you were gonna tell me. You gotta believe me. I wouldn't have done it unless I thought I had to. In fact, I tried to call and tell them to abort their mission after you talked to me. Go back and look at my calls if you don't believe me. I'm sure you had people listening in."

Sloane held up his hand for me to stop blabbering. "Faith, please stop. I had someone sort through your call log, and I did indeed see the phone calls you placed. For that reason, I'm willing to believe you. Now if you would be so kind, tell me about your phone call with Jakob last night."

"Jakob? Oh yeah. Umm, he kept saying something about how someone found my ring and my dad would be mad."

"I read the transcript. I know exactly what was said, and what was implied. It sounds as if REFUGE is under the impression that we discovered the leech you planted. Evidently, you inadvertently turned it off when you reclaimed it and once it stopped transmitting, the technicians at REFUGE assumed it had been discovered. Hence the phone call and secret code."

"I had a feeling that's what Jakob was talking about, but I had to play along so he would stay on the phone longer. I tried to tell him I was okay, and they didn't need to worry about me, but he just thought I was being dense."

Sloane nodded his head. "Yes, I know. You did a fine job."

"So, what about your satellite? I tried to tell them to give it back."

Sloane stood and walked to the window. "Funny you should ask. There has been some disagreement in my camp about the satellite, but I believe we have a solution. A solution that requires your assistance once more."

"Sure. You name it."

"Have you thought any more about our discussion about REFUGE, and their true plans for my satellite?"

I shook my head slowly. "Not really. Been kinda busy."

Sloane turned around to face me. "I know you don't believe my hypothesis, but I ask that you grant me one favor. Please keep an open mind and allow yourself to accept the possibility that what I said has at least a grain of truth."

"Okay, I can do that."

Sloane nodded his head. "Think it through. Can you admit that it is within the realm of possibility that REFUGE is planning to overthrow me by using the satellite to control my military, and use them to usurp my authority?"

I leaned forward and rested my elbows on my knees. "I don't know. It just doesn't sound like the REFUGE I know."

The Chancellor took a few steps closer to me. "You mean the REFUGE they have allowed you to know about? Faith, in order for a plan like this to succeed, they would have to keep it closely guarded, with only a select number of people aware of it. Perhaps your father has been kept in the dark, as have most of the members of REFUGE, and that is why you find it so difficult to believe."

"But the leech wasn't even their idea. It was Jakob's. And it was my idea to be the one to put it on your computer. How could this be their plan if it wasn't their plan, to begin with?"

Sloane smiled. "That's the genius of it, Faith. Aside from using mind-controlling microchips, the best way to get people to do what you want them to do is to make them think it was their idea. I'm certain they had this whole thing orchestrated ahead of time, and if Jakob didn't mention the leech, and you didn't volunteer for the mission, they would have steered you in that direction until you took the bait."

My stomach sank as I began to believe there was a sliver of truth in what Sloane was saying. "I don't know. I guess it makes some sense, but that's kinda out there."

"Faith, consider everything you've already been through. All of it seems out there, does it not?"

I couldn't really argue with that logic. "I guess so. So, let's say you're right. What are you planning on doing about it?"

"I want you to help me test my theory. I need you to place another phone call and tell your friends at REFUGE that I'm willing to give them what they want if they relocate my satellite to its original position."

"What if they say no?"

Sloane smiled. "You do the math."

"Well, they would only refuse if they either didn't trust you...or if..." I looked up at Sloane. "...or if you're right about them."

Sloane stood up and held my phone out toward me. "Care to find out how right I am?"

I took the phone and dialed Charlie's number. Not surprisingly, he didn't answer so I left him a message telling him I needed to talk to someone who could make an important decision. I hung up and shrugged my shoulders. "Now what?"

"Now we wait. Care for some brunch?"

A couple of hours and several pancakes later, my phone rang with no caller ID. I put it on speakerphone so Sloane and Collins could hear too.

"Faith, this matter had better be critical. You're taking an immense risk in telephoning us in this manner."

She didn't have to say her name. It was obvious by her vocabulary that it was Mia. "Yeah, I know. I have important news to tell you. They know about the missing satellite. I promise I didn't tell them anything. They figured it out on their own."

"Very well. This is not an unexpected development. Our mission continues unaltered."

It was a little upsetting that her first instinct was to talk about the mission rather than ask about my safety. "I'm fine by the way. And I have great news. Looks like we really got the Chancellor's attention."

"Go on."

"Well, he wanted me to call and tell you that he's ready to negotiate a truce."

I could almost hear Mia's eyebrows raise through the phone. "A truce? What sort of truce is he proposing?"

I looked at Sloane, who nodded his head, signaling for me to continue. "He's willing to change his laws on religion if you return his satellite."

Mia scoffed through the phone. "Surely you jest. Faith, the man cannot be trusted. Any truce he claims to seek will be broken at the first chance he gets. You, of all people, know how eager he is to say what people want to hear, with no intention of following through on his empty promises."

"I know, but trust me, he's different now. I can tell he..."

"Ms. Webber, you almost sound as if you believe this maniac. Are you in allegiance with him now?"

I closed my eyes so tightly my face contorted. "That's not what I'm saying. I'm just saying, our whole goal is to get religious freedom, and now he's offering that. He has a whole big idea, and he wants me to help him announce it this week. Trust me. You'll see. Why don't you tell Duncan about this and see what he says?"

Sloane and I stared at each other as we waited. Mia's response would tell us everything we needed to know about REFUGE's plan.

"As you wish. Please allow me a few minutes to consult with Duncan. I'm certain he will not go along with this, but I will allow him to make the decision for himself. I will phone you again shortly." With those words, the line went dead.

Sloane rubbed his chin and squinted his eyes as he thought. "Was that Mia?"

I nodded my head. "How do you know about her?"

"Ms. Webber, my intelligence is quite good. REFUGE has many secrets, but we know the key players such as Duncan and Mia."

"What do you know about them?"

"Not much, other than the fact that Duncan is elusive, and Mia is his right-hand woman. We think they may be involved romantically, but the evidence is not conclusive. REFUGE began work as a non-profit medical provider about ten years ago. They were aggressive in their fundraising and amassed a considerable amount of money during that time. Some of which they used on medical expenses, but we believe the bulk of those funds has gone toward their clandestine activities. How do you think they're able to build their bunkers and safehouses?"

"I guess that makes sense."

"We have never seen Duncan out in public, at least that we know of, so we have no idea who he is or what he looks like. I believe our cameras have caught Mia on occasion, but we have never been able to apprehend or question her."

We sat in silence for a few moments as I digested what Sloane was telling me. As much as I hated to believe his conspiracy theory, on some level, it actually made some sense. I still believed REFUGE's intentions were good, but I allowed myself to believe there was a slight possibility that Sloane was right. The silence was interrupted by the sound of my phone ringing again. I answered and put it on speakerphone for Sloane and Collins.

"Hello?"

"Ms. Webber, I conversed with Duncan, and he made me aware of his intentions. We are, by no means, willing to negotiate with Chancellor Sloane. We can ill afford to sacrifice our leverage on a promise that we all know will go unfulfilled. We are going to proceed as planned."

I looked at Sloane, who had a flicker of anger growing in his eyes as he opened his mouth. "Mia, this is Chancellor Sloane. I understand your apprehension, but I give you my word, that I will follow through on this promise. I am willing to step out in faith and offer you the religious freedom you so desperately seek, in return for my missing satellite."

Mia paused for a moment, then replied. "Chancellor, it is an honor to dialogue with you. Please accept my apologies for being so frank, but I know you understand why I responded in such a manner."

When these two talked to each other, it was like a competition to see who could use the biggest, smartest-sounding words.

Sloane's eyebrows furrowed. This was a man who was used to getting his way. "I understand completely. You have no reason to trust me, but do you trust Faith? She believes me, so you should as well."

"We trust Ms. Webber on some matters, but I'm afraid her judgment is clouded on this particular issue. It appears as though you have convinced her that your intentions are noble, but Duncan and I are not weak-minded enough to fall for your chicanery."

Chicanery? Weak minded? I was really beginning to dislike Mia. Not as much as I despised Corinne, but still.

Sloane nodded his head even though Mia couldn't see him. "I see. Are you certain there is no way to convince you that my gesture is genuine?"

"I'm afraid not. Now if you'll excuse me, we have a mission to finish."

I looked at Sloane, who looked at me with an *I told you so* expression on his face. "Well? What do you think now?"

I closed my eyes and shook my head. "I can't believe I'm saying this, but maybe you're right. What are you gonna do about the satellite? They're obviously not gonna give it back, are they?"

"It does not appear so. But, as always, I have a contingency plan." He nodded at Collins, who took out his phone and made a call.

"Hello, Gatlin? It's Collins. We're a go for Project Falling Star."

I looked at Sloane, who had a satisfied look on his face. "Falling star? What's that?"

"We were able to ascertain the location of the missing satellite a short time ago, but we were still unable to communicate with it. Now that we have been locked out, and I know REFUGE will not return it to me, I have no choice but to destroy it."

I nodded my head. "Some contingency plan."

Sloane pushed a button on his desk and a television screen tilted and lowered from the ceiling. The screen was split, with an animation of two satellites on the left side, and a video feed of the Oversight satellite on the right. Within a few seconds, a tiny, animated laser left one of the satellites and created a trail of dotted lines across space.

"Laser away," Collins said as if we couldn't see it on the screen for ourselves. "Destruction expected in approximately twenty seconds."

We sat in silence, watching the dotted line grow longer. Finally, the satellite we had been watching on the right side of the screen was vaporized.

Collins nodded at Sloane, who then looked at me. "Well, that's that."

"Now what?" I asked.

"Well, now that those criminals at REFUGE cannot control my microchips, I can concentrate on locating them and bringing them to justice."

My heart sank. "All of them?"

Sloane sighed. "Only those who are guilty of treason. If your friends and family are innocent, they will escape punishment. I seek to cut the head off the snake, and end this once and for all."

"You mean Duncan?"

Sloane nodded. "Now that you know my intentions, and you are starting to see the truth about REFUGE, perhaps you can help in another way."

"What do you want me to do?"

"I need information. Where have you been the last few days?"

I looked down at my feet. "Uh, well, just here and there I guess."

"And where exactly might that be?" My silence was not the answer he was looking for. "Look, Faith, it's high time you trust me. The faster I can end this conflict, the sooner you and your family get what you so desperately want. What do you know?"

A million thoughts ran through my mind at once. If I truly trusted the Chancellor, I had nothing to fear from him. If REFUGE really was trying to overthrow Sloane, they should be stopped. And stopping them wouldn't stop Sloane from allowing religion again. Maybe I should help after all.

"If I tell you what I know, I want you to promise that my friends and family will be safe."

Sloane held up his hand. "Faith, if they truly are innocent, I give you my word that they will not only be free, but I will invite them here to help us with our announcement."

I took a deep breath in and let it out. "Okay, fine. I'll tell you what I know."

CHAPTER TWENTY-FOUR

Paul and my dad walked into the office where Mia was sitting, staring at her computer screen. She looked up from her screen long enough to wave them in. "Gentlemen, come join me."

The two men sat down across from Mia's desk and waited for her to speak since she was the one who summoned them.

"There has been a development in Washington. The Chancellor has responded to our actions regarding his satellite."

"He destroyed it, didn't he?" Paul asked.

Mia nodded.

Dad cocked his head to the side. "So, it's over? What happens now?"

Mia's smile revealed her confidence. "As I stated, the Chancellor responded. However, his response was not unexpected. Duncan predicted this might happen, so not long after we gained control of the satellite, we transferred everything from that satellite to one of our REFUGE satellites. Call it an insurance policy."

Paul stroked his chin as he thought. "Smart. How long until you're able to use it?"

"We are not able to ascertain that at this time. Our technicians are efforting a solution as we speak, but as of yet, they have not been successful."

"What about Corinne? She worked in the tech group in our agency. She might have some insight on these chips."

Dad's head snapped toward Paul for making such a recommendation. "Absolutely not. She doesn't need to be involved."

Paul shot a glance at my dad that told him he meant business.

"Andrew, she's already involved. So why not get her to help?"

Mia was intrigued. "Corinne? Who is that?"

Paul spent the next several minutes explaining Corinne's backstory while Mia listened. Dad interjected a few unflattering words, but he was shut down each time.

After hearing the story in its entirety, Mia finally spoke. "Mr. Cross, I believe your proposal has merit. I shall speak with Duncan, and with his approval, I will telephone Charlie and have him bring Ms. Maxwell to our tech center."

Dad fidgeted in his seat. "What about Faith? When can we get her out of there?"

Mia pursed her lips as she paused. "Faith. Yes. Well, I'm afraid the situation has grown more complicated."

"What are you talking about?" Dad asked.

"Mr. Webber, you will not want to hear this, but Duncan believes Faith is helping Chancellor Sloane now."

Dad's chin dropped. "That's not possible. Why would she help him? He tried to kill her. More than once."

Mia stood to her feet and walked toward the front of her desk. "She called Charlie and asked him to get in touch with me. I phoned her in return, and she stated that Chancellor Sloane was willing to revise his laws against religion if we relinquished control of his satellite."

"That's great," Dad said. "That's what we've been working for this whole time."

Paul and Mia shook their heads, but she was the only one who spoke. "Surely you cannot be serious. You, of all people, should know that the Chancellor cannot be trusted. He promised to allow religion a few months ago, did he not? And nothing changed. The populous forgot about Faith, and he carried on as if nothing had happened. What makes you think he will do anything differently now?"

Dad nodded. "You're right, but why does that mean Faith's working for him now? Maybe she was acting under duress."

"Possible. But she sounded convinced that she was in the right. It is difficult to put my finger on it, but something about her tone seemed genuine and unafraid. I played a recording of that call for Duncan, and he, like me, believes she has changed her allegiance."

Dad looked at Paul and Mia, who were both staring at him.

"Do you think that's possible?" Paul asked him.

"No. I can't imagine any circumstance that would cause her to do something like that. Not for him."

Mia returned to her seat. "No matter. Just know that we are proceeding as if she were one of the enemies. We have not made this amount of progress without taking the proper precautions, and we refuse to behave in a careless fashion now."

Dad leaned forward in his seat. "I understand that. I really do. But this is my daughter we're talking about. She risked her life to get you that satellite, and now you're just willing to write her off?"

Paul's eyes widened as Mia gathered her thoughts. "Mr. Webber, we are not writing her off. We just cannot afford to take any risks when it comes to her allegiance. If she truly is in league with the Chancellor now, she is likely safe."

"Likely safe? I can't accept 'likely' safe."

Mia frowned at my father's protests. "We must proceed with caution. Sometimes that means making some difficult decisions. But first thing is first, we have a security issue to resolve."

After lunch, and a long conversation with me and Mr. Collins, Chancellor Sloane requested the National Security Council to join him at the White House. I had told Sloane everything I knew about REFUGE's headquarters in Philadelphia, and he wanted to share that information with his military and intelligence advisors. An internet search failed to yield any results about Lennon Linen, but I had given them enough information to narrow down the list of possible locations. Because it was a Sunday afternoon, it would take a couple of hours for the Security Council to arrive, so we had some time to discuss other things.

Now that the threat of REFUGE using Sloane's satellite against him had been neutralized (or so we thought), we could set our attention on the plan for allowing religious freedom in America again. Sloane took advantage of that time to lay out his plans for his Faith in America initiative with me and Collins. Sloane wanted plenty of publicity, but he wanted to avoid the typical hoopla and fanfare that came with his bold new programs. It would be an understated approach, allowing the power of the program to be the star. The cabinet meeting was scheduled for Tuesday, so time was running out.

Collins' phone buzzed in his pocket, and he took it out. "Chancellor, the National Security Council members will be arriving soon. We should leave."

"Very well. Faith, I want you to join us in the Situation Room."

"Me? Why me?"

"We need you to identify the building you were in."

I shook my head. "Yeah, but I never saw it from the outside. All I know is that it's some big laundry facility in Philadelphia. They hid us inside laundry trucks when they moved us in and out."

"I know. But maybe you can provide some details, even small ones, that can help us locate the REFUGE leaders."

I shrugged my shoulders as we stood up. "Sure. I'll give it a shot."

Our entourage proceeded down into the basement of the White House, passing through an endless labyrinth of hallways. Much to my surprise, the Situation Room was more than just one room. It was a series of rooms with the most advanced computer and communications technology I had ever seen. My inner computer geek was in awe. I followed Sloane and Collins into a large conference room with a huge table, cushy chairs, and walls full of display monitors and digital clocks. A group of men and women, some in business attire, and some in military uniforms stood as we entered. We all sat down, and Chancellor Sloane began the meeting.

"Thank you all for coming in on a Sunday. You know I normally refrain from calling weekend meetings, but time is of the essence in this situation. As many of you know already, this is Faith Webber. I tried to execute her a few months ago for treason, but now she has agreed to help us locate the criminals at REFUGE so we can put an end to their planned insurrection."

My face turned flush as every one of these important men and women stared at me.

Sloane continued. "Ms. Webber has been to the REFUGE headquarters, so I invited her here to disseminate what she knows, in the hopes that she can provide some clues as to REFUGE's location. Faith, why don't you tell them what you know?"

My mouth opened, but no sound came out. I cleared my throat to stall until I could regain my composure. "I...um...well, here's what I know. We went to some car repair garage where a guy named Lenny worked. There they put us in laundry bins and loaded us into white cargo trucks that said, Lennon Linen."

Everyone was scrambling to enter my information on their notepads, tablets, and computers as I spoke.

"I know we were in Philadelphia, but I don't know exactly where we were. Once we stopped, they wheeled us out of the trucks, into an elevator, and into some secret rooms underneath some sort of laundry company."

One of the women in the room pushed some buttons and a satellite image of Philadelphia appeared on one of the screens with several buildings highlighted in yellow. "These are all the commercial laundry facilities in the city of Philadelphia whose buildings are large enough to fit Faith's description. My people are searching the traffic cameras in the area for Lennon Linen trucks. All we have to do is locate them and follow them until they lead us straight to REFUGE."

Sloane nodded his head. "Very well, Veronica. Please keep me posted. I want to thank you all for the successful execution of Project Falling Star this morning. It pained me to destroy a piece of equipment like that, but it was our only option. We could not allow REFUGE to use our satellite against us. Now it is only a matter of time before we bring them to justice."

Sloane had barely finished his sentence when Veronica received a message on her phone and sat up in her chair. "Chancellor, I think we have something. We found a Lennon Linen truck matching Faith's description a few days ago, and we tracked it to a commercial laundry facility in west Philadelphia. We can have agents there within the hour."

A wide grin spread across Sloane's face. "Veronica, you have done it again. I want every available resource at that laundry facility. They are not suspecting a raid, so we will use the element of surprise to our advantage."

My heart pounded inside my chest. Had I done the right thing?

The Chancellor must have noticed the look on my face. "Faith, are you still with us?"

I nodded my head. "Yes, sir."

"We couldn't have done this without your help. You have played a vital role in this endeavor. Because of you, we can now eliminate the threat REFUGE has posed for far too long."

"That's what I'm afraid of."

Sloane squinted his eyes and everyone in the room turned their gaze toward me. "I sense some apprehension. Trust me, you are doing the right thing."

"I know...at least I think I know. It's just..."

Sloane looked at the others and said, "Give us the room." Within seconds, he and I were the only people remaining. "Faith, remember our dreams. That's a sign that you should trust me. I want to make things right, but first I must deal with REFUGE."

"I know. I'm just worried about my family and friends. I want you to remember your promise that they'll be safe and won't be in trouble. If REFUGE is really planning what you think they are, there's no way my dad knew about that."

Sloane thought for a moment. "I already gave you my word. But..."

"But what?"

Sloane cleared his throat. "But if they are aware of REFUGE's true plans, he must be dealt with along with the other traitors. How confident are you of his innocence?"

"Confident enough to help you find their headquarters I guess." My mouth said the words, but my heart wasn't as convinced. Working with Sloane to protect my family and friends was still my best move.

Sloane smiled. "Very well." He pushed a button on the table and the others re-entered the room. "Welcome back. Now let's catch some traitors."

Forty-five minutes and lengthy conversations later, the group watched the monitors on the wall. The screens were divided up into smaller sections, each showing live video footage from body cameras and satellites, as well as a video feed showing a computer-generated schematic of the laundry building, with little red dots representing the location of each agent in the area.

Veronica pushed a button on her tablet that allowed her to communicate directly with the agent in charge. "Alpha One, you are clear to proceed. Remember, the targets are several stories underground. No casualties."

A voice spoke through the speakers in the room. "Roger that."

The red dots circled the building, and the room was filled with radio chatter.

"Alpha team in position."

"Bravo team in position."

"Charlie team in position."

"Delta team in position."

Veronica looked at Sloane, who nodded in return. She pushed the button on her tablet again. "Alpha One, you are go."

"Y'all heard her. All teams advance on my mark. 3...2...1, go go go!"

The video screens were filled with chaotic movements, agents in battle gear, machine guns, and converging red dots. The laundry workers all looked surprised and confused, but none of them offered any resistance. Within seconds, the agents had secured the main room and gathered all the workers together in one corner.

"Alpha One to base. Main level secure. Now proceeding to lower levels."

Veronica spoke into her tablet again. "Very well. Proceed with caution."

A handful of red dots stayed behind to watch the laundry workers, but the majority moved on. I had told Sloane we rode in elevators, but he figured there would be at least one set of stairs as well. Building schematics didn't show any stairs, but they didn't show a secret underground bunker either. The red dots spread throughout the building, and the radio chatter continued as the agents searched for a way down. After several minutes of searching and shouting, one of the agents found a stairway. Many of the other red dots joined him, and they made their way down the stairs. I had no way of knowing how far underground we had been, so the agents had to stop at every floor to have a look around. Finally, they reached the bottom of the stairway and ventured out.

"Alpha One here. We've reached the bottom level. There are several rooms, but no signs of life."

Chancellor Sloane called my name. "Faith? Do you recognize these rooms?"

I walked over toward the screens to get a closer look at the body camera footage. "I don't know. There was a kitchen, bathrooms, and living room, but that's all we saw. Can you ask the guys to slow down a little so I can see?"

Veronica spoke into her tablet. "Alpha One, give us a look around. Slowly."

"Roger that."

Veronica did something on her tablet that enlarged the video from Alpha One's body camera. "Alpha One, we're looking for a kitchen, restrooms, and living quarters. See anything like that?"

"Not yet, but we're still moving."

They soldiered on, but nothing looked familiar to me. Empty room after empty room greeted the agents as they circulated.

Sloane frowned. "Faith, I thought this was supposed to be their headquarters."

"So did I. At least, that's what they told us. We never saw anything but the living area."

"Base, this is Alpha One. I think we found something." He turned, and his camera revealed the living area we had been in, the restroom where I colored my hair, and the kitchen. We had the right building, but everyone had vanished.

I looked at Sloane, who had a scowl on his face. "Veronica, tell them to keep searching. Maybe they left something behind."

The agents continued their search but found nothing that indicated the presence of anyone or anything suspicious. After another hour or so of searching, the agents called it quits and returned to the main floor. They questioned the workers, but none of them provided any information that would help us. The people at REFUGE were meticulous in their planning, so it should have come as no surprise that they wouldn't leave any incriminating evidence behind.

Sloane sighed. "Well, either this was not REFUGE's headquarters after all, or they got wind of our plans and cleared the building before our arrival."

Everyone looked around the room, then all stared at me. I glanced around the room a few times before I realized what they were thinking.

"It wasn't me! Honest!"

One by one, the men and women in the room scolded me with their eyes. A few of them spoke, saying things like "How could you?" or "I knew we couldn't trust her." The murmurings built to a crescendo before the Chancellor silenced the group.

"That's enough."

I pleaded at the Chancellor with my eyes. "Chancellor, you gotta believe me. You were with me when I talked to Mia. Did you hear anything?"

"I don't recall hearing anything out of the ordinary. Perhaps there was some sort of code being spoken."

I shook my head and spoke with desperation in my voice. "How would I have done that? I don't know any codes. If I'm helping you, why would I warn them? I want the same thing you do. Please believe me."

Sloane held up his hand to silence my blathering. "All right, all right. That's enough. I believe you. I don't see how you would have warned them during that conversation. There must be another explanation. We all know how paranoid Duncan is. Perhaps they intentionally misled the Webbers into thinking that was their headquarters, all the while concealing its true location."

One brave man in a dark suit dared to speak up. "Chancellor, that's a bit of a stretch, isn't it? Do you really believe that?"

A hush fell over the room, and the brave man's face turned deep red.

Sloane sat with his elbows on the table and his fingertips meeting under his chin. "Mr. Walker, which is more likely? That the powers that be at REFUGE concealed the true location of their headquarters from people they do not fully trust; or that they learned of our impending raid and managed to clear out every remnant of their headquarters and flee in less than an hour?"

"Well...I suppose...I mean..."

Sloane continued. "Think about it. REFUGE may trust Faith's father and her family, but they were also harboring two of our former agents. Two agents who were trying to stop REFUGE just a few short months ago. So, Duncan is well within his rights to be suspicious of Paul and Jakob."

Mr. Walker adjusted his collar to let some of the steam out. "Well, when you put it that way..."

Sloane smiled. "Precisely. There will be no more discussion of Faith's motives. Instead, we must turn our focus on finding..." He stopped mid-sentence and turned to me. "Paul. Jakob. Your family. Where are they?"

The blood drained from my face. "I don't know. I know that's where we were."

Sloane shook his head. "Scour satellite and traffic cameras around that building for the last few hours. Tell me if any laundry trucks left."

Walker looked confused. "But sir, I thought you said..."

Sloane looked at me with anger in his eyes. "If your family and the others are gone too, I'm afraid they may have received a helpful tip after all."

CHAPTER TWENTY-FIVE

The last of the laundry bins arrived in the empty room, and everyone climbed out. My parents, Hope, Alex, and Paul stretched their legs and walked around to get the blood flowing again.

Paul, being the oldest of the group, took a little longer to recover from the long, dark drive. "Andrew, any idea where we are?"

Dad thought for a moment. "I'm not sure. Well, we drove for at least two hours, so we could be just about anywhere between New York and Washington."

Paul twisted and cracked his back several times, causing Hope to squeal in disgust. "You work for these people, Andrew. Don't you know where they have bases?"

Dad laughed. "Not quite. You know how secretive they are. We're only told the information that's pertinent to our current mission. No one knows everything except Duncan and the people close to him."

Paul rolled his eyes and twisted the other way, cracking his back again. "Ahh yes. The mysterious, all-seeing, all-knowing Duncan."

As they wandered around the room, the door opened, and Mia entered with Olivia. "I see you all made the journey without incident. I must apologize for the abrupt nature of our departure, but time was of the essence."

Dad walked up to Mia, with Paul close behind him. "What's going on? Why did we have to leave so quickly?"

"Mr. Webber, Mr. Cross, the three of us need to have a difficult conversation in another room. Please come with me. Olivia, please tend to the Webbers' needs until we return."

"Yes, ma'am."

Dad and Paul followed Mia down a hall and into a conference room.

"Gentlemen, please sit."

The two men sat down at the conference table and waited for Mia to speak. "Gentlemen, I will cut to the chase. It appears as though my suspicions about Faith were confirmed."

Dad perked up. "You're not saying what I think you're saying."

Paul squinted his eyes. "What are you saying she's saying?"

"Mr. Webber, I have a source whom I trust completely. I asked them to either confirm or refute my suspicions regarding Faith's allegiance. They not only corroborated my suspicions, but they also reported that Faith was helping the Chancellor locate our laundry facility so they could move in and arrest us. Hence the reason for our hasty escape."

Paul's ears perked up. "Just who is your source?"

"Mr. Cross, I assure you, it is not one of your colleagues. Let us just say that I know someone who knows someone."

Paul shot a steely glare back at Mia. "That still doesn't answer my question."

Mia felt Paul's gaze but turned to make eye contact with my dad. "I cannot fathom why Faith would do such a thing. My only hypothesis is that the Chancellor has somehow brainwashed her or threatened her into siding with him. But we do not know how he would have accomplished such a thing."

Dad set his elbows on the table and rested his head in his hands. "This doesn't seem right. Are you sure about all this?"

Mia slid her tablet across the table toward my dad. "This is footage from our surveillance videos at the laundry. Play the video."

Paul leaned forward as Dad pushed *play* and set the tablet down on the table. The two men watched as three laundry trucks left the building.

Dad looked at Mia. "Was that us?"

Mia nodded. "Now fast forward eight minutes and sixteen seconds.

Dad scanned ahead as instructed, just in time to see dozens of agents swarming around the building and forcing their way inside.

Mia took a deep breath. "The only explanation for this is Faith."

Dad rewound the video and watched it again. "That can't be true. None of us even knew what building we were in. How could she have given away our location?"

Paul scoffed. "You underestimate the Chancellor. All Faith had to do was tell him we were in a commercial laundry building in Philadelphia, and his people would figure out the rest.

Dad's chin dropped and his heart sank as he started to believe Mia's story. "I don't understand why she would do this. She has to have a good reason. She wouldn't just betray us."

Mia's face showed no emotion. "Mr. Webber, it is not my job to attempt to decode Faith's motives. My job is to protect this organization from every threat, and now that list includes your daughter."

"I still say she's being forced to give them information. What if she's in danger?"

"Mr. Webber, to borrow a line from a classic television show, "Your daughter is not in danger. She *is* the danger. The sooner you allow yourself to accept that the sooner you will be able to help us."

"Help *you*? We need to help *her*. Something's obviously wrong. I'm telling you; she wouldn't betray us without a good reason. Tell your source to figure out why Faith's helping the Chancellor. Or do you not want to know the answer?"

"I understand your frustration. I will indulge you and query my source as you requested. But you must at least acknowledge the fact that Faith presents a danger to us, and we must proceed with an abundance of caution."

Dad shook his head and gritted his teeth. "Fine. Maybe you're right. What do we do now?"

"Now, we wait for reinforcements to arrive."

— • ● • —

Several hours of planning and meeting in the Situation Room had yielded no results. Traffic cameras had picked up the trucks leaving the laundry, but lost contact with them once they left the city. Sloane's people knew the trucks were heading southwest, which meant they were likely going toward either Baltimore or

Washington, DC. That helped, but it didn't give them enough concrete information to act. Sloane's people believed Baltimore was their likeliest destination, and probably the location of REFUGE's true headquarters. It was a large enough city for them to hide in plain sight, and it was close enough to Washington for them to keep a close eye on things at the White House.

The Chancellor asked his people to monitor the traffic cameras in Baltimore, but we all knew it may not help. REFUGE had to know we would be looking for Lennon Linen trucks, so there was a good chance they transferred their passengers to other vehicles for camouflage. It was like trying to find a needle in a haystack; only we didn't know what this needle looked like, and this haystack was the size of a major city.

While we waited for updates on the needle hunt, Chancellor Sloane summoned his closest advisors and laid out his plans for Faith in America. At first, they were skeptical, but they are smart enough not to make a habit of questioning the Chancellor. After a somewhat lengthy meeting, we had laid the groundwork for the program and scheduled a press conference for Wednesday. It was really awkward to sit in on a meeting with some of the most powerful people in the country, but the Chancellor did a good job including me in the process and making me feel at ease. At the end of the meeting, he dismissed everyone but me.

"Faith, I have a surprise for you."

"Oh boy. I don't know if I can handle any more surprises these days."

Sloane chuckled, which was pleasant, but still a little strange. "I think you'll like this surprise. You have been a tremendous help so far, but I have a feeling I'm going to need more than just your insight as we move forward. You were able to hack into REFUGE's mail system before. You know their system, so perhaps you can assist us with your computer expertise."

"Yeah, sure. Anything to help."

"You are a brilliant young woman, capable of doing things few others can do. But this may be a job for two brilliant young women, so I brought in someone to help you." Sloane pushed the intercom button on his desk. "Please send our guest in."

The door opened, and in walked my best friend. I shrieked as I ran to her. "Audrey!" We hugged and laughed, then hugged and laughed some more. "I can't believe you're here."

Audrey took a step back and frowned at my hair. "What did you do to yourself?" Her brutal honesty was one of her defining qualities.

I ran my fingers through my unnaturally blonde hair. "Well, I figured since I was coming to Washington, I'd better look as beautiful as I can."

Audrey wrinkled her nose. "Beautiful?"

"Well, pretty."

Audrey scoffed. "Pretty?"

"Uhh, nice?"

"Nice? I don't know if I would go that far."

I cleared my throat and looked down at my feet. "Well, I wanted to look different."

Audrey smiled widely. "Well, mission accomplished. It's definitely different."

We both laughed and hugged again.

Sloane stood out of the way while we chirped and chatted for the next several minutes. Finally, he had enough of the teen girl talk and asked us to sit on the sofas. "Ladies, I'm happy that you are finally reunited, but we have work to do. I'll give you the rest of the evening to visit, but in the morning, you'll need to get started on your assignment. Agent Martinez will come to your room at eight o'clock and take you to one of our computer labs. There you will work with my brightest minds and see how much information you are able to gather for us."

"What kind of information?" I asked.

"Anything and everything. We know what REFUGE's ultimate goal is, but I want to know how they are planning to accomplish it, where they're hiding, and who's involved. Anything that will give us some insight. Now that they lost access to my satellite, I'm certain they will regroup and work on another plan. That means a treasure trove of communication for you to intercept."

Audrey and I both nodded in perfect synchronization.

"Faith, you were able to accomplish a lot with your personal computer. Just imagine what the two of you can do with my resources at your disposal."

Audrey leaned over and whispered in my ear. "Just imagine the kind of trouble we could cause, too."

Sloane leaned forward. "What was that?"

Audrey's face turned red. "I...uh...I was just telling Faith how excited I am to be here. You have a lovely office."

I poked Audrey in the ribs. "Don't mind her. She says weird stuff when she's nervous."

Sloane stood to his feet, signaling the end of our meeting. "Very well. Please step outside, where an agent will escort you to your room. Whatever you need, just ask."

Audrey and I said "thank you" and walked toward the door. On the way out, I stopped at the edge of the office and turned back to the Chancellor. "By the way, could we maybe get some pizza for supper?"

He nodded. "Certainly. Just let them know what you would like."

As we exited the room I leaned over toward Audrey. "You know, you really should work on your whispering."

•━━━━━━━•●•━━━━━━━•

Corinne entered the conference room with her typical bravado, Jakob's hand securely in hers. "All right, I'm here. What crisis do you need me to solve for you?"

Paul and my dad rolled their eyes while Mia reached her hand out to shake Corinne's. "Ms. Maxwell, thank you for your willingness to assist us."

Corinne used her right hand to shake Mia's hand while using her left to remind everyone that Jakob belonged to her. "Like I told Charlie, I'm only willing if you're able to pay me the extra half-million I asked for."

"I spoke with Duncan, and although he believes your request is rather excessive, he agreed to pay the full amount upon the completion of your task."

"Which is?"

Mia sat down and invited Corinne to do the same. "As you know, we have endeavored to secure control of the satellite Chancellor Sloane utilizes for communicating with the microchips in the heads of his soldiers. Faith was successful, and we were able to relocate that satellite so the Chancellor could no longer reach it."

"Surprised Riley Riley actually came through. Good for her." Sarcasm flowed from her mouth.

Jakob rolled his eyes while Mia blinked hers. "Riley Riley? Who is that?"

Corinne laughed. "Psssh. Never mind. It's a long story."

Mia continued. "Very well. Duncan suspected the Chancellor would rather destroy his satellite than have it used against him, so we transferred the Oversight program to one of our satellites. As it turns out, our suspicions came to fruition. Chancellor Sloane did indeed destroy his satellite, but he is unaware of the fact that we no longer need it. We must take advantage of this fact, and take control of his soldiers before they can be used against us. Unfortunately, my technicians are having some difficulty. They successfully transferred the Oversight program, but they have not been able to operate it."

"And you think I can help because I'm good with tech and I used to work for the government?"

Mia nodded her head. "Precisely."

"Sure, why not. But I'll need Jakob with me. He's my good luck charm."

Dad cleared his throat. "Actually, we need Jakob with us for a strategy meeting."

Corinne glared at my father with more than a hint of red in her blue eyes. "Maybe you didn't hear me the first time. Jakob stays with me, or I walk."

Everyone looked at Mia who sighed and shook her head. "Ms. Maxwell, you're in no position to make demands. You are our guest, and you will..."

Corinne turned her piercing gaze toward Mia. "Actually, I'm in a perfect position to make demands. You said it yourself, your people can't do this on their own. At least not before Sloane finds out the truth. You brought me here because you need my help. So, it seems to me, I can make whatever demands I want."

A hush landed on the room as the two women exchanged intense glares, each waiting for the other to blink.

Mia conceded first. "Very well, Ms. Maxwell. While I have the utmost confidence in my team, time is of the essence, and we must secure control of Sloane's soldiers before he mounts a counteroffensive." She pressed a button on her phone and spoke into it. "Olivia, please come in here and escort our guests to the Technology Center."

Olivia entered the room, and an obnoxious smile spread across Corinne's face as she stood to her feet. "I knew you'd see it my way. Come on, Jakob." She held out her hand and Jakob obediently took it. Without another word, they were gone.

My father rubbed his temples. "She's horrible. Are you sure we need her? Maybe I should call Duncan."

Mia snapped her head toward my dad. "Mr. Webber, firstly, you do not have the means to call Duncan. Secondly, Duncan and I have spoken at length about this, and we agree it is for the best."

"But she's..."

Mia's glare stopped my dad in his tracks. "How dare you question our judgment? Need I remind you, REFUGE existed before your involvement, and your assistance, while appreciated, is not essential for our success." Mia was trying hard to regain some of the dignity she had just lost in her encounter with Corinne.

Dad's face turned flush. Partly with anger, partly with embarrassment. "Look, I just don't trust her. And how do you know she can do what you want her to?"

"Mr. Webber, please do not allow your personal feelings to cloud your judgment. If you remove emotion from the equation and examine this empirically, you will undoubtedly concur with our assessment of the situation."

Dad looked over at Paul, who, until now, had remained an innocent bystander. "Paul, help me out here."

"All right, I'll help you. I'll help you by telling you the truth. You're wrong about this. Corinne has been helpful thus far, and I believe she can do what Mia asked. Would you be opposed to her help if she wasn't flirting with Jakob?"

Dad's mouth fell open, but he didn't speak. He looked down at the table as he thought about everything.

Mia stood and glided across the room toward my father. "Mr. Webber, please excuse the harshness of my words." She put her hand on his shoulder. "This is a time wrought with raw emotions and intense stress, and I spoke out of haste. I stand by the message, but I regret the tone I used."

Dad looked up at Mia and nodded. "Thank you."

Mia smiled. "Duncan may not be here to say it, but we are sincerely grateful for the sacrifices you have made. REFUGE would not be in this position without you and your family."

"Speaking of my family, can we come up with a plan for Faith?"

"What sort of plan?"

"A plan to get her back. If she's helping the Chancellor, we need to get her away from him as soon as possible."

Paul chimed in. "I think you're right. But whether she's helping him or not doesn't concern me as much as the question of what he'll do to her when she accomplishes whatever it is he wants her to do. She's not safe in the White House."

Mia patted my dad on the shoulder and smiled. "Duncan and I were discussing your daughter a short while ago, and he has generated a plan for this very thing. It may not be pleasant, but it should work...as long as your heart is in it."

CHAPTER TWENTY-SIX

Audrey and I had spent several hours eating pizza and catching up in my bedroom. As we sat "crisscross applesauce" on the bed, I told her everything we had been through since my execution. How Paul saved us, how we hid in the bunker the last few months, how we were close to running out of food, and our harrowing escape. Her jaw fell open more and more the longer I spoke. She then told me the story about her arrest, and how Agent Belford used her to trick me into giving away our location.

"I'm glad you're okay, Audrey. It tore me up inside to read your e-mails. I know what these people are capable of, but my dad wouldn't let me reply to your e-mails. I hated that so much."

Audrey laughed and patted me on the knee. "I bet you did. It wasn't as bad as it sounded though. They were pretty nice to me...except for the part where they abducted me from my home and took me away from my parents and forced me to work for them."

"Yeah, those are just minor details."

"But I guess you're glad you didn't reply or else they would have caught everyone."

I sighed. "Yeah, I guess."

Audrey squinted her eyes and cocked her head. "You guess? What does that mean?"

"Well, a lot's changed since I got here. Turns out, Chancellor Sloane's changed."

"So, he's even meaner than before?"

"No. The exact opposite."

Audrey still wasn't sure. "He did seem a little nicer when we were in his office. But can you really trust him?"

"I think so. He said he's gonna give us what we want. We don't have to fight anymore. I just have to convince the people at REFUGE."

"Faith, are you sure about this? I mean, look at his history."

I unfolded my legs to let the blood flow to my feet again. "Yeah, I trust him. He told me he's had second thoughts ever since he thought I was dead. I reminded him of the daughter he never got to raise, and he started thinking about things differently."

"And you believed him? I mean, how do you know he wasn't just saying that to get you to give up information?"

"Well, yeah. We had the same dream on the same night, and he seemed really genuine. Besides, why would he lie to me? Why not just hold me here against my will and threaten me into working for him?"

Audrey uncrossed her legs and let her feet hang off the end of the bed. "That's the thing. Would you truly work for him if he threatened you, or would you be willing to sacrifice yourself for your cause?"

I refused to answer the question honestly because she was right.

"Your silence tells me you know I'm right. He knows he can't threaten you, so his only option is to act nice and convince you to play along."

I shook my head. "No way. What about the dreams? That can't be a coincidence."

"Did he talk about his dream first, or did you talk about your first?"

I thought for a moment and shrugged my shoulders. "I really don't remember. I'm pretty sure he was first, but I'm not positive."

"What if you told him about your dream first, and he just made something up to trick you?"

"No way. I told you, I'm sure he told me about his dream first."

"But you're not positive. Faith, I'd love to believe you, but I don't think you're thinking clearly. Maybe he's just telling you what you want to hear. No offense, but you kinda have a habit of trusting people too quickly. I mean, look at Jakob."

I sat up and huffed. "What about him? We're together now, aren't we?"

Audrey cleared her throat. "I guess, but you trusted him way too quickly and it turned out that he was only there to spy on you."

"But it worked out. He changed, and now we're together. Or at least we were."

"What does that mean? You broke up?"

"No. At least I don't think we did. We had to get his ex to help us, but it's complicated because he never really broke up with her, and now he has to act like they're still together so she'll keep helping us, and now I'm here and he's somewhere with her. It's a mess."

My skin crawled at the thought of Jakob and Corinne together. What were they doing? Were his old feelings coming back? My palms began to sweat, and my breath got shallow.

Audrey reached over and put her hand on my shoulder. "Faith? Faith? Are you okay?"

I wiped my hands on my thighs and smiled my best phony smile. "Yeah, I'm good."

"I don't think so." She grabbed my hands and squeezed them. "Look me in the eyes. You've gotta slow your breathing. Take deep, slow breaths. Like this." She inhaled and exhaled deeply and slowly.

Within seconds, my breathing slowed down and matched hers. Once I calmed down, I squeezed her hands back. "Thank you. I'm good now."

Audrey's eyes expressed her skepticism. "Are you sure? That looked like the start of a panic attack."

I nodded my head. "I think it was. I've been getting those sometimes. No biggie."

"Faith, you're wrong. It's a big deal. You probably have PTSD with everything you've been through."

I squeaked out an uneasy laugh. "PTSD? You mean I can read minds?"

"Stop making jokes. This is serious. When my dad was in high school his family went through a category 5 hurricane. He didn't know it at the time, but it gave him PTSD. He finally told his parents about the way he was feeling, and they got him some counseling. He still freaks out during bad weather, but nothing like he used to."

"Wow, I didn't know that."

"Well, it's not something we talk about outside the family. But I guess you're practically family, so he won't be mad. Just promise me when this is all over, you'll find someone to talk to."

I leaned over and hugged Audrey with all my might. "I promise."

She was the best kind of best friend. The kind of person who will be your closest confidant and support you, but also stand up to you when they think you're in the wrong. It took guts for her to tell me the things she did, but she did it because she believed it was for my own good.

———— • ● • ————

Corinne pounded the desk, startling everyone in the room. "I thought I had it that time."

Jakob rested his arm on hers. "You can't think clearly if you're mad. It's getting late, why don't you take a break or something?"

The look in her eyes softened as she put her hand on his. "Sure. Can we take a walk?"

Jakob looked around. "I guess. But I don't know my way around this place so we may not be able to go very far."

Corinne stood and pulled Jakob up by his hand. "That's fine. I just want us to be together."

They left the room and ventured down a series of hallways, nodding and saying hello to people as they went. Once they were alone in the hall, Corinne gave Jakob's hand a squeeze. "Jakob, I need to ask you something."

Jakob sighed because those words always signaled the start of an uncomfortable conversation. "Sure. what is it?"

"Where do you see us ending up after all this?"

"Probably in jail."

Corinne punched Jakob in the arm, but he refused to rub it even though it hurt like crazy. "I'm serious. We used to talk about our future all the time, but you haven't said anything about it since you got back."

Jakob took in a deep breath. "Well, I guess things have been so crazy I haven't been able to think of anything beyond the current mission."

"Has anything changed?"

"Changed? What do you mean?"

Corinne began to swing their hands forward and backward as they walked. "You're gonna think I'm stupid..."

"Too late for that." Jakob's smile let her know he was only kidding, but she smacked his arm in the same spot anyway.

"See? You're always joking around when I wanna have a serious conversation. Is that a guy thing or something?"

Jakob decided to give his sore arm a rest, so he changed his tone. "I'm sorry. You're right. So why am I gonna think you're stupid?"

For the first time ever, Corinne was at a loss for words. "Well, you remember when you came home around Christmas and told me you had something important to talk about?"

Jakob nodded, unsure where this conversation was heading.

"And you came home to tell me about this important mission you just got? The one where you were going to catch Riley Riley?"

"You mean Faith?"

"Yeah, her. I keep forgetting her name. Well, not to put any pressure on you or anything, but when you said you had something important to talk about...I kinda thought you were gonna propose."

Jakob's body tensed up and he stopped walking in the middle of the hall. "Propose? Really? Wow, that's a big step."

"Just imagine how I felt when you not only didn't propose, but you told me you were leaving for several months to try to seduce this other girl."

"You didn't *seem* mad."

"Well, I was. I was mad, sad, disappointed..." She looked Jakob in the eyes. "...and jealous."

Jakob looked at Corinne with pity in his eyes. "Jealous? Really? You don't seem like the jealous type."

"I know. Sometimes I put on a good front. But anyway, I was disappointed you didn't propose, but once you left, the jealousy really hit me. I know it was just business, but it hurt me to think about the things you would have to do with that girl to get her to fall in love."

"Corinne, please..."

"No, just listen. I know how charming you are, and I knew it wouldn't take her long to fall for you. I just...I just couldn't stand the thought of you kissing her...and doing other things with her."

Jakob blushed. "Well, if it's any consolation, we didn't do anything but kiss."

Corinne sniffed, then smiled. "Really?"

Jakob nodded his head and smiled. "Yeah. They're really religious people, remember?"

"I guess you're right."

Jakob reached up and brushed Corinne's hair away from her face. "You know, being around you again has been great. I was gone for so long I had almost forgotten how much I love you."

Corinne pushed Jakob up against the wall and leaned in close to his face. "I'm sorry, I didn't quite hear you."

He pushed his lips against hers and held them for several seconds before pulling away. "I said, I love you."

Corinne's perfect smile spread across her face. "You know, I believe you this time. It's one thing to hear the words, but I could feel it in the way you kissed me. Well, that leads me to the next thing."

"Which is?"

"The whole time you were gone, I wondered when you'd be home. Month after month went by, and nothing. Then I began to hear rumors."

Jakob cocked his head. "What kind of rumors?"

Corinne frowned. "Lots of things. That you had switched sides, that you had fallen in love with that girl for real, that you had been...I can't even say the word."

"Killed?"

Tears appeared in Corinne's eyes for the first time as she nodded her head. "And now that you're back, I can't lose you again." Her head collapsed onto Jakob's shoulder, and he wrapped his arms around her.

They held each other for a minute or two before they let go and got lost in each other's eyes. Jakob smiled and kissed her on the forehead. "I know. I feel the same way. I'm excited about the future, too."

Corinne smiled in return. "I was hoping you'd say that. Speaking of the future...What do you say we finish what you should have started?"

"Which is?"

"I think it's time you finally propose to me."

Agent Martinez knocked at our door precisely at eight o'clock, just as the Chancellor had said. The three of us walked through a network of halls and into a room filled with people, computers, and giant monitors. Martinez pointed to two empty chairs. "This is you."

Audrey and I sat down and looked at all the technology in front of us. It was far more sophisticated than anything either of us had used, but it wouldn't take us long to get comfortable with it. One by one, the other people in their room introduced themselves. Most of the women smiled at us as they spoke, but several of the men made us feel less than welcome.

Audrey leaned over and whispered in my ear. "What's with these guys? It's like someone came over and punted their dog or something."

One of the women laughed and said, "Actually they're cat people."

Audrey's face turned red. "You heard that?"

Everyone in the room nodded.

I patted Audrey on the shoulder. "Told you."

As everyone else went back to their seats, the woman who made the "cat people" comment walked up to us and held out her hand. "Don't mind them, they're just grumpy because they had to leave their basements and come in early today. My name's Jordan."

Audrey and I shook hands with Jordan and thanked her for her hospitality.

"No problem. Believe me, I know what it's like to work in a man's world." When she said the words *man's world,* she did air quotes with her fingers. It was at that moment I knew I had found a soul sister.

Jordan showed us to our seats and helped us settle in at our computers.

As Jordan wheeled a chair toward us and sat down, a question burned in my mind. "Jordan, I gotta confess, I don't really know what we can do here. I mean, you are all so smart and experienced, and we're not. What can Audrey and I possibly do to help?"

Audrey smacked me on the leg. "Hey, that wasn't very nice. I'm smart and experienced."

"As experienced as them?"

Audrey smiled and lowered her head. "No. But still."

Jordan logged us into our computers. "I can tell you two are really close. How long have you known each other?"

Audrey spoke first. "I can't remember. Faith, how long have your parents been paying me to be your friend?"

"I don't know, ask your parents. They're the ones that gave my parents the money to pay me to be your friend since they felt sorry for you since you had no friends."

Jordan and Audrey stared at me with their mouths open. I've never been good at coming up with fast comebacks.

I cleared my throat. "So, Jordan, how long have you been working here?"

"About two years. After college I worked for a few IT companies, then a friend who worked for the government put in a good word for me. I started at the bottom, and now I'm here."

Audrey was staring off into the distance as she spun in her chair, but I was engaged. "I was thinking about going into a career in computers or programming, but then all this happened."

"I heard you have some skill. Prove yourself, and maybe the Chancellor will write you a glowing letter of recommendation."

"Yeah, I bet he could get me into any college in the country. Then maybe I'll come work with you."

Jordan flashed a pleasant smile. "You never know. What do you say we get down to business?"

Audrey stopped spinning and put her hands on the desk. "About time. I thought you two were gonna flap your gums all day."

I glared at Audrey, then smiled at Jordan. "It's okay. She gets grumpy when she's bored."

"Well, you two won't be bored for long. What did the Chancellor say about your mission?"

I shrugged. "Not much. He just wants information on REFUGE. I don't really know where to look though. Do you have anything to get us started?"

Jorden entered something into her computer and the large monitor on the wall in front of us came to life. "Well, let's see what we can find out together."

After three grueling hours with no progress, we decided to break for lunch. Audrey and I were confused when Jordan told us she would get us lunch from the White House Mess, but when she explained that it was just a restaurant within the building we felt better. My food had a little more garlic than I liked, so Audrey and I made our way to my bedroom so I could brush my teeth.

Audrey huffed as we walked in. "Don't take too long, Faith. I wanna get back to work."

"Yeah, yeah, yeah. Just gimme a minute." I put my toothpaste on the brush and began brushing. While Audrey sat on the bed, I walked over to check my phone. Nobody was likely to call me, but it wouldn't hurt to take a peek. When I read the text message on the screen I gasped, nearly choking on my toothpaste.

"Call me ASAP. It's your dad."

CHAPTER TWENTY-SEVEN

My hands trembled as I dialed the number Charlie had given me. It took forever for him to answer.

"Hey, it's Faith. What's going on?"

"Faith, there's no easy way to say this, but your dad had a heart attack. He's still alive, but he's unconscious."

My heart sprang up into my throat as I collapsed on the bed. "What? When did this happen?"

Audrey saw the panic on my face and sat next to me. "What's going on?"

"My dad had a heart attack. He's alive but unconscious." I put the phone on speaker so we could both hear. "Where is he? What're you gonna do now?"

"As you know, we can't take him to a hospital so he's in our clinic. We have all the tools we need to help him, but your mom's asking for you. She needs the whole family together for this."

That last sentence hit me right in the heart, and the tears began flowing. "Okay. How am I gonna get there?"

"I'll be there at two o'clock. Go out front and start walking through Lafayette Square. I'll text you directions when I'm there."

"Okay. Please tell my mom I love her, and I'll see her soon." I ended the call and fell into Audrey's arms. The two of us sobbed until we were out of tears. I stood up and began pacing the floor. "I gotta get out of here, but what am I gonna tell the Chancellor?"

Audrey squinted her eyes and shook her head at me. "You tell him the truth. I'm sure he'll understand. Your big press conference isn't for a few more days, so it'll be fine. Jordan and I can keep working here."

I nodded my head and opened the door just as Jordan reached up to knock on it. She flinched when the door swung open.

"Ready to...what's going on?"

Within minutes I was seated across from the Chancellor on the sofas in the Oval Office. He listened in silence until I finished explaining the situation in between my tears and sniffles.

"Faith, I understand why you are upset. I would be upset as well. But we must consider another possibility."

"Another possibility? What do you mean?"

"I need you to keep an open mind. Can you do that?"

I wiped another tear from my eye. "I guess so."

"What if this is merely a ploy to draw you away from me?"

I sniffed and wiped my nose with a tissue. "Why would they do that?"

Sloane stood and walked toward his desk. "Think back to your conversation with Mia. You told her that I was willing to allow religious freedom again, but she was unwilling to accept that." He turned and leaned on the front of the desk. "What do you suppose they did after your phone call?"

"I don't know."

"Think for a moment. What was REFUGE's response to that conversation?"

I looked down at my feet as if they had the answers. "Well, it didn't sound like they believed me. But I don't blame them. I didn't believe you at first either."

Sloane smiled at the quasi-compliment. "Yes. And what do you suppose they think about you and your role in all of this?"

"They think I'm either working for you because I believe you, or because I'm being forced to."

"So how does REFUGE view you now?"

I bit my lip as I thought. "They either think I'm a threat, or I'm in danger."

Sloane came back to his sofa, sat down, and crossed his legs. "And what would their response be in both of those cases?"

I looked up and met Sloane's eyes. "To bring me home."

"Precisely. They cannot just call and tell you to come home. They need to compel you to return."

"By telling me that my dad had a heart attack? That's pretty harsh."

Sloane nodded his head. "I know. But they knew they had to come up with something so serious you would not dare question it."

I took a deep breath in and let it out slowly. The worry was still there, but Sloane's theory made sense. "Why walk me through all this? Why not just come out and say it?"

"Because you are more likely to accept the truth if you come to the conclusion on your own, rather than hearing it from someone else."

"What do we do then?"

Sloane glanced at his watch. We have an hour. I'm sure we can come up with a plan."

— • ● • —

An hour later I was sprinting across Lafayette Square with several agents in pursuit, gaining ground rapidly. There was no way I would outrun them, so my only chance was to outsmart them. Up ahead, a large group of tourists gathered around their guide, listening to her speech about one of the monuments. I barged my way into the group, knocking several of them over in the process.

I screamed into the crowd. "Run! Run! He's got a bomb!"

The crowd shrieked and spread out in all directions, impeding the progress of my pursuers. I glanced back as I ran to see many of the agents picking themselves up off the ground, and the others slowly pushing their way through the mayhem. I had bought myself some time, but I needed a place to hide until I heard from Charlie. A loud scream caused me to turn my head back around just before I stepped off the curb and into the street. A man on a bicycle was flying toward me and swerving to avoid me. He yanked the handlebars to the left, causing the bike to lose control, and sending him skidding across the pavement.

I ran up to him and knelt down. "Are you okay?"

His elbow and leg began bleeding profusely. "Ahh, my leg! Why don't you watch where you're going?!"

"I'm really sorry. I just..." I glanced down at his leg, nearly vomiting in the process, then back at the bike. "...I just need to borrow this for a minute."

He reached a bloody hand for my arm, but I yanked it away. "What are you doing?!" he screamed.

I hopped on the bike and began to pedal; glancing back as I drove away. "I'll leave it down the street for you, I promise."

I had no idea where I was going, but my goal was to get as far from the White House as possible. My bomb scare in Lafayette Square had bought me some time, but those agents wouldn't be too far behind. They wouldn't be looking for me on a bicycle, so maybe I had a chance to escape. I flew down the sidewalk, narrowly avoiding pedestrians, trees, and signs in the process. Moments later, I passed through another small park and came to a large roundabout with plenty of streets for me to consider. For no reason, I chose the third street without stopping, sending several cars swerving and honking. All the noise wasn't helping my chances of staying inconspicuous. Several blocks later, I came to another roundabout. What is it with this city and its roundabouts? I took my time so I could avoid calling attention to myself and turned left on a peaceful-looking side street. I cruised down the neighborhood road, looking around for any signs of company until my eyes landed on a house that was painted a strange shade of green. I turned left to hide in the alley next to the unique house and skidded to a stop. The side of the house was painted like a watermelon, seeds, and all. Confident I had evaded capture, I stopped to admire the artwork and catch my breath.

My phone vibrated in my pocket, causing my body to flinch. I took it out and read the text from Charlie.

"Where RU?"

"watermelon house"

I smiled as I imagined Charlie's face when he read that text. He probably thought I was crazy.

"Be there in 5. Stay put."

I was a little disappointed that he didn't reply with a series of questions. Either he already knew where the watermelon house was, or he knew he could find it easily. I was only a block or so off a busy street, so I would need a place to hide until Charlie arrived. I glanced around in every direction then rode my new bike further down the alley next to the watermelon house. Sitting there, hiding between some parked cars, I was reminded of an old riddle my dad asked me when I was younger. *When do you go on red and stop on green?* Once he told me you go on red and stop on green when you're eating watermelon, I finally got it. It was kinda dumb, but it still made sense.

I chuckled as I recalled that old memory, but then it sparked an epiphany in my mind. The watermelon riddle was a lot like my life at that moment. I was going on red and stopping on green. Everything was backward. I was helping the man who had tried to kill me a few months ago, and I was working against the people I had been trying to help. My relationship with Jakob was the same way. He and I were in love, but now that Corinne was in the picture it seemed like everything with us was backward. Now that I was away from the Chancellor and the White House, some tiny shadows of doubt crept into my mind. Was Audrey right? Was the Chancellor using me? Was I really too trusting? He had already convinced me to give away the location of REFUGE HQ in Philadelphia, so what was next? Was the Chancellor right about REFUGE? Were they really plotting a revolution? Were they lying to me about my father's heart attack? Were they going to use the microchips against Sloane, or were they just using that as leverage to get freedom? Too many questions. I had to get some answers, and soon.

After pondering what seemed like a million different thoughts and questions my phone buzzed in my hand. It was Charlie.

"Hello?"

"I'm in the blue van in front of the watermelon house. Where are you?"

"Be right there."

I ended the call and crept out toward the front of the house, leaving my bicycle behind. Sure enough, Charlie was sitting out in the street in the same van I knew so well, only this time it was a navy-blue color. I opened the back door carefully so I wouldn't break another fingernail, and hopped in. Once I closed the door, we were off.

I scooted up and sat right behind the front passenger seat. "How's my dad?"

"He's stable, but still sedated."

"Does that mean he's unconscious?"

Charlie nodded his head. "They're keeping him sedated so his body can heal while they keep running tests. They have to see how much damage his heart attack caused. Then they'll know whether he'll...um...then they'll know more about his situation."

Even though I had doubts about the truth of this story, hearing these words about my father made my heart sink. I needed to change the subject. "Where are we going?"

"I'll tell you in a minute." He pulled the van into a mall parking lot and parked. "Before we go any further, I need to take care of something. Just sit still for a moment."

I eyed him as he got out of the van and closed his door. He walked around to the back of the van and climbed in.

"What are you doing?"

He pulled a wand of some sort out of a work bag and crawled toward me. "I just need to scan you and make sure they're not tracking us."

"Who? Sloane?"

"Yes. Please sit still for a moment. I promise this won't hurt. I just need to scan around you. If this green light turns yellow or red, we have a problem."

Even though I knew there was no device tracking us, it was still nerve-wracking. Like when a police car starts following you even though you know you didn't break the law. I held my breath as he waved the electronic wand around me several times. Fortunately for both of us, the light remained green the entire time.

"All clear," he said as he put the wand away and got back in the driver's seat. He buckled his seat belt, and we were off again. Before long we were cruising down the highway.

"Now can you tell me where we're going?"

"The REFUGE Tech Center in Baltimore. We should be there in an hour or so."

The Chancellor was right, they *were* in Baltimore. "Is everyone there?"

"Everyone?"

"My family and Paul?" I cleared my throat. "And Jakob?"

"Yeah, they're all there."

I waited for a moment, but Charlie didn't mention anyone else's name. That was a good sign, but I had to know for sure. "What about Corinne?"

Charlie paused for a moment. That wasn't a good sign. "What about her?"

"Is she there too, or did you get rid of her?"

"She's there. She's helping our people figure out how to

communicate with the microchips so we can free everyone from Sloane's control."

It sounded like they didn't know the satellite was space dust. "So they're having trouble with the satellite, huh?

"That's what I hear. I'm sure they'll figure it out soon though."

I struggled to keep a huge smile off my face. "Probably. Corinne's pretty smart."

Charlie glanced at me in the mirror. "Speaking of Corinne..."

"Yeah?"

"There's something else you need to know about her and Jakob."

———————————— •●•————————————

The van had barely stopped when I flung the van doors open and sprinted through the garage, my eyes darting back and forth to find an escape route. It didn't matter that I had no idea where I was going; I just needed to see my dad and get some answers.

Charlie caught up to me and grabbed my arm to spin me around. "Faith! Listen for a second. I know you're upset, but you need to try to calm down."

I wrestled my arm free and glared at him. "Calm down? Are you serious? After what you just told me?"

"This is a very delicate situation, and getting emotional won't help anyone. We're not going anywhere until you calm down."

I huffed a few times before finally surrendering. "Fine. Whatever."

Charlie held out his hands. "Take a few deep breaths. When you're ready, I'll take you inside."

I closed my eyes, inhaled, and exhaled several times. My heart rate was returning to normal, and the rage was subsiding. Once I knew I could think clearly, I opened my eyes again. "I'm good. Let's go."

"Are you sure?"

"As long as you don't ask me stupid questions like that." I flashed a half smile to reflect the fact that I was half joking.

Charlie studied me for a few moments before speaking. "All

right. Whatever happens in here; I want you to promise me that you'll stay calm. There's already a lot of tension in the building. Don't need you adding to it."

"I can't make any promises, but I'll try."

Charlie thought for a few seconds. "Fine. Let's go."

I walked with Charlie toward a door on the opposite side of the garage, looking around to see if Lenny was in the area. He was walking way too slowly for my liking, but since I didn't know which way to go, I had no choice but to follow. Charlie touched a sensor next to the door handle, and a green light told us we were free to enter. Like a true gentleman, he opened the door for me, then followed me into a hallway. All these buildings were starting to look alike. Mazes of hallways with one door after another. After what felt like an eternity, Charlie stopped in front of a door.

"Are you still good?"

I glared at him for a few seconds, then decided I was better off being nice. "Yeah, I'm good."

"Just making sure." Charlie opened the door and stepped aside so I could walk in. I stepped inside what appeared to be another conference room and saw some familiar faces staring back at me.

"Hey, Jellybean."

CHAPTER TWENTY-EIGHT

The relief of seeing my dad okay quickly gave way to anger. "You lied to me?!"

Mia sat motionless as Dad stood up and walked toward me with his arms open. "Faith, listen to me."

I brushed his arms aside and stomped off in the other direction. "Why? You're just gonna lie to me again."

"No, I promise I won't do that. Not again."

I turned around and scoffed in his face. "Oh, so you're actually gonna tell me the truth this time? Sorry, but I don't think I believe you."

"We had to get you out of there, and we knew you wouldn't just come back on your own."

I turned back around and faced the wall, refusing to look at any of them. "How would you know? You didn't even ask."

"Because we know what's going on. We know you've been working for Sloane. Somehow, he must be manipulating you into working for him. We don't know how, but we're going to help you get back to normal."

That got my attention. I turned around to face them. "What are you talking about?"

"Jellybean, I'm so sorry. You've been through so much."

"Ya think?"

Tears began to build in Dad's eyes. "If I could wish this all away, I would. But we're in so deep now, the only way out is to keep moving forward."

"Did you hear that from Mia? Or the invisible man?"

"It's the truth."

I turned back toward the wall. "The truth. There's that word again. You know, you wouldn't recognize the truth if it punched you in the face." I stared at the wall in silence for a few more seconds to let my words hit their mark.

"I told you this was a horrible idea, Mia. We shouldn't have lied to her."

"Mr. Webber, extraordinary times call for extraordinary measures. We got what we wanted, did we not? Faith is back where she belongs. With her family. With people who truly care about her."

I whipped my head around and locked eyes with Mia. "Care about me? You sure have a funny way of showing how much you care. You care enough about me to lie to me about my dad having a heart attack? What kind of person does that?"

Dad took a couple of steps toward me, then thought better of it. "Faith, listen. Maybe what we did was wrong, but we did it for the right reason."

"Does that make it okay?"

"It depends on how you look at it. I know you're mad, but we had to get you out of there. This is for your own good?"

"My own good? Just shut up!"

"Hey! You will NOT talk like that to me!" His anger was beginning to match mine.

We locked eyes for several intense moments, each of us waiting to see how the other person would respond.

Mia finally broke the tension. "It is apparent that you are both understandably agitated, so I believe the most prudent course of action is to adjourn for the time being. We may reconvene when our emotions have subsided, and then perhaps our conversation will be more productive."

I kept my eyes on my father. "No. I wanna get this over with now. We have too much to talk about."

Dad nodded. "Me too. Mia, will you please leave us alone?"

"Are you sure, Mr. Webber?"

Dad looked Mia square in the eyes. "Yes. I need to be alone with my daughter."

Mia stood and walked toward the door. "As you wish. I will stand by just outside the door."

Once she was gone, Dad walked back to the conference table

and sat down. "Faith, would you please come sit with me so we can talk this out?"

I crossed my arms like a good teenager and huffed. "I don't know what we have to talk about. Seems like you've said enough already."

"We need to talk about what's been going on, and where we go now. Regardless of how it happened; the fact is you're here now." He paused for a moment. "Speaking of how you got here, how did you get here? I doubt Sloane just let you waltz out of the White House."

"Nope. I didn't waltz...I square danced."

Dad rolled his eyes. "Can you please do this without the sarcasm?"

"Fine. It's a long story, but I convinced Sloane to let me go outside to get some fresh air since I'd been stuck inside for so long. An agent came outside with me, and I started walking around behind the White House. I needed a diversion, so I pointed at someone on the other side of the fence and told the agent he looked suspicious. When he walked over to investigate, I took off. I climbed the fence and landed on the sidewalk before anyone saw me. By then, I had a good head start on the agents that started chasing me. I found a group of tourists and I screamed something about a bomb so they would all run around and slow the agents down. Then I stole a bike and rode it to the watermelon house until Charlie picked me up. So, what else do we need to talk about?"

"Are you serious?"

My eyes burned with rage. "Yeah. I'm not like you."

Dad closed his eyes as he tried to figure out a way to change the subject. "Faith, a lot has changed and I need to bring you up to speed. Will you please sit down?"

I sighed one more time for emphasis before walking over and sitting at the opposite end of the table. "Fine. What are these big changes?"

"Thank you. First of all, I see that your mission to plant the leech was a success. We were able to get the satellite and move it into a different orbit."

"Yeah, I heard."

"But then you called and spoke in some sort of code. It sounded like you were telling us to abort. Was that really the case?"

"Yup."

Dad stared at me, waiting for more information, but I had already answered his question. "Why did you do that?"

"Because we didn't need the satellite anymore."

"And why is that?"

I looked down at the table. "Doesn't matter. You won't believe me anyway."

"Try me."

Satisfied with the verbal smackdown I had given my father, I decided to change tactics so he might believe me. I looked back at him with all the sincerity I could muster. "I know this sounds crazy, but Chancellor Sloane's changed."

"Faith, you can't seriously..."

"See? I told you you wouldn't believe me. Why should I even bother?"

Dad tapped his fingers on the table as he thought. "You're right. That was disrespectful of me. How do you know Sloane changed?"

"Are you actually gonna believe me?"

"Faith, I can't make that promise. But I do promise that I will listen to your story with an open mind."

I thought for a moment, reaching for the right words to convince my dad about the Chancellor. "Well, he said when he first met me, I reminded him of his daughter."

"I didn't know he had a daughter."

"He did, but she died right after she was born."

Dad closed his eyes and shook his head. "I don't understand. How do you remind him of his daughter if she passed away as a baby?"

I blew all the air out of my lungs, causing my lips to flutter. We were not off to a good start. "No, I reminded him of what his daughter could have been like if she lived. It's like he saw an alternate reality or something. Anyway, he said that after he thought I had been killed he kept feeling regret."

"Okay, but if that's the case, why did he have his people shooting at us when we escaped from the safehouse?"

"Once he found out I was still alive he was kinda relieved, but also mad. Even though he felt some regret, he didn't want to give in to it. He just wanted to act like he always had so the regret would go away. But then he saw my face on the TV the other day and things changed."

Dad wrinkled his lips as he digested my words. "I don't know, Faith. I mean, he could just be telling you these things to gain your trust."

The words came pouring out all in one breath. "I know. I thought the same thing. But then he told me about a dream he had the night I was on TV after his speech. He dreamed about a wolf that had been killing a shepherd's sheep, but then he got his leg caught in a trap. He was hurt, but then the shepherd came and felt sorry for him, so he let him out of the trap and took care of his injured leg. Then the wolf stayed with the shepherd and helped protect the sheep. Don't you get it? He's the wolf."

Dad held his hands up to slow down the barrage of words. "I don't know. I see where you're coming from, but how do you know he didn't just make up that whole story?"

"Yeah, but I haven't told you the best part. That same night, I had a dream about a wolf that was protecting some sheep from other wolves. What are the odds that Sloane and I would each have dreams about wolves and sheep on the same exact night? It's a sign that God's in this. Can't you see it?"

Dad rocked back and forth in his chair as he thought. "It could still be a coincidence though. Or maybe he knew about your dream and used it against you. Did you tell him about your dream before he told you about his?"

"Wow, you sound just like Audrey."

"Audrey? What does she have to do with this?"

"Oh yeah, I didn't tell you that she got captured the other day and they tried to use her to lure us out of hiding, but she's okay now. The Chancellor brought her to the White House so I could see her again. So, see? He wouldn't have done that unless he had changed."

Dad closed his eyes to settle his brain. "Whoa, that's way too much information. Let's forget about Audrey for a moment. So, let's say he truly has changed and wants to allow religion; why did he want us to give him control of his lost satellite? If he's changed, he doesn't need to use it anymore."

"He doesn't want to use it. That was just a test. He still thinks REFUGE is trying to overthrow him, so he offered to allow religion again as a test."

"Of?"

"REFUGE's motives. If he's gonna allow religion again, why would REFUGE still need the satellite unless they were gonna use it against him?"

"That's preposterous. Faith, we've already been over this. You know as well as I do, REFUGE isn't planning a revolution."

"Then why didn't Mia give up the satellite when he asked?"

"Because..." Frustration emerged in his voice, so he paused to gather himself. "Mia didn't want to take any chances."

I walked over and sat next to my father. "Don't you get it? All of this. All the secrecy. Refusing to give up the satellite. If they're not plotting a revolution, what's it all for? It's because they need the satellite to carry out their plan."

Dad closed his eyes and shook his head slowly. "We don't have a plan other than applying pressure on Sloane."

"That's not true. REFUGE doesn't have an army, so they're gonna use Sloane's. It's brilliant if you think about it. But don't worry, I convinced the Chancellor that you aren't involved in that part of REFUGE's plan, so you'll be safe."

Dad put his hand on my arm. "You don't actually believe that monster, do you? Duncan won't give up the satellite because it's our only leverage against Sloane. We can't lose our advantage if he's lying about all this."

I yanked my arm away and pounded my fist on the table, causing Dad to flinch. "He's not lying! Why do you keep saying that?"

"Faith, look at yourself. You're acting like *him*. What did they do to you in Washington?"

My teeth clenched. "They told me the truth, which is more than I can say for all of you."

Dad's nostrils flared as my words hit their mark. "I can't believe what I'm hearing. Mia was worried that you had changed sides, but I didn't want to believe her. Now I'm not so sure."

"I haven't changed sides. We've always been on the side of what's good and right, and now we know where those two sides really are. There's still time to do the right thing. Convince Duncan to give up the satellite." I knew the satellite had been destroyed, but I was trying to prove a point.

"This is a lot to think about. I need some time."

"I get it." I reached across the table and put my hand on his.

"You know, I'm still mad you lied to me, but it's good to see you again."

Dad smiled and let out a little laugh. "You too, Jellybean. But I suppose there's someone else you're anxious to see also."

I sighed but didn't say a word.

Dad squeezed my hand. "It's her, isn't it?"

I nodded my head with tears in my eyes. "She's horrible, Daddy. She's sinking her claws into Jakob, and I can't tell if he's really falling for her again or if he's just playing along. I can't really explain why, but seeing him with her makes me see him in a different way. Like, if he's willing to throw away what we have, maybe he doesn't deserve me. If you saw the two of them together, you'd know what I'm talking about."

"I'm afraid I have. She and Jakob are here."

I gave his hand an involuntary squeeze. "What?!"

He let go and shook his hand to get the pain out. "We've been having trouble communicating with the satellite, so Duncan and Mia thought perhaps she could help."

"That's great. I was gonna ask if I could see Jakob, but I don't think I can handle seeing the two of them together."

"I understand. Are you hungry?"

"No, I just lost my appetite. I could use some water though."

Dad stood up and patted my shoulder. "I'll go get some. Be right back."

— • ● • —

I looked around the room for a clock, but there was none to be seen. I had been alone in the conference room for at least an hour, but my dad had yet to return with my water. There was only one door in the room, but it was locked. That didn't stop me from trying to open it several times. I walked over to it again and yanked on the knob, hoping this time would be different, but no luck. I pounded on the door hoping to get someone's attention.

"Hello?! Is anyone out there?! I've been locked in here forever!" I waited for an answer, but none came. I pounded again. "Hello? Dad? Mia? Jakob? It's me. Faith."

I finally heard a voice on the other side of the door, but it wasn't the voice I was hoping for. "Riley Riley? Is that really you?"

My heart sank at the sound of her voice. "What are *you* doing here?"

"I heard you were back, but I had to see for myself. Why don't you come out here so we can talk?"

I pounded my head against the door and let it rest there. "The door's locked, stupid. I don't suppose you wanna let me out, do you?"

"Well, I was gonna let you out until you called me stupid. After all we've been through together, I can't believe you'd treat me like that. You really need to work on your temper."

I tried the doorknob again; not because I thought it would open, but to show Corinne how badly I wanted to get out. "If this door wasn't locked, I'd..."

Corinne cackled. "You'd what? Let me use your face as a punching bag? Remember what I did to you in the van? What I did do to you in my kitchen? Think that was really an accident? Watch what you say, Riley Riley. If you don't learn to close your mouth, I just might have to close it for you. Permanently."

I had a sarcastic response ready, but I held my tongue. She was probably strong enough to rip the door from its hinges and beat me with it.

Corinne knocked on the door. "Riley Riley? You still in there?"

"Yes, Corinne. The door's locked, remember?"

"Oh yeah. I guess I forgot."

"Sure, you did. Listen, I'm really busy in here so why don't you go back to whatever it was you were doing before?"

Corinne laughed through the door. "Sure thing, Riley Riley. No offense, but you're kinda boring anyway. Jakob's much more fun to hang out with. In fact, he and I were just talking about you earlier today."

"Oh yeah? What about me."

"Whether to invite you to the wedding. I didn't really want to, but he insisted. He said you were a nice girl, but I thought it might be kinda awkward. I mean, how does a guy invite a girl he pretended to fall in love with to his wedding to another woman? What's the protocol for that, anyway?"

"Your what?"

Corinne spoke slowly for my benefit. "Our...wedding. Try to keep up. I know you probably don't have time or money to shop, so you don't have to get us anything. Just knowing you're there with us on our special day is the only gift I need."

I scoffed loudly enough for her to feel it outside the door. "Yeah, right. Now I know you're just messing with me."

"Nope. We were talking out in the hall and he proposed. He did the cheesy thing where he got down on one knee and everything. Normally I wouldn't go for that sort of thing, but it was sweet." The cheerfulness in her voice was nauseating.

"There's no way Jakob would marry you."

Now it was Corinne's turn to scoff. "Why? Because he's in love with you? Keep dreaming, Riley Riley. He never really loved you. The sooner you realize that, the sooner you can pick up the pieces and move on with your life. Or what's left of it."

I turned around and leaned back against the door. There's no way she was telling the truth. Even if Jakob did say he would marry her, he was only playing along with her twisted game. "Listen, Corinne. I appreciate you stopping by, and I appreciate the invite to your big day, but I'm pretty sure I'm busy that day. If you're even telling the truth."

"Hey, if you don't believe me, just ask Jakob for yourself. He'll tell you all about it. Peace out, Riley Riley!"

I slid down the door and landed on the floor with a thud. She truly was the worst human being I had ever met. No wonder Jakob wanted to break up with her before all this happened. I sat there leaning against the door for what felt like another eternity, trying to scour the memory of Corinne from my brain. My daze was broken by the sound of approaching footsteps outside. I sprang to my feet and sprinted toward the chairs. In the process, I stubbed my toe on one of the wheels of the chair and tumbled to the ground, knocking several chairs over along the way. The door opened and I peeked up over the table to see a man dressed all in black. Black sweater, black pants, and a black ski mask covering his head. "Who are you?"

A familiar synthesized voice answered. "Hello, Faith. It's nice to finally meet you in person."

CHAPTER TWENTY-NINE

I dragged myself over to a chair and climbed off the floor, too stunned to pick up the chairs I had knocked over. "Duncan? As in, *the Duncan?*"

"In the flesh."

Duncan's presence in the room reminded me of the first night I met Chancellor Sloane. His aura was intimidating, even though he wasn't physically imposing. He was average size, about the same as my father, but I could tell he was important when he walked into the room. "What are you doing here? I mean, Mia told us nobody sees Duncan."

"You are correct. But extraordinary times call for extraordinary measures. Mind if I sit?"

"Sure. I mean, it's your place, isn't it?" I eyed him as I spoke, trying to get a clue about his identity.

Duncan sat in the chair that had been occupied by my father a short while ago. "You may stay over there."

I did what I was told. "What are you doing here? I mean, my dad says he's never seen you in person before."

"You're correct. No one else knows I'm here though. I felt it best that you and I spoke face to face."

"You mean face to mask?" The words slipped out before I could stop them.

"Very well. Face to mask. Surely you understand my need for anonymity. I'm the most wanted man in America, so I cannot be too careful."

I nodded my head. "So why couldn't we just talk on the phone again? Don't get me wrong, it's nice to meet you, but I'm lost."

Duncan folded his gloved hands on the conference table. "Faith, I'm going to be completely honest with you, and it may sound as though I'm being harsh, but please know that is not my intent. It seems as though you have created quite a problem for my organization, and I wanted to speak with you about it in person."

"Okay. But why?"

"I'm going to ask you some difficult, very pointed questions, and I need to see you answer them. I want to read your eyes, your face, and your body language to decipher whether you are being disingenuous."

"What's wrong? Your lie detector's in the shop again?" There my mouth went again.

Duncan let out a disturbing robotic laugh. "I've always admired your spirit. It's one of your greatest assets. I don't trust polygraphs. I trust my eyes and ears."

"Okay, fine. So, what are your pointy questions?"

"I have heard the account of your recent visit to the White House, and your conversations with Chancellor Sloane. Mia also told me about your telephone conversation with her. We have been discussing this situation, and we have come to the conclusion that the Chancellor is being deceptive. And now you're caught in the middle."

I sat up to straighten my posture. "I know you all think that, but you gotta believe me. He's being honest."

"I know you think that, but..."

"It's like you said. When you're in the room with someone, you can really tell whether they're lying or not. No offense, but you didn't see him. I was the one in the room with him for a long time. He's telling the truth. He's changed. His whole vibe is softer and gentler."

"His vibe? You're basing this on his vibe?"

I squirmed in my chair a little. "Well, yeah. When I met him before he seemed hard and cold. Now he's kinda warm and caring. If you were there with me, you'd know."

"So, you walked into his office and he just came out and told you he's changing his stance on religion?"

"Well, technically we were in the solarium, but yeah. And that was before he knew about the leach or the satellite. So, he wasn't just saying that to get his satellite back."

"And what does he want from you?"

I was suddenly aware that my knee was bouncing like crazy under the table, so I put my hand on it to keep it still. "He wants me to be his spokesperson. Everyone knows what he tried to do to me, so if I get out there and show the world that I'm on his side, people will believe him."

Duncan began tapping his finger on the table. "This is precisely why I wanted to speak with you in person."

"What, you think I'm lying about this?"

"Not at all. I sense no attempt at deception on your part. But that's the problem."

"Wait, so you know I'm being honest...and that's the problem?"

Duncan cocked his head to the side. "Yes. The problem isn't what you're saying. The problem comes from the repercussions of what you're telling me."

"I don't get it."

"You just said that you wanted to go out and tell the world you're on his side."

I squinted my eyes and wrinkled my nose. "Yeah? So?"

"You're on his side. That's precisely what concerns us."

"Well, yeah...I mean, I'm on his side with Faith in America. That doesn't mean I'm your enemy though. Don't we all want the same thing? Isn't that what this whole thing's been about?"

"I was under the impression that you wanted the same thing we do, but now I'm having my doubts."

I threw my hands up in the air and huffed. "Seriously? What, you think I've been brainwashed and now I'm trying to help Sloane capture you?"

"Perhaps the word *brainwashed* is a bit strong, but it's obvious that Chancellor Sloane has gotten to you somehow. I cannot begin to fathom how you could take the word of a man who tried to kill you. Not just in the spring, but earlier this week."

"I know how it looks, and honestly sometimes I can't believe it myself. I don't really know how to explain it, but it just feels genuine."

Perhaps sensing my growing frustration, Duncan paused for a few moments before speaking. "I know you believe what you're saying, but I don't think this is really you who is talking to me. Perhaps he has somehow poisoned your mind, or perhaps he has threatened you or your family. We don't know how it happened, but I regret to tell you that you have become a very real threat to us and our plans."

My mouth fell open as he uttered those words. "Wait wait wait. You really see me as a threat? Did you really just use that word?"

"You must believe me; I take no joy in any of this. I had my doubts when Mia spoke with me about you. After all, you have been through so much. But now that I see you in person, and hear your words with my own ears, it seems as though she may have been right."

I shrugged off Duncan's accusations and hurled one of my own in his direction. "Wow. You know, I didn't want to believe the Chancellor, but now that I see you in person, and hear your words with my own ears, it seems as though he may have been right."

"About what?"

"About REFUGE's true plans. You aren't content to just win religious freedom or else you would have taken Sloane up on his offer. And that's why you see me as a threat. Because I know the truth about you. This whole time, you were trying to get control of the microchips so you could steal his military and use it against him."

Duncan's mask concealed his face, but he had to be seething underneath it. He sat there; his gaze fixed on me for several seconds without speaking. His silence told me everything I needed to know about his motives. I was in the room with a madman. A madman with the will, dedication, and resources required to overthrow the government of the United States and take over for himself. A madman who was so threatened by my knowledge, there was no telling what he would do to silence me. I had to find a way to escape before I lost my freedom, and maybe even my life. I sprang out of my seat and lunged toward the door, but he stood up to stop me, holding his hands out like he was about to keep me from scoring a touchdown. Lowering my shoulder into his chest, I knocked him off balance and sent him flying over a chair. I reached for the door, but it was still locked. I turned around in time to see him pick himself up off the ground and start walking toward me, growling like a wounded animal.

I took a step back, but the door prevented me from moving any farther. "Get back! Get back or I'll..."

"Or you'll what?"

My eyes darted around the room, searching for something I could use as a weapon. "I'll make sure you're sorry."

He moved closer, a hungry tiger stalking his prey. "Faith, listen to me. You don't want to go this way. If you stop now, I can still help you. If you don't reconsider your allegiance, I'm afraid you'll wind up paying for your transgressions."

"It's you that needs to reconsider your allegiance. You may have an army, but there are plenty of people out there who'll fight you."

"Do you seriously think I'm afraid of them? They're no match for the power at my fingertips."

Cornered, with nowhere to go, I let out a primal scream and lunged once more at my enemy. Duncan leaned forward to grab me, but I lunged to the right and swept him off his feet with my leg. I guess Corinne was good for something after all. He grunted and hit the ground with a thud. I tried to jump away, but he snagged my foot in mid-air and held on as he pulled me back toward him.

"Get back here you little..." Duncan grabbed my arm and flipped me over so I was on my back like a stranded turtle, pinning my arms to the ground and kneeling down over me. "Are you quite finished, young lady?"

I squirmed, but he was too big and strong to overpower. There was no way to push him off of me, so I would have to try another tactic. I leaned my head over and bit his right arm as hard as I could. The fabric of his sweater was thick, but I still managed to cause some damage. He screamed a robotic scream and pulled his arm away, allowing me to roll over and get on my hands and knees. I scrambled to crawl away, but he grabbed me from behind and his forearm wrapped around me, applying pressure to both sides of my neck. As we knelt on the floor, my hands smacked his arms, hands, and head, but he refused to let go.

"Don't fight it," he said. "Just let yourself fall asleep."

As my arms flailed around, trying desperately to hit or grab anything I could, I managed to grab his mask and pull it off his head. I swung my head side to side, trying to catch a glimpse of his face, but I couldn't see anything definitive. Dropping his mask on the floor, I grabbed his sweater sleeve and pulled it up, exposing his flesh to another bite. I chomped down as hard as I could, eliciting another pained shriek from behind me. Instead of a robotic voice, he now sounded like a normal man. His voice sounded vaguely familiar, but I didn't have time to think about it. As I kept my jaws clenched on his arm like some sort of starving animal, blood filled my mouth. I let go long enough to spit it out and take a few breaths. I looked down to find another place to attack, but my vision was going dark and I started getting light-headed. Despite my limited vision, I could see that a jagged gash had appeared on his forearm. Normally the site of blood makes me queasy, but the fact that I had hurt him actually gave me strength. I held my breath and opened my mouth to bite again, but then everything went dark.

I opened my eyes and examined my surroundings. Gone were the conference room table, chairs, and Duncan. In their place was the compact cot I was lying on, a tiny table, and two flimsy folding chairs. As I stood to my feet, I became light-headed and plopped back down on the cot. I rubbed my temples to soothe the pounding in my head, but it didn't help. There was no clock and there were no windows, so there was no telling what time, or even what day it was. I slowly stood back up again, waited as the room stopped spinning, and shuffled my feet across the concrete floor. If I didn't know any better, I would have thought I was back in the government compound I wrote my confession in.

There were two doors in the room. One was closed, and the other was open. I walked over to the door that was closed and jiggled the handle. No surprise, it was locked. I went to the open door and turned on the light. The ragged blonde hair and pale eyes that greeted me in the mirror startled me. It had been several days, but I still wasn't used to the look. There was no shower, but there was a toilet and sink. I ran my hands under some cool water and splashed my face with it. My mouth was dry, so I cupped my hands and drank several swallows as I tried to get used to my appearance. I wiped myself off with the towel and walked around the room, examining the walls. I don't know what I expected to find, but that didn't stop me from exploring the small space as much as possible. More than likely, there was no way for me to escape, but it didn't hurt to look.

I walked up to a television screen that was mounted on the wall and searched for a way to turn it on. There was no remote, and no power button, so I just left it alone. I sighed and slumped my shoulders as I lumbered back to the cot. My legs gave way, and I collapsed in a heap on the uncomfortable excuse for a bed. My mind raced as I braced myself to cry for the thousandth time that week. To my surprise, there were no tears. I felt no sadness. In fact, I didn't feel much of anything. My mind and spirit were numb from the recent events. It was really getting old that every time I thought I was doing the right thing, it blew up in my face. I had nowhere to turn, so I began to pray.

I had only muttered a few words when the television clicked and flickered to life. My head snapped toward it as the picture came into focus. I gasped as the two familiar faces came into view.

My dad spoke first. "Faith, can you hear me?"

I didn't see a camera, but there had to be one somewhere in the room. "Where am I, Dad?"

"Somewhere safe."

"What's that supposed to mean? Are you trying to protect me from something, or are you trying to protect yourselves from me?" Neither of them answered. "What do you guys want, anyway?"

Jakob jumped into the conversation. "We had to talk to you about everything."

"Sure. Come on over and see how I've decorated my new home. I'd send you my address but I don't know what it is. On second thought, don't bother. I'm not really in the mood to talk right now. Besides, it's not like you'll actually listen to me."

"I know you feel that way, Jellybean. But I need you to see things from our point of view."

"You mean the point of view of the guy who's helping REFUGE take over the country?" I looked down at the cot. "You definitely can't be talking about the point of view of my father who let his people lock me up in here."

"You have every right to be upset. But you have to admit, you've become..." his voice stopped mid-sentence.

I looked toward the screen again. "I've become what? A threat? A problem?"

Dad sighed. "You've become erratic. How else do you explain

what you did back in the conference room?"

"Hey, he had it coming."

A wave of confusion spread across Dad's face. "Who had what coming?"

"Duncan. I hope his arm rots off. Maybe I gave him rabies."

"Faith, what are you talking about?"

I held my hands out with my palms up. "I'm talking about fighting with Duncan and biting his nasty arm. Didn't he tell you?"

Dad and Jakob looked at each other, then Dad spoke. "I haven't spoken with Duncan in days. You're not making any sense."

"Well, what did you hear that I did back in the conference room?"

"We heard about how you tore the room up," Jakob said. "How you were tossing chairs around, throwing things, trying to break down the door. Someone heard the noise and had to give you a tranquilizer. Don't you remember?"

I sighed as I realized what must have happened. "That's not at all what happened. Duncan was there. He came in to talk to me and then we started fighting."

Jakob was taken aback by my story. "Duncan came in and attacked you?"

"No, I attacked him when I tried to escape. He grabbed me, so I bit him on the arm a couple of times, then passed out. He must've put a sleeper hold on me or something."

Dad shook his head slowly. "Oh, Jellybean."

"Oh, Jellybean? What, you don't believe me? Duncan was there. He was dressed all in black."

Dad's face dropped, and a wave of pity appeared. "If Duncan was there, what does he look like?"

I closed my eyes and dropped my head. "I don't know. Normal size, I guess. He had a ski mask on. I ripped it off when we were fighting, but I couldn't get a good look at his face. He was using some kind of voice changer inside the mask so he sounded like he does on the phone."

"Why was he there?" Dad asked.

"He said he wanted to talk to me in person so he knew if I was lying about Chancellor Sloane changing. But after talking to him, I'm more convinced than ever that he really is trying to overthrow the Chancellor."

Tears began to form in my father's eyes. "This is why you're in here. Trashing the conference room, wild accusations, taking Sloane's side..." His voice broke. "It's just too much. I don't know what's happened to you."

"I'm telling the truth. You gotta believe me."

"Were you telling the truth about escaping from the White House?"

"Yeah."

Dad looked down and shook his head. "Faith, when I told Paul how you escaped, he said that wasn't possible. There's no way you could have even made it out of the building, let alone several blocks away. Sloane let you escape because he wanted you to come here and help him catch us."

"How can you say that? Yeah, I'm working with the Chancellor, but only on his Faith in America program."

"I know you believe that, Jellybean. That's why this hurts us so much. Something obviously happened to you in Washington, and until we figure out what it was, we need to keep you out of the way. It's for..."

"My own good? Yeah, I've heard that before. Whatever."

Dad's chin quivered. "I'm sorry, but you're going to have to stay there for the time being. You'll get plenty to eat and drink. I need to go. We'll talk soon." With that, he stood up and walked out of sight of the camera, leaving Jakob behind.

"What about you, Jakob? Do you believe me?"

"I don't know, Faith. I just don't get how you could suddenly be on Sloane's side. Especially after what he did to you. Are you really that gullible?"

"Yeah, I guess I am. Are you really this cynical?"

"Don't start a fight. This isn't really the time."

"Actually, I think this is a perfect time to talk this out. Are you alone over there?"

Jakob looked around the room he was in. "Yeah. Your dad's gone."

"What about Corinne?"

"No, she's somewhere else working on something."

I took a deep breath and let it out slowly. "I need you to be honest. I saw you two together, and I've heard stories about what happened after I left. Please tell me you're only faking your feelings for her."

Jakob looked down to avoid eye contact. "It's really complicated."

"Actually, it's not."

"I really can't talk about this right now. I don't want to get you all worked up in your condition."

My heart sank to the floor. "My condition? Wow, you too?"

"Yeah, your condition. Faith, you've changed. You're not the girl I fell in love with anymore."

I ran my fingers through my knotted hair. "Really? I thought you liked blondes."

"What's that supposed to mean?"

"You know who I'm talking about. She told me about your news. Congratulations. I'm sure you'll be happy together now that I'm finally out of the way."

Jakob and I both sat in silence, each refusing to look at the other. Finally, he stood up, still avoiding eye contact. "I'm gonna go. You need some time to think things over. Maybe you'll come to your senses."

"Maybe I should say the same thing to you. Bye, Jakob."

Jakob disappeared, and the television powered off, leaving me alone again. I tried to take a deep breath, but my lungs trembled, making my breathing uneven. In one short week, I had lost everyone important to me. My father and boyfriend not only distrusted me but had turned their backs on me. They were fine with me being locked up so I'd be out of the way. A week ago, Jakob and I were in love, planning our future together. Now, his future seemed to be with another woman. The only person who really trusted me was the man who had tried to kill me a few months ago. What a sad, strange turn of events. The watermelon metaphor came to mind again.

I closed my eyes and slowed my breathing, allowing my mind to take me back to the White House, and the conversation I had with the Chancellor before I left.

Sloane glanced at his watch. We have an hour. I'm sure we can come up with a plan."

I smiled at the mischievous look on his face. "Sounds like you already have a plan. Spill it."

"I believe we should fight fire with fire."

"Okay, but I don't think I can burn their building down."

Sloane chuckled. "I meant that metaphorically. I propose that I allow you to escape. Of course, my agents will pursue you, but they will be instructed to allow you to get away safely. Just refrain from injuring them. Once you have ventured a few blocks away, call your friends at REFUGE and tell them where to retrieve you."

"Okay, but why don't you just let me leave? Why the elaborate show?"

Sloane smiled and crossed his legs. "You should know me well enough by now to know that I am always thinking several moves ahead. Why do you suppose I would go to these lengths just to let you go?"

I thought for a few moments before the answer hit me. "They think I'm helping you capture them. So, if you just let me go, it'll look like you sent me to spy on them or help you catch them. But if I escape against your will, it'll make it look like I'm not really working for you after all. How'd I do?"

"I couldn't have said it better myself. Once they pick you up, they will undoubtedly scan you for some sort of tracking device. Let them go through their routines, and once they determine that you don't present a threat, they'll take you back. And that's when we spring the trap."

"Trap? I like the sound of that. Just please remember your promise. My family and friends will be safe. You won't arrest them."

Sloane uncrossed his legs and held his hand up as if he were taking an oath. "You have my word." He stood up and began walking toward his desk. "Now, before you go, I have something for you."

I opened my eyes and regained my bearings. I knew what I had to do. I summoned my strength and stood to my feet, dragging myself to the bathroom. I flicked on the light and stared at the battered soul facing me in the mirror. This whole ordeal had tested my resolve, my endurance, and my faith. My hair was a mess. My face wore the pain and stress of my current situation. I turned on the water and splashed it on my face a few times, then took another long drink before making eye contact with the stranger in the mirror again.

I took another drink of water, swished it around in my mouth, then swallowed it. A wave of nausea overcame me as I thought about what was coming next. I took a deep breath and nodded at myself in the mirror. "I think I'm gonna be sick," I mumbled.

A smile appeared on my face for the first time in a long time. "Perfect. I can work with that."

Be sure to check bookstores later this year for the final step in Faith's exciting journey.

Facebook: Richard Hartzer

Twitter: @RichardHartzer

Website: www.richardhartzer.com

Instagram: @RichardHartzer

Richard Hartzer is an educator by day, and writer in his free time. His award-winning first novel, a faith-based suspense story entitled "A Confession of Faith" debuted in 2022. His follow-up novel, "A Test of Faith" is available now, and the final novel in the "Journey of Faith" trilogy will be released later in 2023.

Richard currently resides in the Panama City, FL metroplex with his amazing wife Courtney and tolerable children Emily, Andrew, and Audrey. When he's not making people laugh and cry with his writing, Richard enjoys watching football, spending time with family, and sitting on the back porch doing nothing.

ACKNOWLEDGMENTS

I would like to thank all the people who have supported me so far on my writing journey. Five years ago, when I first told my wife about my idea for a novel, I had no idea I would not only write that novel but then go on to write two more. I appreciate all the love and support I have received from my family, friends, and faithful readers.

When I first put this story out into the world, I had no idea it would be so well-received by my readers. I am humbled by, and grateful for every positive review, and every time someone pesters me to hurry up and release the next story. Knowing that my words have impacted, and entertained other people is a truly remarkable feeling.

Thank you again, to everyone who took the time to read these books. I can't wait for you to see what I have in store for the third, and final book of the series.